Text copyright © 2012 by Tom Schreck
All rights reserved.

Printed in the United States of America.

Published by Thomas & Mercer
P.O. Box 400818
Las Vegas, NV 89140

ISBN-13: 9781612182803
ISBN-10: 1612182801

TOM SCHRECK

THOMAS & MERCER

DEDICATION

For Sue and Annette,
my two best friends.

ACKNOWLEDGMENTS

WRITING CAN BE a lonely business, and it chews authors up and spits them out.

When that happens you're lucky to have friends.

I am a lucky man.

I want to thank my friend Joe Konrath, who very nonchalantly offered to make a call for me. Because of that call you are reading this. It is that simple and I'll never forget it.

I want to thank Ruth and Jon Jordan, who publish *Crimespree Magazine* and who treat me far better than I deserve. The Jordans have this way of letting you know that if you stopped writing you'd let them down. I also want to thank Penny Halle, the world's coolest librarian, and Jen Forbus, mystery blogger extraordinaire, for making me feel like I belonged.

There are also the friends who say, "Sure, I don't mind proofing your three-hundred-page manuscript and adding punctuation to it." Bill Dolan and Ginny Tata-Phillips are that kind of friend. Bill, a gifted axman himself, is so cool that when I offered to rename the Elvis guitarist in the book after him he declined because he thought it would affect the story. Ginny, who writes basset hound haiku (yeah, you read that right), just loves finding errors and therefore loves working on my books.

I also want to thank my new friends at Thomas & Mercer. Andy Bartlett brought me on board and changed my life. The team behind me—Jacque Ben-Zekry, Rory Connell, Jill Taplin, Mia Lipman, Paul Diamond, and everyone else—has been incredible to work with. A special thanks to editors Leslie Miller and Renee Johnson for making my books better and for being such good friends to Duffy and Al. After ten years in this line of work I can't believe how nice an author can be treated. I hope no one taps me on the shoulder and wakes me up.

I also have to thank all my friends across the country, actually the world now, who are involved in basset hound rescue. These crazy people do anything to help a hound no matter where the hound is, how far they have to go, and what it costs. Now, I'm going to tell you a secret. A bunch of these wacky rescue types won auctions to benefit rescue to put their hounds in this book, hence the dog spa scene at the Mandalay Bay. A while back I had gotten pretty down on this writing thing, but I had two hundred pages to go to finish *The Vegas Knockout*. I was going to quit but I couldn't. I had to finish because of the hounds and their crazy hound people.

Thank God for their craziness.

Anyone out there doing basset rescue who thinks I can help, let me know.

Lastly, thanks to my two very best friends, my wife, Sue, and my mom, Annette, for, well, everything.

"I'm scared every time I go into the ring, but it's how you handle it. What you have to do is plant your feet, bite down on your mouthpiece and say, 'Let's go.'"

—MIKE TYSON

"Life doesn't run away from nobody. Life runs at people."

—JOE FRAZIER

"You don't think. It's all instinct. If you stop to think, you're gone."

—SUGAR RAY ROBINSON

CHAPTER ONE

THE MAN IN the tailored suit steadied the gun at the Mexican's head. The Mexican, all 134 pounds of him, shook, tears in his eyes.

"Por favor, por favor..." he said, almost to himself.

"Great, Spanish. You don't realize who you're dealing with, do you?" The suited man's mouth smiled, but his eyes didn't.

"Please, please..." the Mexican begged, tears now running down his cheeks.

"Oh, now you can 'hablar inglés'? You idiot."

"My children..."

"That's just what America needs, more starving Mexicans crowding the streets," said the man in the suit.

He cocked the pistol and smiled at the look of terror spreading across the Mexican's face. He read that look and memorized it so he could recall it when he wanted to.

Then he pulled the trigger and shot the Mexican in the center of his forehead.

CHAPTER TWO

"SO LET ME get this straight. The cops pulled you over at four in the morning, you threw up on your Nikes then fell down, and they say you blew a point two six on the Breathalyzer?" I asked my ten a.m. appointment. Monday morning DWI evals really sucked.

"Yeah, but I fell down because my foot fell asleep and I threw up because I had bad Chinese. I went to the Dragon's Fire Buffet and got bad squid. It was awful. You ever had bad squid?" Wally asked me.

"Walter, what about the blood alcohol content? A point two six—that's pretty high to blow on the Breathalyzer."

"My lawyer is going to contest that. Those things need to be calibrated, you know."

"How many DWIs have you got, Walter?"

"None."

"None? How many times have you been arrested for DWI?" I asked. I had some idea. I'd seen Walter at least three times over the years for this sort of thing.

"Arrested? That's not the same as convictions, Duff." Wally's indignation limped, and he knew it.

"How many?"

"Seven—but that's not supposed to figure into this evaluation. My lawyer told me that."

Wally's lawyer, Martin Mazzarotti, advertised on TV a lot. He was usually dramatically emerging from a fog, or, if it was football season, he was wearing a uniform and saying he was there to "tackle your disability claim!" He looked like a fool on TV, but he was great at getting his clients off and I'd had beers with him a few times. He was actually an alright guy.

"Wally, I'm going to need you to sign some releases so I can get the police report. I'm going to check with your wife and call Mazz, and then we'll see what our recommendations are," I said.

"C'mon, Duff, we've been through this before. I don't need no counseling sessions. It was just *circumstances*."

"Wally, I'm going to level with you. Anybody can use bad judgment and get unlucky—once. Sometimes cops *do* have it in for someone and set them up. And some people wind up having to go to rehab who don't need it," I said, making eye contact with Wally, who was nodding. He had relaxed, believing I was on his side. I gave him a minute to let that sink in before I spoke again.

"But in your case, Wally, I think you are totally full of shit. I think you lie so much that you can't even keep track of what's true anymore."

Wally squinted, the relaxation leaving his face, and turned bright red. I gave him an appointment card for a follow-up and told him to have a nice day.

That's me, Duffy Dombrowski, Jewish Unified Services caseworker extraordinaire, a naturally therapeutic, nurturing, and empathic individual.

It was now 11:15 and that meant two things. It meant that I didn't have another appointment for two hours and that I still had a shot at the leftover donuts in the break room. I grabbed the sports page and went hunting.

There was a single plain donut left on the counter. The tray was dusted with white sugary powder and toasted coconut flakes—there to remind me of how life was a series of compromises and opportunities to settle. I took a bite of the donut. It had a slight crispness to it brought on by the onset of staleness. I liked plain donuts like this, a day or two past their freshness date when the fat in them seemed to congeal. My belly was starting to warm. Though it didn't fill me up existentially, the donut did quell the rumblings.

In the paper the pundits were equating the Yankees' middle-relief issues with Armageddon. The Giants were about to open camp in Albany, and Tiger Woods was struggling at some tournament. Boxing was barely mentioned in a small box under the "Scoreboard" section of the paper that listed the upcoming fights. That was about all the paper ever covered in boxing.

I care about boxing because I make part of my living that way. I'm a pro heavyweight with about thirty fights and a record barely over five hundred, which means I beat most local mediocre guys and lose to up-and-comers. I'm what's called a "professional opponent," the irony being I get paid much more for the bigger-name fights that I almost always lose.

I skimmed through the girls' softball scores and was down to the bottom of my coffee when a small article caught my eye.

"Mexican Lightweight Murdered" was the headline. *Juan Manuel Martinez was found dead with a bullet wound to the head in the desert outside Las Vegas. He was training for the WBO lightweight title elimination bout later this month.*

Geez, the poor guy trains his whole life for a break at the title and shit like this happens.

CHAPTER THREE

"DUFFY!" IT WAS my boss, Claudia Michelin, yelling across the entire office. Let's just say the Michelin Woman and I are not buddies; I have teetered on the brink of unemployment most of my career here at Jewish Unified Services. The fact that last year I saved her from a fire and brought her back to life with CPR hadn't even helped our relationship. I actually think it made it worse, because she wanted to prove that she still was objective about my job performance.

"In here, Claudia," I yelled back. I didn't move. I played a passive-aggressive game of hide-and-seek. Sometimes it's the little victories that bring the most satisfaction.

Claudia was a tall woman with a seventies perm who was approaching maximum density, hence my private nickname for her.

"Duffy!" she yelled again. By this time, I had moved out of the kitchen and snuck around to my cubicle.

"Duffy! Where are you?" She was standing next to my desk.

I came up behind her and said, "Good morning, boss."

It startled her and she jumped a bit, then exhaled with anger and glared at me.

"Take a look at this," she said, handing me a tri-fold brochure. "Paperwork for the Human Services Professional: An intensive two-week-long training in New York's Beautiful Catskill Mountains."

Now, I've been in the wacky field of human services long enough to know a few things:

1. A week with human services professionals is enough to make you require a psychiatric hospitalization. Two weeks would induce suicidal tendencies.
2. You learn absolutely nothing at the trainings except how many simple carbohydrates you can consume in a day.
3. The conferences were always held in awful places. The heyday of the Catskills was a half century ago, and a trip to the Borscht Belt to spend more than a week with the ghosts of Milton Berle and Myron Cohen did not exactly sweeten the deal.

"I want you to attend this training and learn something," Claudia said. About twice a year she tried to fire me for poor up-keep of my paperwork. So far I'd been able to evade her attacks, but mostly from dumb luck. This "invitation" didn't mean she really wanted me to improve; it just paved the way to firing me. You see, if she sent me to this she could document that I had adequate training and that made canning my ass that much simpler.

"Oh, Claudia, you're too nice to me. Why don't you let some-one else go?" I said.

"It is not a vacation, Duffy. Continuing education is a required part of your job. I expect you to attend," she said.

"Uh…" I couldn't think of any way to get out of it.

"It begins on the seventh and I expect you there," Claudia said.

On the other hand, it would get me out of the office for a cou-ple of weeks.

CHAPTER FOUR

I HAD TROUBLE focusing for the rest of the day. I had four other scheduled sessions and none of them showed, which wasn't unusual in the wonderful world of human services. Had I been a reasonably disciplined individual I would've taken that time to catch up on my dismal paperwork. However, I was not even unreasonably disciplined and besides, the Michelin Woman was sending me to that conference anyway so I didn't want to get started only to find out that I wasn't performing my charting optimally.

Last year Jewish Unified Services finally got some technology, which meant I now had a computer on my desk hooked up to the Internet. The beauty of that was that I could be typing away, staring hard at the monitor, and it would appear like I was doing something they paid me to do. I don't know how much I was fooling anyone looking at Fightnews.com, but the murder of the Mexican guy had me curious.

Martinez had been a lefty, like me, but he fought in the lighter divisions, mostly in California and Nevada, so I didn't know a whole heck of a lot about him. He was fighting a title eliminator, which meant if he won that bout he would get a shot at another fight to win the title. Fightnews.com said he had been training in

Johnny Tocco's gym with a whole team of Mexican fighters and, lately, with Boris Rusakov and his entourage. Rusakov was this month's heavyweight sensation from Russia or Croatia or In-your-crack-istan or one of those Eastern Bloc countries.

Rusakov was 24–0, but he had only fought in the States twice, and both times he fought against guys who were past their prime. It was the usual ploy smart promoters made to get their boy noticed. It's not dangerous and they have zero chance of losing. Then you get to say, "I beat so-and-so who beat, say, Holyfield." In cases like this they hope people forget that the guy beat Holyfield when Holyfield was fifty-six years old and had a bad shoulder.

Boxers getting murdered outside the ring wasn't all that unusual, but it made me feel bad for this guy who spent all this time getting to the top just to have it taken away from him. I think I was pondering that deep existential point when Monique broke in. She was the other counselor in the clinic and had her shit together as well as anyone I knew.

"I hear you're getting the next couple of weeks off," she said. She was dressed all in black with a rainbow pin on her lapel.

"*Hooo-ha!* A whole two weeks of paperwork technique—yippee!" I said.

"Duff, try to go to *some* of it, will you?" Monique rolled her eyes.

"'Nique! I'm offended."

* * *

Surfing the Internet barely got me through the rest of the day. When four thirty finally came around I got out of there as fast as I could. I had to stop at home before I headed over to the Crawford Y for a workout. My roommate, Al, sometimes got destructive if I didn't visit with him enough, and in the last few days I had been out a lot. I should mention that Al is a large, disagreeable basset hound. He belonged to a client of mine who got sent off to jail five or six years ago for ripping off the dollar store for some hair extensions. Before she went in, she made me promise to take care of Al and then she went and got murdered. Since then the hound and I have been roommates.

When I came through the door Al was asleep on his back with all four paws straight up in the air. He's conditioned to respond when I come through the door, but he was a bit slower today. He rolled over, slid off the couch, sprinted toward me, and then jumped up and tried to kick me in the nuts. I was ready for him, blocked it, and went to get his leash. He set off barking. As soon as you grabbed a leash it was *on*.

He barked incessantly with no tune or beat. He got so excited he spun around, grabbed a sneaker, and ran through the house. When I tried to get the leash on him he head-butted me hard enough that I saw a flash of light and stepped backward. This must've meant to Al that the walk was being delayed, because he objected by jumping up and getting me in the nuts again.

"Fuck!" I yelled, doubling over. My verbal enthusiasm conveyed to Al that I wanted to play some more so he got me in the nuts again. I threw the leash against the wall and went to the bathroom to sulk and rub my nuts.

As I walked past my phone I noticed the red light was blinking. I hit the message button and kept walking to the head.

"Duff, get to the gym ASAP," the message said. It was Smitty, my trainer and manager, and a man with total economy of words. I couldn't remember him ever telling me to get to the gym "ASAP," but when Smitty said to do something, I did it.

CHAPTER FIVE

AL OBJECTED TO the loss of his walk, especially after being teased with the sight of the leash, but I decided I could walk him later. I threw some gear in a bag and made the ten-minute drive to the Crawford YMCA.

No matter how many years I've gone to the Y, every time I walk through the doors I notice the smell that goes with the place. It's a combination of chlorine from the world's most disgusting pool, stale sweat, and Pine-Sol. I headed downstairs and, like every day, I felt that little twinge of excitement with a touch of fear that I got when I approached the gym. Someone was working the speed bag and another fighter was hitting the heavy bag. I could tell all that just from the sound echoing off the stairs.

I recognized the speed bag sounds as Carlos, the teenage welterweight, and the heavy bag as Piggy. Piggy was an on-again-off-again amateur who, you might have guessed from his nickname, was a heavyweight and not a very well-conditioned one. He had a flat, turned-up nose and inconsistent hygiene. He answered to "Piggy" and didn't take any offense by it.

The din of the work stopped as the round bell sounded for a minute's rest. Smitty had used the term "ASAP," and so instead of changing into my gear first I sat down in the one old wooden chair with the two missing back slats outside Smitty's small office. I watched him talk to Malik, an amateur with two fights under his belt. Malik fought at 154. He worked hard and was great in the gym, but it all seemed to fall apart for him in competition. Smitty would work on that. If Malik stayed with it he might conquer that block. Maybe—some guys never did.

Smitty did another round with him without acknowledging me. Carlos worked the speed bag like he was automated while Piggy labored with hard but wide-looping hooks that would never land on an opponent. They made a cool sound on the bag and he had a smooth rhythm going, but it was work that was actually counterproductive to real boxing. It ingrained bad habits. When you're under the stress of the ring the body reverts to what you've programmed it to do.

The bell rang ending the round. Smitty gave a couple of instructions to Malik on feinting, Piggy headed out, and Carlos took his spot on the heavy bag. Piggy nodded to me.

Smitty walked toward me still concentrating on his work. He got within a foot of me, wiped a drop of sweat that was hanging off his nose, and exhaled.

"Duff—let me see you in the office," he said. I followed him and waited for him to sit down behind the battleship-grey metal desk. I sat on the old chipped corner stool that was there for guests.

"I got a call from some Russian fight manager. Guy's name is Milcavecov or something like that," he said. His hands were now folded in his lap.

"Okay," I said, not knowing where this was going.

"They're looking for sparring."

"Gleason's or the place in the Bronx?" I said. Gleason's was in Brooklyn, the oldest boxing gym in the world. The PAL gym in the Bronx was a great gym where lots of pros trained.

Smitty just shook his head. "Duff, I don't think it's a good idea for you. I'm not crazy about your head yet." A while back I had gotten a medical report that showed I had some abnormality in my brain from a series of concussions. I had taken a couple, well, maybe more like a *few* knockouts in a row both in sparring and in fights and Smitty was being his overprotective self. He claimed that my balance was off and that I was, as he likes to delicately say, "A little fucked up mental-wise." I've always been a little fucked up mental-wise so I didn't give it a lot of concern. Besides, the last two times the boxing commission docs checked there wasn't any evidence of problems.

"Smitty, the tests have been okay, you know that. Besides, if it ain't going well I tell them I'm done and I drive home."

"They don't want you in New York."

"Where then?"

"They want you in Vegas. It's for Rusakov. They want a south-paw. He's fighting for the title in two weeks." Smitty scrunched up his forehead.

"Vegas! Smitty, I can't turn down Vegas. Are you kidding?"

"I knew you'd react like that. Kid, you make your own deci-sions, but I can't go with you. I think they want you there for a while and I can't leave this place for that long. But I don't like not being there to keep an eye on things," Smitty said.

He was looking directly at me, probably more like studying me.

"I'll be fine—holy shit, Vegas!"

"It's a big-time fight card, heavyweight title plus a couple of big lightweight fights. I got to admit, these Russians got some cash and they don't mind paying for what they want. The money's good," he said without emotion.

"How much?"

"Two thousand dollars plus a place to stay, use of a car, and meals."

"Holy shit! I'm in."

"I knew you would be," Smitty said.

CHAPTER SIX

I RUSHED BACK home to call my new bosses. Al was even more wound up—he started barking the second I pulled in the driveway. My inconsistent attendance in Al's eyes pissed him off the most, and my running home then going to the gym had him in a mood.

To quiet him down I gave Al a big bowl of dog food and sweetened it with a can of sardines. I wanted to call Las Vegas, but Al consumed food like it was an Olympic event so I only had a minute or to two to make the call in any kind of peace. I dialed the number for Steel Hammer Boxing, which, according to the card, was headquartered in Las Vegas. A very corporate-sounding operator answered on the first ring.

"Good afternoon, SHB," she said. The initials threw me for a second.

"Uh, Mr. Mil-ca-veco…" I tried to pronounce his name.

"Milcavecov? One moment please."

I waited and listened while the hold music played an incredibly lame version of "Viva Las Vegas."

"This is Stan," the voice said. It had just a hint of Russian or Eastern Bloc accent.

"Hi, this is Duffy Dombrowski, I'm calling to—" I didn't get to finish.

"Duffy! We want you to come work with us. We need a south-paw with some moves for Boris. Will you come help us?"

"Sure, I'd love to."

"Boris asked for you especially. He likes the way you work. We can't wait for you to get out here."

I've had a few fights on TV, but they were unspectacular and I usually lost. I didn't quite get why a guy fighting at the championship level who was from the other side of the world would know who I was. I also wasn't sure why they would give a damn about bullshitting me. The sparring money was good enough. I was used to being treated like a piece of meat.

"Can you be out here in a couple of days?"

"Sure," I said.

"We have a perfect place for you to stay. Mishka will call you tomorrow with your travel arrangements," said Stan, my new best friend.

After giving me a few more details he hung up. Al was sitting still and silently staring. He knew something was up. I got up to get his leash, but he did none of the usual frantic antics. He just stared at me with big, sad, brown eyes. He couldn't have understood the conversation, could he?

I hooked the lead to his collar and enthusiastically said, "C'mon, boy!" Al pulled back with his body and lay down. I pulled and he resisted.

"What? You think I'm taking you to Vegas?" Despite what other dog owners may say, I felt foolish having a conversation with my dog.

Al stared at me.

"You can't. How could I even get you on a plane? You can't," I insisted.

He continued to stare at me. He fixed his eyes right on mine and didn't break his glare. I tried to stare him down using my human dominance but I looked away first.

"I'll see what I can do," I said. Al immediately bounded up, tail wagging, and we went for a walk. I wasn't sure how one accomplished air travel with a near-ninety-pound basset hound nor how one just appeared at one's new employer with such an uninvited guest. Al didn't care. He was accustomed to getting his way.

We did our customary walk down Route 9R. The sun was going down and the waning sunlight glimmered off my home in an iridescent kind of way. That is one of the benefits of living in a converted Airstream trailer. I had christened it the "Moody Blue," after Elvis's last hit. I saw Al do his telltale rounding so I stood and sort of meditated while he made like an oversized Play-Doh machine. I think that was the first time it dawned on me that I had just agreed to go to Vegas during the same period I was supposed to be at a compulsory paperwork festival or something.

This was going to take some creative problem-solving.

In my life, creative problem-solving meant one thing. It was time to go to AJ's.

CHAPTER SEVEN

AJ'S WAS THE bar I hung out in. It was about a hundred years old and smelled like a century of stale beer. It had that old bar feel, not because AJ III was big on ambience; rather because it was an old dive and nothing was ever done to it. It had that look on the inside that mall bars go for but never come close to getting. The other reason I loved AJ's was because they served Schlitz, my beer of choice.

The Fearsome Foursome were there when I came through the door. No surprise there. These guys were always at the bar, like it was some sort of time-warp phenomenon. As usual, they were deep in an intense discussion. On this particular night it had something to do with cultural differences in regard to criminal justice. That's about the nicest way I could phrase that.

"That's why they cut off the right hand," Rocco was saying. Rocco was pushing eighty, drank draft Genesee, and, let's just say, he didn't have any problem with being adversarial.

"What if the guy was a natural left-hander? Did that make a difference?" TC asked. TC worked for the state, drank B&B, and didn't always track well.

"Hold up—I wasn't paying attention because of the TV. You're saying that in Iran they'll cut off a guy's right hand because that's the hand you eat with. That in turn forces people to eat with their left and that's the hand that they wipe their ass with?" Jerry Number One said.

"Sounds like shit to me," said Jerry Number Two. Jerry Number One was a fiftysomething draft-beer-drinking guy who told bad jokes and held political opinions that made Pat Buchanan look like a Green Party candidate. Jerry Number Two looked like he got back from Woodstock last week. He drank cosmopolitans, lived on the computer, and preferred tie-dyes accentuated by the red cosmo juice that dribbled off his chin.

When they were this far into a discussion they didn't bother to say hello to me.

"Damn it, it's true. Those people eat with their hands, and so if you cut off the nonwiping hand you're screwed, nutritionally," Rocco said.

"Why don't they just use TP?" asked Jerry Number One.

"They ain't got it," Rocco said. His face was getting redder.

"So they wipe their ass with their bare hand? Remind me to not order pizza from Andy's anymore. The guy rolling out the dough is some sort of Arab," TC said.

"Rico is Puerto Rican," Jerry Number Two said.

"How come the pizza tastes like shit, then?" TC said.

"It's a cultural thing. In that culture it is seen as proper to wipe your ass with your hand," Rocco said.

"I got to believe there's some mavericks over there listening to rap music and wiping their ass with Cottonelle," Jerry Number One said.

"They'd probably cut off both hands of that guy," TC said.

"Can you imagine the itching after about a week?" This was Rocco.

"Beats running one of those cold hooks up your ass," Jerry Number Two said.

"So Rocco, you're saying if you get in trouble they do away with your food hand and make your shit-wiping hand do double duty so no one ever invites you over for Thanksgiving," TC said.

"You're an asshole," Rocco said.

"I'm an asshole? How would you like to be a one-handed, hungry, skinny bastard who smells like shit and has no friends?" TC said. "Then I would feel like an asshole!"

Apparently at his limit, Rocco turned to me. "What's up, Duff?"

"I got the shits, Rocco. High five!" I said and raised my left hand.

Rocco just shook his head in disgust.

"Hey, guys—check this out. I'm going to Vegas," I said. AJ, who had refrained from joining the Iranian hygiene discussion, slid a bottle of Schlitz in front of me. The condensation beaded down the side of it was good enough for a print ad.

"Vegas? What for?" asked Jerry Number One.

"I'm gonna spar with that Russian heavyweight to get him ready for the title shot."

"Why you?" TC asked.

"Aside from my outstanding boxing skills, they needed a left-handed guy."

"I wonder if there are any left-handed fighters in Iran?" Jerry Number Two said.

"Iranian athletics ain't worth shit," Rocco said.

Almost in unison, the Foursome stopped to sip their drinks. It was like a collective exhale, a natural punctuation point for the group. It was the perfect time to ask a question.

"Do you guys have any idea how I could get Al on a commercial flight?" I said.

They just looked at me.

"Al, the basket hound?" TC said.

I didn't take time to correct him. "Yes."

"You put him in baggage in his dog house thingy, don't you?" Jerry Number One said.

"I don't see Al diggin' that or for that matter spinnin' around the conveyor belt," Jerry Number Two said.

"He might like it. It would be kind of like an amusement park for him," Rocco said.

"I thought I could get him on the plane with me," I said.

"Cost you at least the price of a ticket, and I think the canine can only be the size of one of those yippy dogs," TC said. Using the term *canine* gave the first part of his sentence some authority. Adding the adjective *yippy* to the second part ruined it.

The group took another sip and let the topic die. Their problem-solving efforts seemed a bit less energetic than usual. They were probably distracted by the whole mention of Las Vegas. TC broke the silence.

"Where you staying?" TC said.

"I'm not sure," I said.

"Probably in some skanky casino. They'll have you beating up card counters in a back room with no windows," Rocco said.

"I don't think so—I don't think I'm staying in a casino. You know, they said something about having a whole house to myself. You guys up for a road trip?" I asked.

They all got quiet and looked at each other. Without a word being spoken I knew what they were thinking. *Leave town? Us? There's alcohol and television here and no guarantee in Las Vegas that we'd get to sit in the same order of barstools. It sounds unpredictable and dangerous!*

While they were quiet, a rare occurrence, Kelley the cop came in. It was his off night, so he had on jeans, running shoes, and a T-shirt. He'd been lifting more and it showed—not in that bodybuilder way, but in a way that was all about useful muscular function. As always, he took the seat to the left of me, closest to the

TV and two stools away from the Foursome. AJ opened a bottle of Coors Light and placed it in front of Kelley, who was staring at the screen.

"Let me bring you up to speed. You missed a discussion on the challenges left-handed amputees face in Iran because their remaining hand now has to do both ass-wiping and feeding duties," I said.

"What makes you think I 'missed' that conversation?" Kelley said, still looking at the television.

"That, and I'm going to Las Vegas to spar with some Russian big deal training for a title shot."

"Really?" Kelley asked. This time he looked at me.

"Yeah, you wanna come along? There's a free place to stay," I said and lifted my eyebrows.

"You're serious?"

"Why not? I mean, you only box for about an hour a day and that leaves an awful lot of time to, I don't know, play baccarat or something."

"Baccarat?" Kelley asked.

"I've always wanted to say 'pass the shoe' like Sean Connery," I said.

"Let me think about it. I got plenty of time that I haven't taken, and it wouldn't be the worst thing in the world to get out of this town," Kelley said.

That was Kelley's version of ventilating his feelings. A romance he recently had with a conservation cop had soured. He didn't talk about it at all. One night I asked how she was and he said, "That's done." That was all he said, and I knew better than to ask anything else.

The Foursome had moved on to oil reserves and wind-powered automobiles when Rocco interrupted.

"Hey—Duff, it's a good thing you're not Mexican," he said.

I was confused until he nodded at the TV. CNN was on because the Yankees game hadn't started yet—they were playing Anaheim later that night. The square-jawed reporter looked very serious.

"The body of a twentysomething Mexican male was found in Red Rock Canyon fifteen miles east of Las Vegas today. It is believed that he was an undocumented street worker passing out advertisements for Las Vegas escort services. These undocumented workers are found all over the Las Vegas Strip passing out these ads. Despite the city's attempt to remove them, they remain a fixture on the Strip and the subject of outcry from politicians with quality-of-life concerns. This is the third such worker found dead with a single gunshot wound to the head. Police officials are downplaying speculation of a serial killer and are attributing the killings to gang disputes."

"There you go, Duff. You can start solving crimes again—this time in Sin City," TC said.

"Crime solving? I'm no cop," I said.

"Uh-huh, what do you call saving Shondeniesha from that porn ring?" TC said.

"Or finding out who was killing the kids at Crawford High?" Rocco said.

"Or foiling that terrorist group?" Jerry Number One said.

They were all staring at me. I just shook my head and sipped my Schlitz. They were full of shit.

CHAPTER EIGHT

I HEADED HOME to the Moody Blue tired, with just a trace of Schlitz buzz, listening to Elvis sing "Good Luck Charm," again. My '76 Eldorado had started to stall out when I idled at lights. Every time that happened, the eight-track in the player would skip to the next track. For a week I had missed Elvis doing "Such a Night" because it would kick off and play "Good Luck Charm" instead. I didn't mind "Good Luck Charm," but it was a softer commercial song and I preferred "Such a Night." The Drifters and Johnny Ray did a pretty good cover, but it kind of goes without saying that Elvis did it better.

When I got home I went straight to bed and found Al had beaten me there. He was on his back with all four feet in the air snoring at the decibel level of a fifteen-amp, ten-horsepower chainsaw. He was also lying at an angle, maximizing the square footage he covered on my bed. I slipped both hands under him to flip him over but the fat of his belly made leverage difficult. He interrupted his snoring just a tad, to register a low growl that was supposed to serve as a warning. I ignored it and went to flip him but only managed to set him on more of an angle across the bed. He kind of coughed a half snore, half growl, without opening his eyes.

I got my hands underneath him again and this time tried to do the flip as quickly as possible. Al's legs lowered toward the mattress but then bounced back to the center like they were affixed to some sort of hydraulic spring.

"C'mon, Al," I heard myself say, as if he would respond to reason.

He farted loudly.

It was hard to believe he didn't do it on purpose.

"You're an asshole," I said.

I started to head for the couch, but just when I got to the door, Al rolled over to the left side of the bed and let out a baritone hum. I just shook my head and crawled into my side of the bed. I tried not to concentrate on the canine flatulence that filled the air.

The pleasant Schlitz buzz that I had hoped would carry me off into a blissful delta-state sleep was now gone and I found myself staring at the ceiling and wincing at the stench. I pondered making a run to the kitchen but didn't want Al to wake up. He believed any time I was in the kitchen it was time for me to fill his dish and crack open some sardines. I rolled over and noticed for the first time that the light on my answering machine was blinking. I hit the button.

"Duffy, this is Claudia. You will need to be at the conference training center in Valatia at seven thirty a.m. Monday morning to pick up your registration packet. I want to remind you that this training is part of your performance improvement plan and shouldn't be taken lightly. As you continue to have paperwork challenges this training is essential and if missed will lead to further disciplinary action and possible termination based on your disciplinary history with regard to your record keeping."

It was always good to hear from Claudia. Somehow in all the excitement about Vegas I forgot about the paperwork festival I was supposed to attend. It didn't matter—there was no way in hell that I would miss the Vegas opportunity. The trick was going to be making the Michelin Woman believe I went to the bullshit thing, or that I had some sort of emergency that legitimately prevented me from attending.

The problem was I had no legitimate chance of bailing on it. I'd lied and schemed my way out of things before, but I'd gotten caught enough that it was getting harder and harder to pull off. I'd gone out on BS disability leaves before and it was a tactic that worked some of the time. One time I went out on a fibromyalgia leave to take a fight and that worked until the fight was broadcast on national television. Irritable bowel syndrome worked, so did depression. Epstein-Barr disease, post-traumatic stress syndrome all worked, along with a few others.

My chronic health problems didn't necessarily fool Claudia, but because of my friends in the medical profession I always had documentation and she couldn't dispute them. The problem was I had gone down this path so many times even my doctor friends were backing off a bit. As I lay in bed not sleeping, bogus ways of getting out of work ran through my head.

There was family leave, but I lived alone. There was bereavement leave, but I didn't know anyone who died. I had a friend or two at the *Union Star* newspaper and I wondered if they could doctor up an obituary so it said I was a relative of someone. You know, you could take someone who only got a few lines who had no local relatives and say they were Duffy Dombrowski's dad or something. That seemed a little shady even for my purposes.

I also could just concoct some outrageous crisis story where I, like, save a family burning in a car, but I didn't know how to stage that or work it into a two-week furlough. I could get kidnapped and they could hold me for ransom then call Claudia with the demands.

That just seemed a little over the top.

I could stage a maternity leave. All I would have to do is find a pregnant chick and give her a few hundred dollars to claim I was the one. Then in the confusion I could say it got cleared up with DNA tests. I didn't like the feel of that one or the karma it would bring.

Then it dawned on me.

They couldn't bust me if I was there, right? And the proof of being there amounted to my name on the sign-in sheet and a body in a seat. They wouldn't do roll call, so all I needed was for someone to sign my name and take up my spot in the room. People there who knew me wouldn't know the difference because there would be a lot of faces they didn't recognize. They'd just assume that the guy in for me was someone else from Buffalo or something.

Could it work? It had to work better than the truth.

Now I had to find someone willing to spend two weeks at a conference who would fit my general description and who could keep his mouth shut and not give it away.

Like when the apple landed on Newton's (or was it Einstein's?) head, it came to me as clear as possible.

Cheese Roucquefort.

CHAPTER NINE

JEFFREY ROUCQUEFORT HAD been a year behind me at McDonough High. He was a stoner famous for a couple of things. For one, he was famous for his commitment to drop acid every single day of his senior year in high school. He was famous for being a junior in high school for three years running, and he was famous for streaking a homecoming football game and running into the metal cable at the end of the gridiron. Ol' JR cut up his thighs pretty good, and it took all the attention away from the McDonough football team, who went on to lose that night by twenty-six.

But there was something else that Jeffrey was famous for, and it was how he got his nickname.

Jeffrey "Cheese" Roucquefort farted more than anyone else.

He could fart at will and on command. He could do them so loudly it would startle an entire classroom. He could also drop a covert stench bomb and then leave the room. Once the room filled up with malodorous gas it didn't matter if Cheese was nowhere to be found. Everyone knew who did it.

Unfortunately, farting on command is not a marketable skill. Cheese, as you might have guessed, didn't turn out to be one of McDonough's great achievers. The last I knew, he was getting fired from the Price Gobbler. He had been the assistant night produce manager, but apparently it was his own homegrown herb that had been the focus of attention. Cheese got canned for sparking a fatty on his break, and though he claimed the pot smell was the off-gassing of the fresh basil delivery, no one believed him. Last I heard, he was back home living with his folks listening to his Phish bootlegs and tinkering with his hydroponic gardening system.

He was in the basement when I called and got his mom. She put down the receiver and screamed, "Cheese! Cheese! It's for you!"

It struck me as odd that his own mom called him by the nickname he had earned for flatulence.

"Yo, this is Cheese," Jeffrey said.

"Cheese, it's Duffy Dombrowski. You remember me?" I said.

"Sure, Duff, what's up?"

"Cheese—you been working?" I asked.

"Nah, I got canned at the Gobbler. That gig sucked anyway."

"How would you like to make five hundred bucks for two weeks' work and all you got to do is sit around?"

"What do I gotta do?"

"Look, you remember people used to say we looked a little alike? Well, I'm supposed to be at this training, but I can't go. All I need you to do is show up and sit there for two weeks. You don't have to do anything. You just sign in every day and sit there. The lunch is even free," I said.

"What do they got for lunch?"

"I don't know, but it's usually good shit—you know, cold cuts, dessert, you know, whatever," I said.

"It's not like bullshit mac and cheese and crap like that, right?" Cheese said.

"No, man, it's usually pretty good. Cheese, this is important. I'll pay you five hundred dollars for it and all you got to do is show up."

"Wow, dude, I can show up. What else do I got to do?"

"Nothing man, I swear. It's going to be boring as shit, but you just got to sit there with other people," I said.

"What kind of other people?" Cheese said.

"Social worker types."

"Man, those people are fucking boring!"

"I know, I know, but I'm paying you half a grand, Cheese."

"Yeah, but you didn't say they was social workers. I want seven hundred fifty."

"C'mon, Cheese!"

"Take it or leave it, Duff. Those people get on my nerves," Cheese said.

"Alright, alright." I couldn't believe Cheese Roucquefort was holding me up. I paused before I made my next point because I wasn't sure how to broach the subject.

"Cheese, there's something else," I said.

"Yeah?"

"Yeah, well, it's important that you don't call attention to yourself, you know."

"So…I got that, Duff," Cheese said.

"Well, Cheese, then, you know, you can't let them go during the training."

"You mean fart," he said.

"Yes."

"Well, what the fuck am I supposed to do, blow up?" Cheese said with more than a little indignation.

"Uh, well, okay, just don't do any just for fun. Like if you get bored, don't do them on purpose," I said.

"On purpose? I'm not in high school anymore, Duff. That was a long time ago."

"Sorry, Cheese."

Cheese assured me that he'd do his best to hold it in and that he would just show up and keep his mouth shut and, well, that he'd keep himself shut too. That was all I needed—at least from Cheese. Next I called Trina, the office manager at the clinic. She and I were not only coworkers, we were friends, and on occasion a little more than friends. She was the Michelin Woman's gal Friday, but she knew the score and was loyal to me. She also knew I was an idiot.

"Are you out of your mind?" she asked after I told her my plan.

"C'mon, it's genius and you know it," I said.

"You don't think everyone will notice that 'Duffy Dombrowski' is now 'Cheese the Fart Machine Stoner'?"

"They don't have to know it's me. He just fills a spot and signs my name. As long as he keeps his mouth shut, no one will pay attention to him," I said.

"And what if he, you know…uh…lives up to his nickname?" Trina said.

"Geez, Trina, he was in high school—that was a long time ago," I said.

"Uh huh," she said.

Some people just never get off a guy's ass.

CHAPTER TEN

MILCAVECOV'S SECRETARY CALLED and gave me the flight information. She told me there would be a car waiting for me at McCarran Airport. I was to fly out tomorrow at 12:55 and that would get me to Vegas around four, their time. I packed four sets of training gear, my own sparring gloves and wraps, headgear, and boxing shoes. I was getting my Hawaiian shirt collection ready when I noticed Al at the foot of the bed. He was growling at me and the suitcase. The TV was on and set to CNN.

"What's your problem?" I asked. I had arranged for Trina to come and visit him three times a day. She would feed and walk him and, knowing Trina, give him spa treatments.

He growled at me again. He knew every time I took out a bag and put things in it he was going to be left alone. He didn't like that idea.

"*Grrrr…*" Al said.

I tried to ignore it.

"Woof! *Aroooo…*" Al said.

"Look, it's hot as hell out there and I'm going to be busy," I said. "Besides, you love Trina."

"*Grrr…*"

"And how the hell would I get you on the plane? There's no way you're going to stand for being put in luggage," I said.

"*Grrr…*"

I did my best to ignore him, but he knew he would outlast me when it came to that. I was gritting my teeth so hard my jaw ached and my temples throbbed, but I didn't want to give Al the satisfaction of screaming at him. Besides, Trina would take care of him and he'd love that.

"*Aroooo*, woof! Woof! Woof! *Grr…*" Al said.

I turned and looked at the TV and turned up the volume.

"*And in Las Vegas, two more itinerant, undocumented Mexicans were found murdered in Red Rock Canyon. It appears that each was killed execution-style, with a single bullet hole in the temple area…*"

Al continued barking at me.

"*We turn to our former FBI profiler, Marcus LaFontaine. Marcus, your thoughts on just who might be committing these murders?*"

The square-headed dude with the pale skin and grey hair picked it up from there.

"*Clearly, it is not coincidental that the victims apparently have all been migrant workers in the country illegally. With the victim number now approaching ten, and with all the victims having similar backgrounds, it seems quite possible that the perpetrator has a racial motive.*" No shit, Sherlock. I wondered how he got to be an FBI profiler and thought about looking into exploring this career option when I got back from Vegas.

"*Aroooo, Arooooo, Aroooo…*"

That is if I didn't get a brain hemorrhage first.

"Alright, I'll call the freakin' airline, but you're not going in with the Samsonites, I'll tell you that right now."

I called Southwest Airlines and navigated their phone messaging system for about thirty-five minutes until I got a live person. I asked about bringing a dog on a flight.

"If the dog is over thirty pounds it needs to go in a carrier and will be put with the luggage," the woman said with contrived kindness. Al hadn't seen thirty pounds on the scale since he was in puppyhood.

"Uh, are there any exceptions to that?" I said.

"Well, not unless your dog is a service dog."

"You mean like a seeing-eye dog?"

"Yes, but also dogs used for other medical conditions."

"Really?" I couldn't believe I was having this conversation. "Like what other medical conditions?" I asked.

"Well, heart conditions, seizure disorders, and even anxiety," she said.

"No shit?" I said.

"Well, yes, sir."

"What does the passenger need to bring a service dog on board?"

"A doctor's note of service dog certification," she said.

I just sat there on the phone, thinking. Al was quiet also, staring at me, his tail thumping.

"Sir, will there be anything else?" she asked.

"No, thank you," I said and hung up.

I had to get over to the hospital right away to see Rudy.

CHAPTER ELEVEN

RUDY WAS MY landlord, he worked the corner of my fights fixing cuts, and he was a doctor of internal medicine at the Crawford Medical Center. The Moody Blue was a gift, of sorts, from Rudy. An uncle of his had died and left him this Airstream that Rudy had no idea what to do with.

His office was in the building adjacent to the hospital. When I came to the door and looked in he was where he always was, doing what he always did. He was hunched over the computer monitor, his back to the door, cursing at the screen while he fiddled with his reading glasses. His underarms had deep pit stains because, well, they always did.

"You know, when I see you like that with your back turned toward me I just want to rip off your sweaty shirt and run my hands through all that glorious back hair," I said as I entered his office.

"Go to hell, Duffy," Rudy said without even the slightest effort or reflex to turn around.

"Hey, I need a favor."

"Now there's something new. You know how I could tell you were going to ask me for something?"

"How?"

"You're here, that's how," Rudy said. He still hadn't turned around. "Shit, this goddam thing," he said to his monitor. Finally he spun around on his office chair. The buttons down his coffee-stained dress shirt were under maximum stress, and it looked like any minute there could be a fabric-and-belly-fat explosion.

"I need you to write a pass so Al can be considered a service dog," I said.

Rudy stared at me like I had just landed from Mars. He sort of squinted. Rudy knew Al.

A moment went by.

"I'm serious, Rudy," I said.

"I have no doubt you're serious. You know I've met Al. What type of service will he be providing? On-demand slobber? Room deodorizing? Leftover waste management?"

"Look, I got a chance to go to Vegas to be a sparring partner for that Russian guy that's making all the noise. I gotta get Al on a plane."

"Hold it—you're going to be a human punching bag after what you went through? Kid, you're out of your mind," Rudy said.

He was referring to the head thing. When I took those knockouts a while back, Rudy, the nosy bastard that he is, found out Smitty didn't want me fighting. He also made a big deal about a few mental lapses I had and claimed I was a little wobbly when I walked.

"The last two tests—"

Rudy cut me off. "Fuck the last two tests! We're talking about your brain, dipshit." He shook his head.

"Rudy, you know me and you know I'm going. If you don't write me whatever the hell it is I need then Al's going to have to stay with you," I said.

Rudy looked up at me, frowned, and pursed his lips.

"Fuckin' Polack," he said almost to himself. He took out his letterhead, loaded it in his printer, and typed something on his computer. After he printed it out he signed it, stuffed it in an envelope, and handed it to me without looking at me.

"Lay off the eight on the craps table," he said.

"Thanks, Rud." I hesitated for a second. "Why don't you take a few days off and come with me. I supposedly have a whole house to myself," I said.

He finally turned to face me, a blank expression on his face. "Yeah, right, Duff," he said and turned back to his computer. "Do you have any idea how much paperwork I gotta do? I don't have time to be following you around Vegas loaning you blackjack money."

He let out a big exhale and went back to his computer.

CHAPTER TWELVE

IT WAS HOT in front of the Flamingo.

Jorge and Manuel stood in the sun all day long with their head-phones on handing out the cards. They'd slap them twice against the meat of their palms and then hand them to the tourists walking by.

Jorge had a Lakers cap on and Manuel wore a Notre Dame cap. They were very thirsty. The cards had two photos. One was a blonde woman wearing nothing but thigh-high boots, pouting at the camera from a slouched pose on a chair, her legs spread. In quotes it said, "I'm lonely. Call me!"

The other photo was a very young-looking Latina bent over naked, looking back at the camera. Her quote read "Hola! Let's go south of the border!"

The bottom of the card had a message that said, "We can be in your room anywhere on the Strip in half an hour!"

About every tenth tourist accepted the card as they walked by, but most immediately threw them to the sidewalk. By nightfall, the cards littered the entire length of the Strip.

Jorge and Manuel were thrilled at the twenty-five dollars a day they received. They'd come here for a month, make a few hundred, and return back to Sinaloa to feed their families. Then they'd cross the border again. Getting in wasn't that difficult in terms of getting caught, but the heat and a night and day in the desert were brutal.

At midnight they headed to the motel room that they shared with six others who'd made the trip. It was eight miles south of the Strip, but they didn't mind the walk. Sometimes they splurged on a city bus, or if they were lucky, they came across an unattended bike. The walks were easier when Jorge and Manuel split a fifth of tequila or at the very least a forty-ounce St. Ives.

Today was especially hot and the two were drained. Two miles from the famous "Welcome to Las Vegas" sign they were walking slowly, sharing their bottle, when a white Lincoln Navigator pulled over to the side of the road in front of them and sat there, idling. The windows were tinted completely black. Jorge and Manuel didn't pay it any attention.

They were within ten feet of the car when a man got out. He was in a black suit with a black shirt and wore black sunglasses. He didn't say a word. Jorge and Manuel continued walking forward, veering slightly to the right to avoid the man.

"Do you know who I am?" the man in black shouted.

Jorge and Manuel kept walking. Manuel held the tequila, but he didn't sip it. The man in black made him uneasy.

"Dirty, stupid leeches!" the man yelled.

Manuel looked at Jorge. Jorge stopped to look back at the man, who had started following them.

Jorge looked back at Manuel, concerned. Jorge was five years older, and Manuel deferred to him when it was time to make decisions.

"Vamos," Jorge said quietly.

Jorge started to run, but gunfire cracked and he fell facedown. He screamed in pain. Manuel looked at his friend, who was now gurgling blood through his mouth and grabbing at his stomach.

A second shot rang out.

Manuel was hit in the side and went down.

Now the man in black was over them.

"Ayudame...Ayudame..." Jorge whispered. Manuel writhed in pain.

The man in black now stood directly over Jorge. He looked up at the man wondering why.

"No! Por favor..." He spat up blood.

The man in black smiled. Then he shot Jorge in the face.

Manuel screamed as he watched.

The man in black smiled then laughed at Manuel. Turning, he shot Manuel twice in the head.

CHAPTER THIRTEEN

I DROVE TO the Albany International Airport. Apparently having a few flights to Chicago and Baltimore qualifies an airport to use the "International" designation, because near as I could tell you couldn't get to another country by flying out of Albany.

There was a constant jangling sound coming from Al, who was seated in the passenger seat of the El Dorado. He found the "Service Dog" vest I got overnighted from Amazon uncomfortable and was digging at it with his back paw. As Al dug, it kicked up the hound funk he had going on, and the interior of the car began to smell like a huge, hollow basset. Perhaps that was his "service" to me. Rudy had written an official medical letter that I had something called a "Generalized Anxiety Disorder" with acute schizotypal symptoms. I didn't mind Rudy assigning me an official mental illness; after all, he told me I was fucking nuts to my face every time he saw me.

I had Al's documentation on me and felt pretty proud of myself for thinking of such a clever and easy ruse. My pride faded a tad when Al went through the double doors into the terminal and immediately started barking. He was relentless and was going on like a crazy dog. I've learned over the years that certain things set Al off. He always barked at people pulling squeaky-wheeled luggage, he always barked at people with headphones, and he barked at people who seemed to be wandering aimlessly.

Once you take into consideration the people fitting those descriptions, who is left in an airport *not* to bark at?

We got in the line for Las Vegas with about two hundred other people, and even though it was early in the day a group of twenty-something guys had already been drinking and were being loud. Al objected to their social insolence. He pulled the leash out of my hand and went over and attacked one guy's knapsack that was on the floor next to his feet. Al had the corner of it and started to thrash it back and forth like it was small prey whose neck he wanted to break. He let out a low but intense growl while he was at his business.

"Yo, dude, your dog is, like, out of hand," the slacker said. He had that perfectly styled messed-up hair, a T-shirt that was a size too small, jeans that hung off his ass, and flip-flops designed to look ratty.

"Sorry," I said. I didn't really mean it.

"Well?" the slacker said with just a hint of attitude that I didn't really care for. His friends got quiet and looked at me with that semiaggressive macho guy thing.

"Well what?" I said.

"Dude, make him stop or I'll have to," Slacker said and bobbed his head.

I hate airports. They make me tense. Just the same, I kind of figured knocking someone out in one would probably upset the TSA or something, so I decided to refrain from doing anything. I just wanted to get on a plane and head to Vegas. I tugged a little on Al's leash.

Unfortunately my anxiety-calming service dog was making a little bit of a scene. Over the years I've also learned that he can sense vocal tone shifts, and the slacker just gave him one. Al stopped working on the corner of the knapsack, but for its owner it came a few seconds late. There was a new two-inch hole in the corner of the bag.

"Dude, that fucking dog ruined my gear!" Slacker said. He took a step toward Al with his leg cocked to deliver a kick to Al's midsection. A few years back, a biker had laid into Al like that and Al never forgot it. He freaked if he thought someone was going to give him the boot.

Al dove in and pounced on the guy's stationary leg, biting him hard on his exposed big toe. The guy went down ass-over-teakettle, grabbing his wounded digit instinctively, which was unfortunate because it twisted his body in a weird way and he wound up cracking the side of his head on the tile.

Al started going ape shit with the barking, probably out of pride for scoring a knockdown. The rest of the slackers started making noise and doing that guy thing that cowardly guys do when they think they're supposed to fight but don't really want to. That is, they start talking loud and stupid and hunching their shoulders and breathing hard. I stood there without moving but with my senses sharpened just a bit.

"That's fucked up, man," one of the astute slackers observed. Another gave me a glare that I'm sure he'd studied from his Vin Diesel Netflix rentals.

Al had returned to the bag and started rummaging through it when the TSA cops showed up. They weren't really sure how to address the issue. I'm guessing their training on basset hound service dog management was only a small part of their overall coursework. Al made their focus a whole lot clearer, however, when he pulled out a nickel bag of pot from the bag.

CHAPTER FOURTEEN

THE FIRST COP there, a young, muscular black guy who took himself very seriously, said, "Who is the owner of this piece of luggage?"

No one said anything. So I spoke.

"Sir, my medical service dog has had training in drug detection. He was coincidently put in close proximity to that bag and he instinctively pursued what he sensed."

I felt so official.

The black cop reached down and read the Southwest paper name tag that was hanging off the knapsack. The second cop to arrive was a tall, thin white guy with a shaved head and a perfectly honed look of great intensity. I guessed you got intense from inspecting shampoo bottles that held more than 3.5 ounces of liquid.

"Are you Brendan Noonan?" the black cop asked, straightening up. He looked down at the guy who was rubbing his head.

"Don't I have, like, you know, the right to remain silent or something?" my new friend Brendan asked. His buddies had very worried looks on their faces.

"Clearly you have the right to be an idiot, don't compound that by adding asshole to it," the black cop said. Noonan frowned.

"I will need to see the four of you in the TSA detainment room immediately," the cop said, starting to herd the men in the direction he'd come from. "Bring your bags. You will not be making this flight and I doubt you will be traveling at all today," the black cop said.

"Uh, officer, can't something, you know, be worked out?" one of the other slackers said. As he spoke he slid a twenty in and out of a small pocket in his T-shirt.

That's right, I said a twenty.

During all this Al had fallen asleep on the tile floor and had rolled over on his back. The black cop looked over at him.

"Can I ask you a question?" he said to me.

"Sure," I said.

"Any chance this dog was once in the FOI?" The FOI stood for the Fruit of Islam, the security arm of the Nation of Islam.

"Yeah, as a matter of fact—"

He didn't let me finish. "AK?"

"Yep," I said. Al was indeed a member of the Nation of Islam. He had flunked out of a drug detection/man-trailing security program because of some hygiene issues and was adopted by my old client Walanda, the one who got murdered.

Al rolled over, woke up, and did that turbo basset thing where he shakes and twists and flings his drool all over the place.

"AK baby, AK baby!" the black cop said.

Al's tail went crazy and he started barking. The white cop even smiled.

"He still shittin' and pissin' all over the place?" the black cop asked.

"Of course," I said.

He smiled.

"Take good care of him, huh?" he said. Then he nodded to the white cop and they ushered the slackers to what I'm sure was going to be a poor substitute for their Vegas vacation.

Al and I moved up in line. He was awake and sniffing and twisting and turning again. The next guy in line was a beefy middle-aged salesman type who just stared at us.

"What was that all about?" he asked.

"My dog found some pot," I said.

"No, the Nation of Islam part."

"Oh, my dog was part of their security force for a while as a search-and-rescue, bomb-sniffing, and drug-detection dog. He got thrown out of the force for bad hygiene, but one of the members kept him as a pet. When she got murdered I adopted him," I said.

The guy just stared at me again.

"You lead an interesting life, don't you?" he said.

I just smiled.

CHAPTER FIFTEEN

SINKOFF DIDN'T MIND the heat. It reminded him that he was a soldier and one with a job to do. He also didn't mind the long ride for his twice-a-month shift guarding the border. Somebody had to stand up.

He was in charge of the four men who traveled with him. Two were ex-military, and the two others were young guys who were gung ho but didn't have the training. They were raw, unproven, and eager, but Sinkoff just didn't give them as much responsibility and treated them as junior members.

The rules were clear: Each member carried a flashlight and a walkie-talkie. If a Mexican national was spotted attempting to enter the country illegally the members were to ask him to halt (which they knew would be futile) and then call their captain on the radio. The captain would then immediately alert the US Border Patrol. The crew would then decide if they would intervene in an orderly and lawful way by making a citizen's arrest. These arrests were to be non-violent and as nonconfrontational as possible. In a sense, they were to ask the Mexicans to detain themselves.

Though it was the official line, the members groused about it. Sinkoff didn't in front of the men who reported to him, but among the organization's officers he often spoke off the record about taking "real action." Everyone knew what he meant, and all of them felt the same way. Sinkoff was confident that he knew what was right and that he had God's blessing to do so.

This was the first patrol in which he carried a gun. In the past, there were rifles in his trunk—all legal and none requiring registration. They were there for hunting and practice on the range. He never mentioned them to the men, though when he went into the trunk to get something out of the cooler he didn't try to hide them either. It was his tacit way of letting people know how he felt.

The small-caliber pistol was concealed in an ankle holster that chafed his skin already dried by the desert air. Sinkoff didn't think he'd use it, but it made him feel better to have it and less impotent. He felt more authentic with a sidearm when it came to being a military man, and he spent time working up scenarios in his mind about what it would take for him to draw it.

He thought of a scenario where one of his men was in grave danger and he needed to kill an alien. He thought of a case where the aliens drew on him thinking he was unarmed. He thought about aliens entering the country with the intention of committing other crimes and forcing them to stay put while he held the gun on them.

But that wasn't all Sinkoff dreamed about.

He loved his country and he hated the way it had been bastardized. He hated the nerve of "undocumented" workers taking jobs away from real Americans and having the nerve to claim they should receive the privileges of real Americans. He hated their total lack of effort to learn English and their refusal to adopt the American culture. They wanted the benefits of this country without the work and with continued loyalty to the land they had escaped from.

Sinkoff ran this through his head as he walked along the border; the dust and sand caused his eyes to water and his skin to tighten. He fantasized about drawing his weapon and taking matters into his own hands. He dreamed of doing the right thing—even if it meant *going outside the law—because it meant serving the greater good of the country he loved. He thought about defending his country and his fellow Americans from the erosion of values that he held dear.*

And he fantasized about shooting and killing the Mexicans that no one would ever miss.

CHAPTER SIXTEEN

DESPITE HIS HERO status, Al still hadn't settled down. He was distracted, looking back and forth and stopping and starting as I left the ticket counter. Thankfully, once they checked my tickets and ID and looked over his service dog documentation, they paid very little attention to us.

The airport was set up with the ticket counters on the first floor and the security checkpoints and the gates on the second. I was wheeling my bag and leading Al on his leash, which wasn't the easiest thing in the world to master. Al kicked up the challenge factor by wanting to run behind me and confront every suitcase that was demonically rolling on wheels. Each time he did, my rotator cuff nearly tore off. As we approached the crowded escalator, Al surged at a gigantic wheeled duffel bag being dragged by a college kid. It spun me around and my feet got caught up in my own suitcase and I fell on the ground.

"Jesus fuckin' Christ!" I yelled at the top of my lungs. I had let go of Al when I fell and he had seized the opportunity to jump on the duffel bag. That was inappropriate enough, but Al had just gotten started. My anxiety service dog then started to hump the poor guy's defenseless bag.

Tom Schreck

"What the hell?" the college kid said. He said it without anger. More with amazement.

I grabbed Al by the collar and dragged him off the traumatized duffel.

"What the hell is the matter with you?" I yelled.

Al turboed the slobber out of his cheeks, and part of it landed on the duffel, part of it on the kid, and the rest of it on me. Reflexively, I went to wipe it off, and with that Al sprang on the duffel bag again and started working his basset lovetron. A semicircle of harried travelers had stopped rushing to their flights to look. It was like the proverbial bad car wreck and they had to look.

I wound the leash around my hand and pulled back hard, trying to stop Al's unrequited love actions.

"Stop being such a fucking asshole, would you!" I yelled at him. His service dog vest had flipped around and now covered his belly. I bent over to right it and Al abruptly sat up and head-butted me in the forehead.

"Motherfucker!" I yelled and grabbed my head. Al sprinted away from me—probably after another really hot piece of luggage. As the stars faded in my head, I looked around to see a whole host of people looking at me like I was some sort of scientific curiosity. "Man dominated by hound" or something like that.

I could hear Al's barking echoing across the tiled airport. I grabbed my bag and headed off in his direction. I was trying to figure out a polite way of getting through the crowd to the escalator when the group of people in front of me let out a collective *"Ugh!"*

The crowd separated, with each traveler's face a mask of disgust. As the crowd parted, there was Al, my anxiety service dog, in his trademark squat, leaving a five-pound present for all the busy sojourners to forever treasure.

Al was bent over and squinting the last pound of waste from his innards. He took a meditative cleansing breath and then confidently strode away from the big steaming pile with pride.

Let no one say that Al had not accomplished anything today. With apologetic smiles I took care of the cleanup and joined Al at the TSA checkpoint.

At the security stop they actually patted Al down. He growled but didn't bite anyone and passed through remarkably quickly. Fortunately Al didn't have a nail clipper, a cigarette lighter, or a five-ounce container of shampoo, because that undoubtedly would have caused a ton of trouble.

We got inside of the plane early because, well, I was a passenger with special needs. I took the very first seat on the aisle and got comfortable with Al at my feet. He immediately commenced with his chronic sleep apnea–induced snoring and proceeded to roll over on his back with all four legs in the air. I wasn't exactly sure how this was supposed to "service" my post-traumatic stress, but I was feeling okay for the time being.

Then the non-special-needs passengers started to file in with their suitcases, briefcases, and duffel bags, and Al sensed danger. The first group in was three Franciscan friars decked out in those brown getups that looked like dresses. It dawned on me that they'd make damn good travel gear and I made a mental note to think about getting me some for the next flight. There had to be a Franciscan.com outlet store or something. They took the three seats in the row across the way from me and immediately buckled in.

Al rolled up and did the turbo slobber removal thing all at once then alternated between growling and barking at each person who boarded the plane. A group of those older women who wear purple outfits and big red hats got on the plane, all of them in a spirited mood. The first one through was another croissant short of three hundred fifty pounds. She thought it was cute to start singing "Hound Dog" when she saw Al. Al loves Elvis, but he hates to be patronized, and he gave her several aggressive barks to let her know he didn't care for her condescending attitude.

"Isn't he a cute, fat little thing," she said, oblivious to the irony.

The big purple lady went to scratch Al under the neck.

"Please don't—" I didn't get to finish, though I'd tried to warn her.

You see, I once left the TV on while I took a shower, and when I came out, Al was snarling, growling, and showing his teeth to Barney the dinosaur on public TV.

He hated Barney.

Al took the well-intentioned neck scratch as an affront to his canine identity and dove for the fat around the woman's ankles, or where they should have been. Her stovepipe legs were ankle-less and the fat gathered around the top of what had to be quadruple E flats. Al took a quick snap, and the woman screamed and tipped over into the row of Franciscan friars across from me.

"Jesus H. Christ!" the aisle seat father said. I had to believe the good Lord would've forgiven him. She ain't heavy, she's my red-hat sister notwithstanding, the guy was now supporting about three hundred fifty pounds on his lap.

"Oh my God! He bit me!" my new friend said. Her red hat was in the space in front of the second friar and her purple stretch pants and purple blouse had separated to reveal a milky white, doughy midsection with more rolls than a Chinese acrobat. Al had backed off but was still humming a low, level growl, and he remained hypervigilant, just in case the Barneylike creature disrespected him again.

I think every traveler should have an anxiety-calming service dog.

Miss Barney eventually righted herself and took her seat after she gave Al and me a dirty look. Al was panting, but other than that he actually seemed pretty pleased with himself. All the excitement had taken its toll and by the time the plane taxied to the runway Al was snoring over the roar of the jet engines.

CHAPTER SEVENTEEN

THE FLIGHT GOT a little bumpy over the desert, but other than that it was pretty smooth sailing. Because we were the first ones on we were the first ones off, and deplaning went smoothly. Al had a prance to his step and was excited at all the new sounds, sights, and especially smells.

It goes without saying that McCarran Airport is much busier than Albany International Airport, Albany's "International" status notwithstanding. We were just off the plane and walking past the second gate from where we landed when I saw a Mexican-looking guy holding a handwritten sign that said, "D. Dombrowski." It was on a card that featured the letterhead from "Appaloosa Ranch and Spa."

"I'm Duffy Dombrowski," I said. The guy nodded and turned and started to walk. I assumed I was supposed to follow him.

We took a tram to another part of McCarran to get my bags, and when I went to get my bag off the conveyor he grabbed it out of my hands. He didn't do it like a servant, nor did he do it with resentment. He was comfortable with his job, but it still made me uncomfortable.

Al snarled at a wheeled bag or two, and once or twice I had to pull hard to get him away from a good-looking duffel bag, but mostly he was agreeable. The baggage area had a really high ceiling and all around it were advertisements for the shows on the Strip. One big billboard featured an ad for someone who called himself "Better than the Original—The King at a New Level." The photo was of a guy who looked remarkably like Elvis.

The billboard was offensive.

I don't expect everyone to get that. Elvis has meant a lot to me for a long time and I take how he is treated personally. This rubbed me the wrong way.

My chauffeur—and boy, let me tell you, this was the first time I'd been able to use that expression—led us through some sliding doors where his black Town Car waited. Al and I went through the doors into the afternoon sunlight and *pow!*

The heat punched me as hard as any fighter. It was the kind of heat you feel when a city bus starts up in front of you on a hot summer day. I could feel the skin on my palms tighten.

"Holy shit, it's hot!" I said, just to say something.

"One oh three today. They say tomorrow it will be one eleven," the driver said. They were the first words he said to me.

"You're telling me it's getting hotter than this?"

He just smiled.

He opened the back door for me. I felt a little confused then realized I was supposed to sit in the back. Al didn't hesitate, apparently far more comfortable with the lifestyles of the rich and famous than I. He jumped up ahead of me, spun around twice, and rested his nose on the backseat air-conditioning vent. I got in behind him.

We went through a covered area of the street leading into the airport and then took a right onto the arterial that brought us out onto the highway. That was the first time I saw the Las Vegas skyline, and like whenever you see something that you've only seen in pictures and TV, it looked odd. From a distance it looked like some force dropped this playland from outer space into the middle of the desert. There was no green. The desert and mountains of red rock formed a backdrop for shiny, mirrored skyscrapers.

I recognized the Mandalay Bay and the hotel next to it, the Luxor, which was a gigantic black pyramid. For whatever reason it had a sign for Absolut Vodka draped over one entire side of it. The enormous emerald-green MGM was right next to these two, and the New York-New York with its weird facsimile of the Manhattan skyline—minus the World Trade Center—was across the street. In the distance I could see the iridescent Mirage, an Eiffel Tower, and, way off, the Space Needle–type design of the Stratosphere.

I couldn't believe I was here to work.

The driver skipped the exit for Las Vegas Boulevard and continued out onto another highway. I was under the impression that I was staying on the Strip, or at least by it, in some sort of compound for fighters. As we drove we went past more casinos like the Palace Station and the Orleans, but he didn't slow down at all.

"Hey—where are we going?" I asked, trying not to sound ungrateful.

"Paradise Springs. It's about thirty minutes away," he said.

"I'm not staying on the Strip?"

He looked up into the rearview mirror, shook his head a little bit, and smiled.

We drove out away from the Strip through a barren area. The desert was like something I'd never seen before. It was stark, but beautiful in a way much different than the Catskills or Adirondacks that I was used to. Al was snoring and it seemed like a long ride, but when I looked at my watch we had only been driving for twenty-five minutes.

We pulled off at a small intersection and headed around a turn onto a one-lane road. I saw a small sign that said, "Appaloosa Ranch, two miles." We headed in the direction the sign pointed and soon, coming into view in the middle of nowhere at the bottom of a small hill, was what looked like a camp made up of trailers, doublewides, and modular homes. There looked to be about seven or eight buildings with a couple more in different phases of development. The camp was surrounded by a chain-link fence on three sides and, strangely enough, a white picket fence done up in a kind of Old West fashion in the front. The front gate was Texas-style ornate, and where the gates came together it spelled out two lines of script. The top line read, "Appaloosa Ranch and Spa."

Underneath it, in slightly smaller script, was one word: "Brothel."

CHAPTER EIGHTEEN

SINKOFF FINISHED OFF *his third Red Bull, looked at his watch, and realized it was almost dawn, the time of day that he had to be most alert. As president of the Men of the Moment movement he was conscious of his role as a leader and role model, and no matter what the conditions, he had to stay alert. They would come at dawn or just before so they could get in undetected. They would come in groups, not because they were united, but because it was more difficult to apprehend a large group all at once. They must figure that they would be able to run so that the weaker and slower Mexicans would get caught. They were animals.*

Sometimes they were dangerous animals. Sinkoff had been assaulted by the illegals he was trying to guard the country against. He'd been pushed to the ground by several of them while they ran away, and one time he got punched right in the face by one right in front of what had to be the man's children he was trying to smuggle in. It had angered and embarrassed him so much that he thought about getting all this over with by getting his firearm and wasting every one that he saw at the border and on the streets of his hometown.

Sinkoff's thinking was distracted by a shuffling sound and distant whispering. He turned to his left and shone his flashlight and saw them—six or seven men in dirty jeans and T-shirts, all wearing baseball hats.

"Alert—we have a code M." Sinkoff spoke quietly but deliberately into his walkie-talkie. He gave the men the coordinates of where he spotted them. Sinkoff then called the Border Patrol and ran to stop the illegals from coming in.

He trotted with his backpack riding uncomfortably up and down his back and his flashlight shining up and down the dusty landscape. "Halt!" he yelled as he approached the men. Usually this just made them all scatter and run faster, but this time the seven of them—he could tell now that there were seven of them—froze and looked in his direction. He could hear his men running behind him to catch up and offer him assistance.

"You are on US soil illegally," Sinkoff said as officially as he could. "You will be detained."

The men talked quickly among themselves and then, unexpectedly, they all charged Sinkoff. The seven men bolted right toward him, closing on him much faster than Sinkoff's own men, who were still off in the distance. The biggest of the Mexicans was heading toward him screaming in a crazed state.

"Freeze!" Sinkoff yelled, but even as he did he sensed his own panic.

The Mexican man leaped and tackled Sinkoff and threw him to his back. The air rushed out of Sinkoff and he felt the tight pain of not being able to breathe. Then the Mexican threw three punches to Sinkoff's face while Sinkoff's men were still fifty feet away. Sinkoff remained conscious, but just barely, and blood flowed from his lower lip and from his eyebrow.

"Ahora!" one of the other Mexicans yelled, and with that the attacker sprinted away from Sinkoff in the opposite direction from the approaching men. Sinkoff was still struggling to breathe and he couldn't yet stand up when the first of his men reached him.

"Andy, my God, are you alright?" he asked Sinkoff. He looked down and noticed that Sinkoff had wet himself during the beating.

"I'm alright," Sinkoff managed. The four other men gathered around him.

Sinkoff was able to sit up and finger the blood from his face. His men formed an uncomfortable circle around him. Not one of them had any idea what to say.

Sinkoff swore he would never feel like this again.

CHAPTER NINETEEN

"HOLD IT. THIS isn't right," I said. "This isn't the right place."

"Yes it is, sir. These were my directions," the driver said, looking straight ahead. He seemed very bored.

"*Yo no horneo para su* hookers," I said, hoping my attempt at his native tongue would help to reason with him.

"What?" The driver wrinkled his brow at me in the mirror, shook his head, and looked annoyed.

"I'm not looking to get laid. I'm here to box."

"Yeah, I know." The driver got out and grabbed my bag from out of the car. Al sniffed at the desert.

"You're sure?" I said. "*Ese es un casa?*"

"Look, this is the place. You speaking the worst Spanish ever isn't going to change this place from a whorehouse." He raised his eyebrows as if to say, "You got it?"

"Follow me," he said and headed for the gate.

He hit a buzzer and the gates opened. I followed behind and Al came along, reluctantly leaving the new and fascinating smells. The main building was a prefab house on a slab of concrete painted a faded pink. The windows were all covered with burgundy draperies so you couldn't see in. I guess this made sense.

We went in the front door and I immediately noticed the temperature dropped about twenty-five degrees. I also noticed the stale smell of smoke that used to permeate every New York bar until the no-smoking laws took effect. The place was deodorized with a very heavy lilac scent that hung in the air. The foyer, if you could call it that, was a small, draped-off area with the same burgundy-colored fabric that I saw through the windows. A printed sign said, "Welcome, your pleasure is our business." And in very small letters underneath that title it read, "Management reserves the right to refuse any patron for any reason."

Good to know, I thought.

The driver picked up a wall phone and said, "He's here," followed by, "Okay." He led me through the curtain to a sitting room lobby area where the lilac smell was even heavier. Two women were sitting on an overstuffed, gaudy, dark blue velvet couch that had to be from "The Classic Whore Collection" at Raymour and Flanigan. One of the women wore a bright white spandex bodysuit with platform silver shoes. She had impossibly black hair, a dark complexion, and dark red lipstick outlined with pencil. She was about thirty pounds overweight and slouched back on the couch.

Her friend wore a red baby-doll kind of thing like Ginger from *Gilligan's Island*. She was skinny and blonde with pale white skin and very large, very circular, and very unreal-looking cleavage. She was sitting with her legs tucked up underneath her, smoking a cigarette. As she took a drag I couldn't help but notice that she had very prominent front teeth.

Next to the lobby and down a couple of stairs was a bar with about ten stools. Behind the bar was a heavyset black woman also sporting a very large set of breasts that were stuffed into a halter top. Her belly fat spilled out over a rectangular belt buckle that read "SEXY." At the bar was an older but fit redhead dressed in a cowgirl getup complete with a gingham blouse tied above her belly button. She was smoking a cigarette and leaning her head into her hand while her elbow rested on the bar. There was a big guy in a grey suit jacket, black shirt, black pants, and Gucci loafers reading the sports page at the stool closest to the waitress railing. His hair was thinning and he looked like he could've been Ernest Borgnine's slightly stronger and better-looking brother. He looked up from the paper.

"Duffy?" He said it with a mild Eastern Bloc accent.

I turned in his direction.

"Yeah," was all that came out of my mouth.

"You brought a dog?"

"Yeah," again was all I could muster.

He shrugged as if to say, what the hell.

He was out of his seat and walked over to me. He looked me up and down, which was something I guessed he did a lot of considering he hung around a brothel and booked sparring partners. He extended his hand and shook it with a firm grip that let me know this was a guy who had some power.

"I'm Stan," he said. He didn't smile, but that was okay, a lot of guys in the boxing business didn't smile.

"Nice to meet you, Stan. Thanks for calling for me, though I have to admit I didn't realize I would be staying in a, a…uh…"

Stan finished my sentence for me. "Whorehouse. That's what it is. It's a whorehouse. They're legal here. It's just like owning a fish market," he said. I found the choice of "fish market" a curious one.

"Where's my room?" I asked.

"Room? Son, you don't have a room. You have a three-bedroom doublewide. It's going to be the party house when it's done, but until then it's where the sparring partners will stay," he said. The irony that Stan was in both the boxing and prostitution businesses was not lost on me.

He told me to follow him and we went out a side door marked "Emergency Exit Only—Alarm Will Sound." Nothing sounded. We crossed a dusty twenty-by-twenty space with some sagebrush to a stark-looking prefab. It was one of those you see up on blocks in a parking lot with ten other models. For a guy who lives in a converted Airstream trailer it was a step up.

Inside it smelled of new carpet and sawed wood, which set off Al's nose again. I had a spacious bedroom with a king-size bed, refrigerator, dresser, and a window air conditioner. I also had a mirrored headboard, a mirrored sliding closet door, and a mirrored ceiling. I love myself, but not that much.

Al stared suspiciously at the identical basset in the mirror and started to growl, warning the son of a bitch that he better back off. When he didn't, Al lunged and bonked his nose, yelped, spun around, and lunged again. Al didn't appreciate this interloper in his territory. He was about to do it again when I spared him and the mirror any further damage by sliding the closet door open. Al looked confused, barked twice, and then swaggered away knowing he had scared his opponent away.

"Here's how it works," Stan began. "I'm gonna pay you after each sparring session, but only two hundred fifty dollars. That'll come to about five hundred per week. Then if you don't run out on us, give us good work, and don't get hurt, I'll give you the balance of the two grand at the end of camp."

"Sounds cool with me."

"Another thing—and this is between you and me. If you knock him down, legitimately knock him down, you get a bonus. How's ten grand sound? It'll make you work hard."

"Ten grand sounds great." The fact that Rusakov had never been dropped by much better fighters than me left me less than totally optimistic.

"Be ready to go to the gym in a half an hour," Stan said. He didn't ask, he didn't offer, he commanded.

Well, I was here to do a job, not to see the sights, so I guessed it was time to go to work. I unpacked my gear and rearranged my duffel bag to bring to the gym. I felt more like getting a beer and seeing what Las Vegas was all about, but I guessed there'd be time for that later.

CHAPTER TWENTY

HE WAITED OUTSIDE *Johnny Tocco's underneath the small awn-*
ing at the bodega. The awning only covered half of him and he could
feel the heat come through the soles of his running shoes. He watched
them come to the gym in the middle of the afternoon at the hottest
part of the day, oblivious to the heat and oblivious to the fact that
their careers in boxing were not going to get them anything more
than punch drunk.

A couple of lightweights came around the corner. Even though it
was over one hundred degrees outside, they were wearing brand-new
Everlast warm-ups. The famed boxing company gave their gear to
up-and-comers they thought might make something of themselves,
usually focusing on tough guys who had very little defense in the
ring. That was what "real Mexican" fighters did. They kicked ass, got
their asses kicked, and wore the scars and deformities on their faces
with pride. It was yet another reason to hate them.

They were the brothers, Jesus and Hector. Jesus was already a
champion, and the younger brother, Hector, was on his way up. They
called Jesus the "People's Champion" or "El Campeón del Pueblo."
The two made big money for Mexicans who bet on them, but because
they weren't heavies or pretty-boy welters or middles they didn't get
paid much. He smiled as he felt the ankle holster on his right leg. It

itched, but he liked the minor discomfort because it reminded him that he had the piece with him. He smiled again knowing what was coming. His reverie was jarred when a white Escalade pulled up in front of the gym.

The driver did a three-point turn right in front of the entrance so that the passenger side was closest to the doors. The license plate read "SBH-1." From the passenger side a large, muscular man emerged wearing a blue Boss warm-up. He barked something short to the driver, who responded by quickly pulling away. The big man disappeared inside.

He wondered how this would complicate his plan. Then he realized it could only sweeten the deal. Ten minutes later, an Econoline van with the plates "SBH-7" pulled in and another large white man got out. He wasn't as big as the last guy and, in contrast to the last man in his stylish Boss warm-up suit, this guy had on cargo shorts and a shirt that said "Schlitz Happens."

The man shook his head. He found it interesting that a couple of Anglo heavies were training at Tocco's. But this was Vegas and things often didn't make sense. He thought again about the gun and the lightweights and making another trip to Red Rock Canyon that night in the cool of the evening.

He smiled and walked away.

CHAPTER TWENTY-ONE

JOHNNY TOCCO'S IS one of those legendary boxing gyms. It opened in the fifties and it remains a gritty, *real* place to train. It was very much like Gleason's in Brooklyn or Kronk in Detroit, not so much in appearance but in feel. I was proud to be here and to be here because I was *hired* to be.

"I'm Duffy Dombrowski," I said to the first guy who looked like a trainer. He was a fortysomething black guy with thirty pounds of hard fat over what used to be a fighter's frame. His eyebrow formed a thick ridge with scars breaking up the pattern of the hair. Looked like he had more than fifty fights and cut a lot for a black guy, which was kind of unusual.

"Hey, nice to meet you. I'm Frankie Camden. You train with Smitty back east, right?" he said. He wiped the corners of his mouth with his thumb and index fingers. His hands were huge, almost like talons, and they looked like they were formed with the exclusive purpose of making a fist.

"Yeah—how do you know Smit?" I asked.

"I fought in New England when I was in the game. He usually handled guys who would come over from New York."

"You must've fought the Horn brothers at some point. You fight at middle?"

"I started at one forty-seven and finished at one seventy-five but did most of the work at one sixty. I fought Frankie a couple of times and sparred with Chris once. I won one and drew with Frank." He paused to check out what was going on in the gym. A couple of small Mexicans were finishing up.

"You better get loosened up. I think you're going to work soon," Frankie said and nodded to the ring.

"Who do I report to? I'm supposed to work with Rusakov," I said.

Frankie looked like he ate some spoiled meat.

"What?" I asked.

"Russian motherfuckers...pain in my ass," he said and shook his head. "You probably want to check in with Constantine. He's the one over there that looks just a little more miserable than the others." He pointed to a group of four men who formed a semi-circle around a big fighter getting taped.

"Thanks, Frankie, nice meeting you," I said.

He nodded and headed over to the locker room.

I walked over to the group and introduced myself.

"Hi, I'm Duffy," I said.

I got no response or acknowledgement from any of them.

"Should I get loose?" I said.

One of the four men looked at me like you might if your attention got diverted by an insect.

"Excuse me, I—"

The guy in the middle cut me off. "Get loose," he said without looking at me or taking his eyes off Rusakov's hands. He looked sixty with a hard face that looked like it was in a perpetual scowl. He had black hair combed straight forward and cut in a bowl shape. He wore black dress pants, a plain white undershirt, and dress shoes.

The other three guys wore cheap dress clothes, like the kind of shirt-and-pant combinations you get at Kmart. They all did the same funky comb-forward thing with their hair and as a group they stank of cigarettes.

I decided that I shouldn't wait around for hugs and started to wrap my hands. Rusakov got into the ring and started to move around. He wore a team tank top from when he was in the Olympics. He won the silver but was universally acknowledged as the best heavyweight. The Cuban won a bad decision that year.

I didn't have an Olympic team uniform.

I was loosening up in my Schlitz Happens T-shirt, and in the heat it wasn't long until I broke a sweat. My muscles still felt cramped and I was a little dehydrated from the plane and probably from the change of climate as well. When Boris or Vladimir or whatever the hell his name was called for sparring to begin, I was a little startled. None of my new Eastern Bloc best friends offered me any help getting laced up so I called to Frankie, who came right over. "Ray of fuckin' sunshine, ain't they," he said.

"Money's good," I said.

"Look, Duffy, these motherfuckers do it differently. Be ready the second you get in there 'cause he gonna come right for you."

CHAPTER TWENTY-TWO

I WASN'T SURE what that meant. The boxing world is full of unspoken codes. One of them is that when you spar with someone for the first time, especially when you're helping someone get ready for a fight, the process starts out slow. You get to know each other's styles and you pace yourself into a workout. Sparring is preparation, and sometimes hard preparation, but its point is different from that of a fight. In other words: sparring gets you ready for a fight, but it's not the fight.

Frankie buckled my headgear and got me laced up with a pair of eighteen-ounce Everlasts. They were the best safety sparring glove and they felt good on the hands. Back home we made do with Title or Ringside gloves, which did the job but were much cheaper. It was like the difference between a Chevy and a Caddy and I could feel it.

I climbed through the ropes in the blue corner. Rusakov was taking instructions from his chief second with his back to me. The bell for the next round sounded and somebody yelled, "Work!"

Before we started, I offered my glove to touch up, a universal sign of respect. Actually it must not be universal in Eastern Europe because Rusakov didn't bother to tap my proffered glove. That's okay, I didn't need any more friends, and boxing was filled with weirdos from top to bottom. There's no doubt the guy was a specimen, though. He was at least six feet four inches and he was cut like a bodybuilder. He also had a bad case of back acne and a jawbone that looked like he had a plumber's wrench stuck in his lower teeth. Maybe his mom looked the same way, but it signaled to me that his nutritional plan included more than just vitamins. He was probably a Barry Bonds fan.

He moved like a Euro, though. That is, he was stiff and deliberate and tended to stalk without throwing punches and his guard was high. Neither of us had thrown a punch when I noticed something that pissed me off.

He was wearing ten-ounce gloves.

They had me in eighteens, and even though I was paid cannon fodder, this was bullshit. A ten-ounce glove is a competition glove, and for folks who have never had a pair on, you should know that they're about the size and density of ski mittens. Like it wasn't enough that the guy outweighed me by forty pounds.

"Whoa, whoa, whoa..." I said and put my hands up to signal to stop.

Rusakov stepped in and threw a jab at me that I was able to block only by flailing my left hand in an off-balanced way. He ignored my request to hold up.

I decided to stop trying to communicate my concerns, not out of a lack of assertiveness, but out of self-preservation. Rusakov threw another jab, this time doubling up on it. The first one landed hard on my gloves, but the force of it rocked me back on my heels. I wasn't ready for the speed of the follow-up jab, and it landed solidly on my left cheekbone. It burned like getting stabbed, and I felt almost immediately the usual warmth that comes before swelling. Worse than that, the thud ran down the back of my head and down my neck. This was a shot I'd feel for a few days.

I didn't have a ton of time to think about the swelling on the left side of my face or the dull ache in the back of my head because just then he threw a three-punch combination—a left, right, left to my body. These weren't just sloppy wingers, these were precise punches meant to do damage. The first left hit me on my right side. The right hit the floating ribs on my left side, and the last left hit me in the pit of the stomach and knocked the air out of me.

I was on my hands and knees trying to catch my breath. For about ninety seconds it felt like the world was going to end. Though over the years it had happened to me a bunch of times, it wasn't something you ever got used to. It also wasn't something that logic could overcome. As I tried to tell myself that it would only last a couple of minutes, I gagged, partly because each second of pain had the perceived duration of a week. Despite the boxing gym shame that comes with rolling over on your back, I did just that to make the breathing easier.

My eyes caught Rusakov. He was smirking.

I was glad he was having a good time.

I also guessed that in Russia or Crack-of-my-ass-istan or wherever the fuck he was from, the universal rule of allowing for a bit of warm-up wasn't observed. So much for the celebration of diversity.

I climbed to my feet just as the timer ending the first round buzzed. The little Russian mafia gathered around Rusakov, apparently to go over the strategy for the second round. I listened through the clackity-clack of the consonant-rich conversation and a few laughs. I figured that either someone had just told a how many Crack-of-my-ass-istans does it take to screw in a light bulb joke or I was the subject of the amusement.

I walked over to the corner.

"Hey, fellas, I know you're paying me and all, but I got a request."

The five of them stopped and looked up at me like I was from Mars.

"Any chance your guy here could wear sparring gloves—you know, sixteens or eighteens? Shit, even fourteens would be better," I said.

The four looked at the guy in the center with the Moe Howard hairdo and waited for him to speak. His face didn't change expression.

"Rusakov wears the gloves he wears for the competition in the final two weeks," he said. He didn't look at me, not because he was avoiding a confrontation but rather, it seemed, because I wasn't worth the caloric expenditure to move his head and neck.

The buzzer for the second round sounded and I got my guard up.

Vegas was going to be a real barrel of laughs.

CHAPTER TWENTY-THREE

WE DID EIGHT rounds.

It felt like I had been repeatedly whipped with a gigantic sack of bowling balls. My face hurt and was swollen all over with a few abrasions from where my new buddy Rusakov ran his cuff up the side of my face.

I was standing in the ring pulling my gloves off by myself. It wasn't easy, but once you got the first one off and had a hand free the other one wasn't a big deal. While I wiggled my way out of the various gear, I looked across the ring and saw Rusakov had one guy for each glove, a guy undoing his headgear, a third squeezing the water bottle, and the fourth, the head guy, talking to him.

I was using my teeth to get leverage on my left glove when a guy I hadn't seen in the Russian posse came up from behind me.

"Here," he said and handed me an envelope. "You did okay, but tomorrow we don't want you to lose energy," he said. He was about five feet eight and weighed about three hundred pounds. His face was all pockmarked and his hair looked like Nixon's. I figured him for sixty. Like the rest, there was no introduction, no invitation to go for a candlelight dinner, and no holding hands at sunset.

There were two hundred and fifty dollars in the envelope.

"Whatya get?" Frankie Camden said. He came from the side of me and like a good fighter moved with such economy I didn't see him until he was right next to me.

"Two fifty, but I get two fifty more per session at the end of all this." I didn't mind telling Frankie because it was a fighter-to-fighter question, not a salary question between two working stiffs. Knowing the going rate was kind of how the informal sparring partner union worked. If we all knew what each other made, then there was less of a chance of us getting ripped off collectively. Frankie wasn't a fighter anymore, but I bet he helped guys who made their living being human punching bags.

"Nice. 'Course, you have to deal with those motherfuckers," Frankie said.

"I can deal with it. At least it's very clear they're assholes. I'd rather know they are assholes and deal with it than work for a lot of the fucking phonies in this business," I said.

"Yeah, I can't count the number of guys who slapped me on the back while picking my pocket," Frankie said. "Kid, just be careful. Money isn't everything."

"Yeah." I was pulling my sweat-soaked shirt off and he was walking away. "Hey, Frank," I called to him as he walked back toward a Mexican who was doing a footwork drill. He raised his eyebrows.

"Thanks, man," I said.

He gave me a nod.

I walked over to Rusakov and his group to find out what happened next. They were sitting in a semicircle around him. I went up to Constantine, the main coach, and spoke directly to him, looking him straight in the eye. Even though I knew his name I wanted to fuck with him a little.

"What's your name?"

He was a little thrown by my directness, like I was suddenly changing the rules on how this relationship was going to be. He looked me up and down, sizing me up, and he seemed to be strategizing how best to answer the question.

"I am Constantine," he said with just a bit of hesitation.

"When do we work again, Connie?"

Though I didn't think it was possible, his face went even flatter than it had been. He was off guard and he didn't like it.

"Tomorrow," he said.

I smiled.

"See you mañana," I said.

You gotta pick your victories.

CHAPTER TWENTY-FOUR

THE GYM WASN'T exactly right off the Strip, but now that I was a highly paid fighter I called a cab and told him to take me to there. Because there wasn't a window with a good view of the street, I went outside to bake in the sun and wait for my ride. The sun seared every trace of hydration left in my body, and there was no awning in front of the main entrance, so I just stood there while my body further dehydrated.

My tongue was starting to stick to the roof of my mouth when two Mexican guys came around from the gym's parking lot. They were in the new Everlast warm-ups, which just made me crazy to even think about in this heat, but I forgot about that when they got close.

It was Jesus Medina and his brother Hector. Jesus fought at 135, and to boxing insiders he was considered one of the best pound-for-pound fighters in the sport. He was from Chihuahua, Mexico, and was easily the most popular Mexican fighter. Hector was Jesus's younger brother and a well-respected top-ten light-weight fighter in his own right. Both of them were fighting on the same card as Rusakov a week from Saturday.

I loved watching the brothers fight. Jesus was already a champion, but Hector, a left-hander, was especially fun for me to study.

I had learned a lot from how he turned his opponents and how he never got in position to get hit. The two of them did everything right with a total economy of movement. No one ever accused me of doing everything right in the ring…or for that matter anyplace else.

"Excuse me, Jesus, Hector," I said, not caring that I sounded like a sixteen-year-old girl waiting at Justin Timberlake's dressing room. "I'm Duffy Dombrowski, a heavyweight from New York. I really admire both of you. You two are role models for me in boxing." I realized I was talking too much and I already felt embarrassed.

"Nice to meet you, man," Jesus said, and he took the time to shake my hand and give me that street half-hug move. Hector shook my hand.

"I'm Rusakov's sparring partner for a couple of weeks," I said.

Jesus raised his eyebrows and shook his head while looking at his brother, who also raised his eyebrows.

"That guy is no joke, eh?" Jesus said.

"Yeah, I just found that out," I said.

Jesus slapped me on the back and wished me good luck, then he and his brother went into the gym. I couldn't believe how cool they were despite not knowing me or being great with the English language. Meeting those two had just made my day.

Right after the Medinas went inside my cab pulled up. When I got inside, the air-conditioning felt as great as a cold shower. The driver had grey hair tied into a ponytail and leathery skin like he hadn't never ever heard of sunblock. He asked me to be more specific about where I wanted to go because the Strip was four and a half miles long. I asked him to take me where the action was, and he sort of shook his head like I was an idiot. He drove on and told me he'd leave me at the Flamingo, which was right in the center of everything.

The Flamingo sounded good to me.

He came up from the back of Las Vegas Boulevard by the tram that ran the length of the Strip, and made a right at the corner where Bally's and Bill's Casino were. It seemed to me that the marketing department at Bill's really wasn't on the day they came up with the name for their casino. We made a right-hand turn and there was Caesar's Palace, which was just gigantic, so big that it didn't look like it could possibly be real. It was now after five o'clock and the streets were packed with people in all shapes and sizes, just a constant river of activity moving up and down the street. Ponytail left me off in front of that really cool red-and-orange sign that you see on TV that cascades up into the word *Flamingo*. It looked just as impressive in person.

I decided to just walk up the street and sort of take it all in. There were groups of guys walking with gigantic plastic containers of frozen margaritas strapped around their necks. There were fat people wearing Tevas and T-shirts, sweating in the sun and looking miserable. There were young blondes with enormous boobs sporting tight shirts with sparkly gold lettering on them that spelled out suggestive things like "Easy," "Trouble," or "Expensive."

I wasn't sure what the place was all about, but there was one thing I was absolutely certain of.

This wasn't Crawford, New York.

The casinos were built flush against the sidewalk on this side of the street and frigid air-conditioning blew out of their wide-open entrances, so much so that I actually had a chill. You could walk right off the sidewalk into a casino and a blackjack or craps table without even thinking about it—which I guessed was the point.

I went past the Imperial Palace, which didn't look all that royal up close. In the front of the place you could get your photo taken next to a grotesque-looking statue of John Belushi and Dan Ackroyd as the Blues Brothers. No matter how drunk you were or how poor your vision, there was absolutely no way in the world you could ever think that these statues looked real. I didn't get the attraction. Still, there was a line in front of the place for free photos. People would take shit in a bag if the word "Free" was stamped on it.

I headed back to the Flamingo, and I must've slowed my stride a bit because before I knew it four Mexican guys, each wearing headphones and caps, were handing me what looked to be baseball cards. They had this way of snapping them in their hands with this certain beat and then handing them over. I looked down to read the top one, guessing it was going to entitle me to a two-for-one frozen daiquiri or a picture with the Blues Brothers statue.

This baseball card didn't have a single batting average on it, nor could it be redeemed for a free drink or a five-dollar steak. Instead, it showed a blonde woman who promised me that she and her "Hot Latin Girlfriend" could join me in my room anywhere on the Strip in thirty minutes or less.

CHAPTER TWENTY-FIVE

I turned the card over, and this side featured a very tan woman without a single tan line with her legs in the air and her hands holding her ankles. A strategically placed star kept her photo from being completely gynecological.

"Check it out, man. Check it out, man. She do you right. She do you right," said the short, pudgy Mexican wearing a Knicks hat.

I looked at him as the crowd passed by, some folks bumping into me. Most of the crowd didn't take the cards when the Mexicans went to hand them to them.

"These are hookers, aren't they?" I asked. The question put me in line for the Most Obvious Question of the Year award.

"*Que?*" my new buddy queried.

"These girls are hookers," I said and looked right at him.

"Check it out, man. Check it out, man. She do you right. She do you right," he went back to his refrain.

It dawned on me that my amigo wasn't fluent in English. He had just learned a few catchy marketing statements. I looked down the street and saw there were four or five Mexicans every hundred feet passing out these cards. As I looked on, a fat, drunken college kid with a mop of red hair walked by and yelled "Yeah!" for no reason at all. He was by himself and had a big red stain on his

"Free Mustache Rides" T-shirt. As he staggered from side to side it dawned on me that the cards probably brought in some okay business.

I entered the Flamingo right off the sidewalk, and a few things assaulted my senses all at once. One was the chill in the room from air-conditioning that must've been set at fifty-two degrees. Apparently hot, sticky tourists don't gamble as much as freezing ones. That, or erect nipples were good for that Vegas image. I also noticed the smell of stale cigarette smoke mixed in with a tropical air-freshener smell that was tougher to identify. It might have been coconut or eucalyptus. There was also the ringing and dinging of slot machines, the occasional cheer from the craps table, and the overall chaotic cloud of activity, energy, and frustration that seemed to never leave the casino. The people seated in front of their slot machines pulled the levers and stared like robots while the wheels went around. They weren't the beautiful people laughing and hugging that I've seen on commercials. No, these folks were heavy, wore shoes that closed with Velcro, and more than a few of them were on electronic scooters.

James Bond, Frank, Sammy, and Dino weren't in the house.

I started to move in toward the craps table, but I could still hear my sidewalk friend chattering, "Check it out, check it out." I guess when you only know one phrase it is tough to diversify your pitch. I lingered around the craps table for a few minutes and realized I didn't have the time or the energy to figure out what they were betting on so I did what came naturally and walked back to a small bar in the middle of the casino. It had about eight stools and a bartender with a Hawaiian shirt.

"I'm guessing you don't have Schlitz," I said to the twenty-something. His name tag said both "Eddie" and "Toledo."

"What's that?" Eddie from Toledo said.

"Never mind. I'll have a draft of Bud," I said. "Hey, Eddie, what's with the Mexican guys with the cards outside?" I asked.

"The slappers? Pain in the ass. They litter the place with thousands of those cards."

"People must respond."

"It's Vegas! Of course they respond. And the few bucks the slappers get per day is a fortune to them, so they're not going to stop any time soon."

Eddie from Toledo went down to the other end of the bar to wait on an older couple waving coupons.

The place was hopping, but I was getting that weird feeling you get when everyone around you is partying and having a good time and you are all alone. Vegas was wild, no doubt, but being here by myself was already beginning to feel like an opportunity lost.

I got out the cell phone and dialed AJ's.

"Yeah." AJ picked up on the first ring with his less-than-Dale-Carnegie greeting.

"Hey, it's me," I said.

"Yeah."

"The boys in?" I said.

"Hang on." I heard him pass the phone and then someone dropped it and said "Shit!"

"Who's this?" TC said into the receiver.

"It's me, Duff," I said. It was getting hard to hear with all the casino noise.

"Huh?"

"It's Duff," I said as loudly as I could.

"You comin' in?" TC asked. The collective memory of the Foursome wasn't substantial.

"TC—I'm in Las Vegas. That's why I'm calling."

"Broke, huh? Look, Duff, I'm strapped myself," TC said. "Here, I'll put Rocco on."

"Who's this?" Rocco said.

"Rocco, it's me, Duff."

"You comin' in?"

"Rocco, I'm in Vegas."

"Bullshit."

"I told you guys that the other night."

"Maybe Jerry remembers, hang on." Rocco passed the phone to one of the Jerrys, who dropped it.

"Shit!" I heard two people say together.

"Hello?" Jerry Number Two said. "Who's this?"

"Jerry, it's me, Duff. I'm in—"

"You comin' in?"

"Jerry! Listen to me. Just shut up for a second and listen!"

"Hello?" Jerry said.

"Jerry, get the guys to come out to Vegas. I have a…er…a house all to myself—you guys can stay for free."

"Really?" he said. Then he yelled into the receiver. "Hey! Duff wants us to go to Vegas—says we can stay with him for nothin'!"

There was a weird silence. Probably the idea of leaving AJ's set them off into a panic. It messed with the intricate structure of their time management system.

"Uh, Duff, I'll see what I can do with getting the boys focused."

I wasn't optimistic.

CHAPTER TWENTY-SIX

HE BOTH LOVED and hated the Strip.

He loved the casinos, the history, and the way the money flowed like it was nothing. The expansive casinos, every one more opulent than the next, were amazing products of American disposable income. America was truly the greatest country on the planet.

He loved the smells of the casinos and the technology. He was also fascinated with casino security personnel. They were invisible to the tourists, but they were always there. He saw them because he knew where to look, and when you did what he did you had to be aware of such things.

He loved the women too. Tall and blonde, spilling out of their low-cut dresses and just reeking of sex. They weren't like the conservative women he grew up with who hid their sex behind religion while being sluts on the inside. Here in Vegas, women didn't mind showing the world the sluts they really were. He liked that. He loved having sex with them, but he had no use for them as people.

He neither loved nor hated the much-talked-about desert heat because he was used to it. He laughed at the dehydrated tourists sick from it and took some pleasure in their often drunk discomfort. There were even outdoor bars that had air conditioners here—outside. This was an unbelievable place, the resources unlimited all because of one thing—money.

But he didn't love all of it. The part he detested the most was right in front of him as he walked past Bill's toward the Flamingo. It was the Mexicans, the dirty, fucking illegals passing out advertisements for escort services. They would do anything for money, for shitty money, including shilling for whores. Escorts, my ass.

The chatter, their rhythmic way of slapping the cards against their palms before they handed them over, he hated all of it. Like they took pride in the nasty thing they were doing. It made him sick.

He passed by four of them in a row, all of them wearing flimsy headphones connected to cheap CD players and radios. They were so poor and stupid that they acted like they were living the high life with their headphones on standing directly in the sun in the 110-degree heat. You couldn't see their eyes behind their dark sunglasses, and somehow to them that made them cool, like they had it going on. It angered him.

He focused on the short one with the Knicks hat on. I bet he is a big Carmello Anthony fan, he thought. He listened as he repeated this staccato verse.

"Check it out, man. Check it out, man. She do you right. She do you right."

He had fashioned it into a sort of bullshit Mexican rap, and you could tell he took pride in it. The tourists laughed as they walked on, but the Mexican was too stupid even to know he was being laughed at. He could feel his hand ball up with raging tension. He was good at making a fist, and the desire to use his fists right now was so strong that it felt like a natural drive.

He watched as a man approached the Mexican. He didn't look like a tourist, but he didn't look like a Vegas citizen either. He was in workout gear. He had an athletic build with a flattop hairdo and pale white skin just beginning to show the hint of sunburn. He looked familiar somehow, and then it came to him that he was the fighter he saw earlier at Tocco's. He was asking the Mexican something, like he was curious what the Mexican was doing.

Idiot. He should know the Mexican might as well be mute. He was more like a human parrot that had memorized a few human phrases. He should know to ignore them.

After a quick interaction the white guy turned and walked into the Flamingo and left the Mexican on the sidewalk.

"Check it out, man. Check it out, man. She do you right. She do you right."

It annoyed him more and more as he watched and listened, and he knew he had the rest of his night planned. He hated having to wait, but he knew he had to. It was too light out and there were too many people to see, but it wouldn't be hard to find this man again.

When he returned, just after one thirty, he could feel his breath quickening. He followed the men as they walked away from the Flamingo. They walked down the side of the casino where the trucks unloaded kitchen supplies. How fitting, he thought.

The one he wanted, the one who made that obnoxious chatter, broke away from the others after they said their good-byes.

Perfect.

He ran just a few steps to get within firing range, and before the Mexican left the darkened unloading area he was within fifteen feet of him.

"Hey!" he called to him. The stupid Mexican actually stopped, turned around, and raised his eyebrows as if to ask "What?"

"Check it out, man. Check it out, man," he said to the Mexican.

The Mexican looked confused then startled when the gun came out.

"I'll do you right. I'll do you right," he said in mock mimicry.

The Mexican froze in front of him, making it easy.

Then he shot him, first in the stomach so it would be painful. Then he took a moment to relish what he had done before shooting the crying Mexican once in the forehead.

CHAPTER TWENTY-SEVEN

IT WAS A good thing that I was now a high-priced professional fighter because the two hundred and fifty bucks I got just five hours ago, plus the four hundred I brought with me, was now down to two hundred. I didn't expect to lose a hundred and twenty dollars on the video poker machines built into the bar. I didn't understand how they worked, but I got the impression that if I played them I would drink for free. Three Buds for $120 worth of hitting buttons on a video screen. The problem was that even when I had to give the machine another twenty for one hundred "credits" and then again and again, it didn't seem like gambling.

I also didn't count on the $175 ride back to where I was staying. The cabbie said going to any of the "Ranches" constituted a premium ride and I had to pay more. I did get to listen to Roy, my seventy-two-year-old cabbie with two teeth, age-spotted skin, and shaved head, give his advice about the employees who shared my new residence. Apparently Mona, who I figured out was the woman with the really black hair, was overweight but "as tight as a gnat's chuff." I didn't have any idea what a chuff was, but I had a decent guess. Louise, referred to as "the colored girl," got "as wet as a drowned rat," and Marilyn, the buxom blonde, could "suck the fuzz off a tennis ball." The beer buzz was fading and the cerebral exertion I had to extend to get my head around Marilyn's skill sobered me that much faster.

We pulled up to the ranch, and I had to admit that at night the place looked a little more like, well, a whorehouse should. The neon stood out against the pitch-black sky and the full moon that evening cast a certain glow to the entire desert surrounding the Appaloosa. I went through the front door just to see what the place was like at night in what had to be prime time in the whoring business. Of course, never having procured a professional, I only assumed this was prime time; for all I knew, lots of guys liked to get off right after they watched *The View* because Barbara Walters got them hot. Maybe they would then ask their hooker to speak to them in a lisp or something.

I came through the funky foyer and was hit immediately by the strong smell of smoke combined with that even stronger lilac deodorizer and heard the chatter of a busy bar. It was darker than it was in the afternoon, which I guess made sense. To my right I could see the small bar full of girls talking to the men. It struck me as odd that there was so much talking going on. The guys were actually flirting and trying out their best lines on the hookers while they bought them drinks. I felt a strong urge to remind them that they didn't really have to work up a really great line to score here because just about any line would work as long as you brought your wallet.

It was right around then that through the chatter and the piped-in eighties music I heard a familiar humming. I identified the song, "Sister Christian," and made note of the title's irony while the hard drive in my head spun around trying to figure out what the humming was. The sound started to intensify and I turned to my left to find its source and all at once I knew that all-too-familiar sound.

It was Al. He was lying on his back on the blue velvet sectional. On his left was Mona, whose incredibly dense cleavage was defying gravity as she leaned over and scratched Al's favorite neck spot. She had on a red stretch one-piece jumpsuit and her black Bettie Page hair fell across her shoulders. Al's leg did that crazy spasm thing as he hummed.

Al hummed when he was too tired, too relaxed, or not worked up enough to bark. He was looking at me, but he made no effort to bounce off the couch and greet me as was his custom.

Louise, the dark-skinned black woman with the very large but well-formed backside, joined Mona on the couch. She wore Lycra jeans and a tube top and her hair was in a Pam Grier–style afro.

"How's the stud doing?" she asked, half of Mona and half rhetorically.

Al's hum morphed into a purr. I squinted hard in that way people sometimes do to make sure that what they are seeing is actually happening and not the type of hallucinations that schizophrenics experience.

"He liked his steak, I know that for sure," Mona said with a thick Southern drawl.

"He's feeling sleepy, isn't he," Louise said as she tickled Al's lower belly. "Goochie, goochie, goochie goo!"

Al's purr morphed into a moan. He gave me a look as if to say, "Duff, don't wait up." I started to head back to my doublewide.

"Hey, fighter guy," I heard a female voice call to me.

I turned. It was the redhead who worked the bar.

"You look like you could use this."

She handed me a rocks glass of bourbon. She sort of smiled, sort of smirked at me.

"It shows that bad?"

"I got a half brother who was a pro. Did a lot of sparring for money."

I raised my glass and took a sip.

"Our two businesses have a lot in common," she said, this time with a full smile.

"Hopefully yours is easier on the body."

"Depends on how busy a day," she said. Then another girl at the bar called for her.

"I'm Robin."

"I'm Duffy," I said.

"I know."

She stood looking at me just a little longer than she had to.

After I finished my drink, I continued on to my trailer. As I walked across the bare dirt that separated my house from the business I noticed that I was starting to tighten up. Rusakov could hit, and when I looked at my face in my trailer there was evidence to support my belief. I had three different pinkish spots on my face with a little glove rash on top. It looked like someone had run some sandpaper over my mug in strategic spots, and my entire face felt 15 percent bigger than it usually did from the usual day-of-sparring swelling.

The frigid cold of the casino air-conditioning had my shoulders and back in knots. It was always tough to sleep on nights like this because the body fought the relaxation by pinching me in different joints and muscle groups. It wasn't just exertion, it was also stress to the body and, if I'm truly honest, probably the emotional tension you get from being in the ring with a guy who can really hit. Make that a guy who can really hit who insists on wearing ten-ounce gloves and it's no wonder I felt this way.

I stood in front of the mirror before I went in to the shower. There was even glove rash on several parts of my upper body, on my calves, and under my shoulder blades. Body shots through a sweatshirt, I reasoned, plus the worn-out ring ropes against the back of my legs and back from being worked over in the corners was the probable explanation. It felt like I had been kicked down a long flight of stairs. For five hundred I'd do that, but it might be nice if I kept a little bit more of it.

I bent over to turn the water on and the blood rushed to my head. Nothing strange about that, but when I stood back up it didn't go away. I had to brace myself against the wall. A wave of vertigo swept over me and I almost felt like throwing up. It came with that odd sort-of-in-my-body-sort-of-not-in-my-body feeling and it scared me.

It scared me because I knew it was happening again.

CHAPTER TWENTY-EIGHT

"You wobbled," I heard the female voice say from behind me. I was still standing in my boxers in front of the mirror.

"A knock would've been nice," I said. It was Robin.

"I knocked a bunch of times. When you didn't respond I let myself in. I wanted to make sure you didn't go the Sonny Liston route."

Liston, the former heavyweight champ and the baddest man on the planet before people called themselves that, either committed suicide, OD'd, or was murdered in Vegas, depending on who you believed.

Robin had on jeans so faded there was just a hint of blue left in them. Both of the knees had holes with white strings protruding. The holes were authentic and the skintight jeans hugged her without the contrivance of Lycra. They had that earned comfort look to them. Her cowboy boots and a plain, form-fitting white blouse were about as understated as a hooker gets.

"Heavyweights don't have to make weight like the other divisions. Your body isn't as cut as a middleweight's," she said. I wasn't quite comfortable getting appraised like this.

"Sorry."

"It wasn't a criticism. It was an observation. I like the way you look."

She said it without flirtation. It was odd. It was dispassionate, but it wasn't without interest. Just the same, I put on the robe that hung on the back of the bathroom door.

"I didn't mean to make you uncomfortable," she said. "Is your head okay?"

"My head's fine."

She frowned slightly and nodded.

"My brother was the same way. He's been done for seven years and still gets headaches. Says it's his sinuses. Loses his car keys three times a day."

I took a sip of the bourbon she had poured for me at the bar. The ice had melted, and it had that cool but watery taste.

"What are you doing in here?"

She smiled out of one side of her mouth and then raised her eyebrows.

"I got a thing for fighters."

I just kind of squinted at her.

There was an awkward pause between the two of us.

"I'm sorry. I'll go." The mischievousness left her face.

She turned to the door. Something didn't feel right.

"You don't have to, at least not for me," I heard myself say.

She turned but looked at the floor.

"I'm on my break and I'm sick of the other girls and everyone else who works here. You mind if I have a beer?"

"Beer?"

"Your refrigerator's stocked. You didn't know that?"

She opened the half-size refrigerator that was across from the bed by the TV. Sure enough, it had four or five types of beer, a couple of bottles of wine, and some champagne.

I sat down on my bed, leaning against the headboard with the cheap Southwestern theme. She handed me a Bud without asking. I immediately held it to my forehead.

"My brother used to do the same exact thing."

"Yeah, comes with the business," I said.

She turned on the TV, and there was some late-night infomercial with a British guy bragging about a steam cleaner. She didn't bother channel surfing.

"Don't you want to know about my work? What it's like to fuck for money? What's the weirdest request I get? How much money I make?" She was smiling.

I sipped the watery bourbon and chased it with the cold Bud. The contrast was nice.

"Not really," I said.

She seemed disappointed. I waited for a second. "Actually, there's something I'd like to know."

"Go ahead." She seemed to sit up just a bit straighter.

"Why do you do it?"

She seemed let down by the question. She also didn't seem to like it.

"It's easy. The money's good. Beats the hell out of retail."

I didn't say anything. I just looked at her. I probably looked at her too long.

"No, I wasn't abused by my daddy. No, I didn't run away from home. No, I'm not addicted to crack."

I didn't say anything.

"That was what you wanted to know, right?"

She was right. It just didn't seem right to ask.

"How did you start?" I asked.

She snickered.

"Same way you started. Stan asked me to." She pushed her hair off her forehead. "He saw me at the bar at the Flamingo with some friends and asked me if I wanted to be a cocktail waitress for him. I did, at a strip club. Eventually I started dancing and from there..." She made a sweeping motion with her hand.

It seemed like the story had been told a million times. I got the sense it was sanitized with repetition.

"Stan seems alright to me, so far."

She snorted.

"He did at first to me too."

I let that hang.

"That fuckin' asshole is a pig. He's less than human," she said.

I didn't say anything, but my expression must've changed.

"He was real sweet to me in the beginning. Then one night after dancing a six-hour shift he forced himself on me. He was too big to fight off, and I was too tired..."

"I'm sorry," I said.

"Oh, fuck you. 'Sorry?' In this line of work you get used to it. You learn to shut your mind off." She seemed to anger a bit, almost imperceptibly. "He still demands a blow job when he wants it. The sick thing is I don't even think it's about sex. He doesn't get off half the time. It's something about the power. The ability to be able to do it."

I didn't say anything. I felt a little sick.

She was quiet. She stayed like that for a long time. I still didn't say anything. I couldn't.

"Don't give me that pitying look. You're doing the same exact thing for him," she said.

"Huh?"

She smiled. "Oh, come on, Duffy. He's using you for your physicality. You get used and abused and then they pay you good." Her eyebrows went up. "Tell me you don't get a feeling in your gut when you're done sparring. Like a not-so-right feeling."

I didn't have anything to say.

"It takes something from you. It's something you can't get back," she said.

CHAPTER TWENTY-NINE

WHEN I WOKE up the next morning I thought I'd better go check on Al. He needed to be fed by five thirty a.m. or he alerted the entire western hemisphere. I threw on some cargo shorts and a T-shirt and walked over to the main building with my sneakers untied. I was tight, but I've had it worse. I thought a few Advil would probably do the trick.

I came in the back door by the Dumpsters and walked past the business office. There was actually a time clock with punch cards. It was too early in the morning for me to think about how hookers punched in and out. I came through the set of curtains that separated the business from pleasure parts of the building.

The bar was open and there was a girl and a guy sitting there with no bartender. The guy looked like he was sent over from central casting after someone requested an average-looking man who would be believable in the role of account executive for some nondescript company that shipped consumerables. It was five forty-five a.m. and that was the extent of the action. Maybe this was a town that never slept, but it sure did take a nap because there wasn't anything going down at this hour. That depended, of course, on what deal Willy Loman worked out with his new friend.

I walked to the bar and the girl raised her eyebrows at me in place of saying, "What's up?" I hadn't been introduced to her yet. She seemed to be the youngest of all the women I had seen in the place. She didn't exactly look virginal, but she had the least worn look of any of the women I had seen so far.

"You're up early," Robin said, appearing from the back of the bar.

"What, do you work twenty-four hours a day?" I asked.

"Pretty much. I didn't mean to get all deep on you last night."

"I enjoyed the company."

"Yeah, well, thanks for saying so," she said.

"Hey, have you seen my dog?"

"Last I saw, Mona and Louise were fighting over who was going to sleep with him."

I wanted to respond, but the situation just seemed a little too absurd. Al was in bed with one of two prostitutes. It was early and I had had no coffee, but I'm not sure if I had several gallons of espresso in me it would've made a difference.

"Uh, has he eaten?" I heard come out of my mouth, the double entendre unintended.

"About three thirty he was snorting down a bunch of shrimp cocktails that some guy from Fresno sent the girls. He loved the cocktail sauce." Robin smiled as she spoke.

"Excuse me?"

"This one gentleman always brings some sort of gourmet food with him for all the girls. It's always way too much, so the girls let Al have a feast," Robin said.

I just looked at her.

"After that he was really tired and the place slowed down, so Mona and Louise went to bed and wanted to cuddle with Al," she said.

"Well, then, I guess he's safe," I said. I had eaten a slice of cold pizza in the food court inside the casino before I got in the cab and had slept alone on my lumpy mattress dizzy from being beat up all day. Al was sleeping with one of two professional sex workers because he was tuckered out from eating too much shrimp.

That seemed just about right.

"You must be the fighter," a voice said from behind me. I turned and saw a stocky, middle-aged woman who had to be just a shade under six feet tall. A cigarette dangled from her lower lip. She was wearing a white stretch pantsuit with a pink blouse that her quadruple E cups just spilled out of, and she had red curly hair in that fake auburn color that was so popular. She had on too much makeup and her lipstick matched her blouse. She held a cup of coffee that said "Boss" on the side.

"I'm Duffy Dombrowski," I said and extended my hand.

She left the cigarette in her mouth and shuffled the coffee to her left hand so she could shake. Her impossibly long nails matched the blouse-lipstick combo.

"Lucille Michelin," she said by way of introduction. "You want some coffee?"

I froze. She was the same height, the same build, and her hair was curly. She was just as gruff…but, no, it couldn't be.

"Boy, you want coffee or not? You've been hit too much, ain't ya?" she said. "Honey, fetch Rocky here a coffee, would you please, darlin'," she said, looking toward the bar. Robin went around the bar and disappeared behind a rack of liquor bottles.

"You got any family back East?" I asked.

"Uh-huh, I do. But I don't think you should ask me any more personal questions, boy. We don't even know each other," she said.

Robin handed me a black coffee and smiled at me.

"Look, Rocky, you're part of the business here, so let me give you the official orientation." I marveled at her ability to sip her coffee without removing the cigarette.

"You're welcome over here to have yourself a drink and make yourself at home. You can talk to the girls, but do me a favor and don't fall in love, okay? Above all, keep your eye on the men, but don't ever make them feel uncomfortable. If someone gets really out of hand, straighten their ass out fast with a minimum of disturbance. In other words, hit 'em in the body so it don't show."

"You mean part of this gig is being a bouncer here?"

"We're all bouncers here. We got each other's backs. It's the nature of the work. Just keep your eyes open," she said and exhaled. "Do whatever you want over in your ranch house. We don't care what goes on as long as it isn't loud, doesn't affect business over here, or causes legal trouble," she said.

"I was thinking of having some friends come stay with me," I said.

"I don't give a shit, but the same rules apply. They get no freebies over here, you understand?" I formed a mental picture of the Foursome at the bar with the ladies making Foursome conversation.

"There's food in the kitchen, and feel free to order yourself a beer on the house. Don't get crazy with it because that goes against our bottom line too. There's a shuttle going from here to the Strip from noon to midnight and then it's on call so feel free to get a ride, but just remember, if it comes to you or a customer you'll have to wait," she said. All of this ran off her tongue like it was automatic.

I looked at her and tried to put Claudia's hair and clothes on her. It seemed to work, but I couldn't tell how much I was forcing the image. It felt like that *Seinfeld* episode where they met the bizarro versions of themselves, only this was far more bizarro than that.

"We straight, Rock?" Lucille said. Her cigarette was down to the filter, and she gulped her last sip of coffee. I got the impression that we had to be straight because the end of her caffeine and nicotine meant she was moving on to something else. Before she did, there was just something I had to do.

"Uh, Lucille, can I ask a favor?"

Her eyebrows went up, but she didn't say anything. I got the impression that most people knew better than to ask Lucille for favors.

"I like to put together scrapbooks of my travel. Can you and I get a photo together?"

She looked at me like I was a freak but shrugged and said okay. The bartender did the honors and told me to pick up the print in the business office. If nothing else, Trina would get a kick out of it when I got back.

With that over, Lucille got back to business.

"Girls, girls, get your pretty asses out here. The breakfast club will be coming soon!" she yelled.

I got a refill of coffee and headed to my ranch house.

CHAPTER THIRTY

I WAS HOPING the coffee would wake me up. I also hoped it would kind of normalize how I was feeling. Twenty-four hours ago I was in the humidity of the Northeast working my bullshit human services job and boxing at the Y. Today I was in the heat of the desert, living with a bunch of hookers, and boxing with the very best in the game. My roommate had also left me for the comforts of at least two call girls.

Come to think of it, I didn't think the coffee was going to help me sort everything out. That was a lot to ask from caffeine or, for that matter, any substance.

I crossed over to my house and noticed I had left the door open. Ordinarily that might have been cause for concern, but considering the tight security here at the ranch I didn't give it much thought. As I got closer, I heard the sound of singing, and I stopped at the threshold and just listened.

It was the most beautifully melodic sound I had ever heard coming from a woman's mouth. She was singing "Amazing Grace," and it just came out of her effortlessly. I leaned against the door-jamb and watched as she made my bed and sang at the same time.

She was dressed in the type of maid's outfit that they wear in hotels. It was light grey with white trim around the neck and cuffs.

As she shook a pillow into a fresh case she turned slightly and caught me watching her. She gasped and dropped the pillow. She still had a hand on her chest when she looked at me.

"I'm sorry, I didn't mean to stare. Your voice is beautiful," I said. She had light brown skin and her hair was pulled back in a bun. She had angular features and looked like she could be Salma Hayek's prettier sister.

"No, I am sorry," she said, and she turned away so as not to look me in the eye. "I will hurry and finish up to not inconvenience you," she said. She spoke with a faint accent, but her English was very good.

"You're not inconveniencing me. I'm a little embarrassed, to tell you the truth, having you clean up after me," I said.

She gave me a confused look but went back to changing my pillowcase.

"You don't have to change that. I just slept on it last night."

"We are to change bed dressings daily," she said. "Besides, there was some blood."

"Blood? Oh yeah, this thing opened up a little bit," I said and pointed to the glove rash on my cheek. I didn't remember it bleeding.

"Were you assaulted?" she asked.

"Yes," I said. "But I am a professional boxer."

She made a clicking sound and shook her head.

"What?" I said.

"Nothing," she said. "It is not my business." She changed the second pillow.

"No, go ahead. I'm guessing you don't approve of boxing," I said.

"In Chihuahua, where I am from, all of the young men took up boxing because Carlos was a grand champion. Many got hurt and many failed and were ridiculed. I think it is barbaric," she said.

"A lot of people think it's too violent. Some think it's barbaric. In lots of ways it is. It doesn't bother me, that you think that way," I said. There was something different about her face that made me stare. Then I realized it was her blue eyes that sparkled like they were electric. Against her soft brown skin it made for a striking look.

"The Medina brothers are also from your hometown. They are two—"

She didn't let me finish. "I know of them. I have a little brother who worships them. He looks very much like Jesus and tries to act just like him," she said.

"I know they are heroes."

She shrugged.

"I am sorry to make you wait. I will be done in a moment," she said. She looked shaken.

"Is something wrong? I know I startled you, but you seem very uncomfortable."

"I am not married. To be alone in a man's bedroom is not comfortable for me. Also, I stopped for a moment to look at the newspaper and it upset me. I should just be doing my work," she said. She wore a simple cross around her neck.

"Don't be ridiculous," I said and went over to look at the paper. The headline read: "Mexican Slapper Murdered on the Strip."

There was a series of photos of what seemed to be a dead body in the center of a taped-off crime scene. Another photo showed people who could have been friends or family of the dead man. The third photo was a close-up headshot of the man at the morgue with a hole in his forehead. It was the size of a dime, and I was amazed at how neat and surgical the bullet hole was.

Then it hit me. I got that sick feeling climbing in my stomach. It's that feeling you get when something wrong has happened.

The dead man was the guy from in front of the Flamingo. Someone had killed the "Check it out, man" guy.

"My God, I met him last night," I heard myself say. I looked at the article without reading it. After a long moment I broke my stare.

She was folding a blanket and not facing me.

"Did you know him?" I said.

She stopped what she was doing and looked up at me. Tears ran down her cheeks. She did nothing to hide them or wipe them away.

"I know a thousand like him," she said.

CHAPTER THIRTY-ONE

.

I FOUND OUT her name was Angelina. I was dying to know more about her, but she seemed to like her privacy, so I let it go. Having a maid clean my room felt weird, like having a driver, and I didn't like the feeling.

I didn't want to admit it to myself, but part of my discomfort stemmed from the fact that Angelina was simply beautiful. She had that look that stayed with you all day—not in a cheap sense but in an elegant way that had you longing to be in her presence again. She was physically beautiful, but she was also strong with…I don't know…a certain class to her. I know that sounds funny since she was a maid, but even Al would have approved.

Seeing her cry over the guy in the paper had made me think. And I wanted to get to know more about her.

At around ten thirty, Al waddled into the room. He looked at me briefly, stretched, yawned, and lay down by the air-conditioning vent, first on his side and then completely over on his back. The snoring commenced. I didn't want to think why the basset hound I live with would be exhausted after a night in the Appaloosa Ranch. There are just some things that I refuse to visualize.

It was heading toward eleven and I realized I didn't know what to do with myself. I was a half an hour from the most exciting city in the world living in a house where sex went on constantly and I had nothing to do until two o'clock when I'd go in to the city and get my ass kicked. Life can be strange.

My deep thoughts were interrupted when my cell phone rang with the opening guitar riff of "Don't Be Cruel." It was Trina from the office, and I smiled when her name came up on the ID.

"This conference isn't going so well," she said.

"Cheese isn't showing up?" I said.

"Oh, he's showing up. That's not the problem," Trina said.

"He isn't, is he?"

"Oh, he most certainly is," Trina said.

"How do you know?"

"Monique has a buddy taking the class from the Schorie County Center. She said the class broke up into groups of three to discuss something and one of the women in Cheese's group threw up all over her desk," Trina said.

"Oh, geez," I said.

"And apparently the woman had gone to town on the tabbouleh vegetarian offering at lunch and then, well, Cheese did what Cheese does, you know, er, uh, making the air unbreathable. It made a wicked mess. They had to end early for the day so that the custodian could run that high-powered carpet thing around."

"Did they know it was Cheese?" I said.

"Well, if there was any doubt, he erased it by laughing so hard that he fell out his desk chair."

"Oh, no."

"Then he sweetened the deal by saying, 'Good point, can you bring that up again.' Cheese thought that was a riot," Trina said.

"Oh, no."

"So basically, Duff, it was another of your classic good ideas. And the Cheester has four full days left."

"Oh, no."

"Just thought you'd like to know." Trina switched gears. "How's Vegas?"

"Hard to describe, actually. I got a whole house to myself."

"Wow, right on the Strip?"

"Not exactly." I didn't want to get into a full description of life on the ranch, so I kept it light. I signed off with Trina and immediately called Cheese's cell.

"Yeah," Cheese said when he answered. It might be hard to understand, but with that one-word greeting it was completely obvious that he was baked.

"Cheese, it's Duffy," I said.

"Oh, hey, Duff."

"Cheese, I got word that you're letting them go at the training. We talked about that, man."

"Oh shit, who ratted me out?"

"Never mind that. You gotta stop, Cheese."

"Dude, these people are whacked. They're all self-important and shit and they never stop talking, especially about themselves. It's fuckin' brutal. And I got four more days of this shit."

He was right, of course.

"Look, Cheese, everyone thinks you're me. You can't be laying bombs."

"Duff, this one really fat lady said I had unresolved transference or some shit. She was all confident and was treating me like I'm an idiot. They let these assholes work with people? I just had to send one in her direction, man. I couldn't not."

As strange as it sounded, I agreed with him. Give social workers a chance to talk about themselves and your issues and it gets pretty stinky.

"Was this the lady you made puke?" I said, almost with some admiration.

"Oh yeah, Duff, I got her good. It was the only thing that kept her from fuckin' talking."

I sighed. "Look, Cheese, do your best, huh? I can't have people think I'm the farting social work guy, okay?"

"Alright, Duff, but if she starts talking about my issues again, no promises," he said.

I figured that less-than-iron-clad commitment was the best Cheese was going to do.

As soon as I closed the cell phone it rang. This time it was Jerry Number Two.

"Well, we're comin'," was what he said instead of "hello."

"Jerry, that you? Excellent!" I said.

"Yeah, as soon as I told the boys about the free luxury accommodations, they were in."

"I don't remember saying anything about luxury accommodations," I said.

"Duff, you know the boys. It has to be a super deal or they ain't getting off of their barstools," Jerry Number Two said.

"But Jerry…"

"I'm sure it will be fine, whatever it is," he said.

I wasn't quite as confident as Jerry, but I agreed to meet them at the airport at seven forty-five so we could all hit the Strip together.

Las Vegas would never be the same.

CHAPTER THIRTY-TWO

I THREW SOME clean gear into my duffel and got ready to go to the gym. I had gotten very little direction on how things were supposed to go from my new employer. Whenever that occurred in my life I tended to try to get in a routine. Having been here at the Appaloosa for about a day didn't exactly constitute a routine, but yesterday when I went to the gym I first met Stan at the bar in the main house. That was enough of a routine for this pug, and I headed over. Rusakov's fight wasn't far off, and that meant there was about a week or less of sparring left. Most camps cut sparring way down the week before a fight to reduce the chance of injury and to let the body heal.

Robin was still at the bar, but she had on a new outfit. She wore only a black leather vest up top and a matching skirt with side vents drawn together with leather laces that went all the way to her waist. I did some mental gymnastics and came to the conclusion that this meant Robin had dispensed with undergarments. Her black motorcycle boots finished the ensemble, and all of it against her white skin was a quite dramatic contrast. She caught me staring.

"You like?" she said and did an exaggerated pirouette that eliminated my embarrassment for locking my high beams on her.

"Very nice...Do you know where Stan is?"

Before she could answer, the phone rang, and she raised her index finger to tell me to wait while she answered.

I took in the scene in front of me. There were three men at the bar, each with one of the girls. The men were all giddy and smiles and the girls played right along. I took the last seat at the bar away from what was going on and waited. After what seemed like a long few minutes Robin came down my way.

"Stan doesn't check in with us. Can I help?" she said.

"I got to get to Johnny Tocco's gym. Yesterday we left right around this time and I just figured he'd be around again today."

"Hang on." She went behind the bar and made a call. She was on the phone for less than half a minute. She walked past the customers, smiled and winked and held up her index finger to let them know she'd be right back. Then she came over to me.

"Lucille says to take one of the cars. There's a wall of keys outside her office. Go take a set. The cars are out back beyond your place behind the garage," she said. "And Duffy—keep your guard up, huh?" She smiled.

Having a call girl flirt with you is a strange feeling, but not an entirely unpleasant one. Maybe it becomes a reflexive manipulative thing that they do with all men all the time. Maybe it's a needy thing that has something to do with their choice of profession.

Or maybe she liked me.

I went back and picked a set of keys out of the eight pairs that hung on the wall. I headed over to the garage, but I didn't see any parked cars until I walked around the side of the building. There they were, six polished and gleaming 2011 Lincoln Town Cars. They were gorgeous, and oh yeah, they were pink with "Appaloosa" painted on the rear panels. The keychain had "App5" written on it, and I found the Town Car with the matching plates.

I went to put my key in the door and realized that I had to push a button on the keychain to unlock the driver-side door. The unlocking made a solid clickety-clack sound as all the doors simultaneously unlocked. The interior was immaculate and the leather upholstery was everything that the ads said it would be. The dashboard was not like my '76 El Dorado, but I guess I should have known that technology meant new car controls had a different look since Gerald Ford left office.

And right here is where I'm supposed to talk about the new car smell. Well, it had a little of that new car smell, kind of like the smell of a new leather jacket, but the overpowering aroma was that sickening lilac that permeated every square inch of the Appaloosa Ranch. There must've been some sort of pheromone in the spray that induced horniness in whoever came in contact with it. Actually, now that I thought of it, if you were a passenger in this vehicle you were already pretty horny, so maybe the pheromones were there to induce the reckless spending of money to sublimate one's horniness. That, or maybe the scent somehow induced a feeling within the sniffer that he wasn't a lowlife loser who needed a moral scrubbing.

Driving a Town Car through the desert with the windows up and the air-conditioning on is something for the senses. The ride in this vehicle was absolutely silent except for a little hum from the engine and the whooshing fan sound from the air-conditioning system. The windows had that dark tint that back home was utilized by gang bangers, pimps, and wannabes, but here in Vegas it was clear that shielding one's eyes from the sun wasn't as much about posturing as it was about not having your freakin' retinas burned off. The polarized tint made the beauty of the desert that much more surreal as did the silent, effortless movement of the Town Car through the landscape.

The beauty of the desert stands in stark contrast to the city of Las Vegas in the daylight. Las Vegas is one of the fastest growing cities in the country, and because of that a good deal of the construction is new, almost new, or certainly not older than twenty years. That means everything is devoid of character, what I think of as the strip mall effect or the prefab feeling. When you go through the parts of the city that aren't inhabited by casinos, everything is flat, bright, and boring. Nothing but concrete, steel, and plastic— no ivy, cobblestones, or architecture. Nothing but a sea of Outback Steakhouses, Red Lobsters, and Olive Gardens.

Driving along the highway that runs along the back half of the Strip is weird too. These glorious structures complete with volcanoes, fountains, and fake Eiffel Towers are really just behemoths of cinder block and concrete. The sides that face away from the gamblers look like the back of a gigantic grocery superstore; in other words, it's all shit and shinola without any real beauty holding it up from its core. In many ways, these buildings were exactly like the women at the Appaloosa.

CHAPTER THIRTY-THREE

LONG DRIVES MAKE me philosophical, and for a while at least I was fascinated by my own deep thoughts and all-around brilliance. It doesn't take long, however, for me to start to bore myself with my pseudo-existentialism and to start focusing on the things that really drive Duffy Dombrowski. Namely, I had already started focusing on what I would eat after sparring, how cold the beer would taste, and how cool it was going to be sitting around all of the gorgeous silicon-enhanced women of this fair city.

I passed the gym and took a left down the side street that bordered it leading to the small parking lot. There were a couple of nondescript cars in the lot and the big Escalade with the "SHB-1" plates. That let me know that my new best buddy, Rusakov, and his homeys were inside and waiting for me. I felt my stomach go a little sour from the thought of boxing today.

As much as fighters will deny it, there is often a feeling of dread that goes along with getting in the ring. Part fear, part realization that you're doing something that isn't good for your health, and maybe part laziness fills me before I get in the ring. Often those feelings are then replaced by the exhilaration of the actual fighting and the energy and, frankly, the sheer terror of what I'm doing. But there are other times when the feelings don't entirely go away, and the whole exertion seems like an absurd pain in the ass and a foolish way to spend my time.

I was feeling more like that today than I was all psyched up. Of course, none of that mattered really because I was here as an employee. It was my job to show up and literally serve as a human punching bag for this other guy who got the better hand in the five-card-stud gene pool game.

I could hear the muffled gym sounds as I approached the door. The rat-a-tat-tat of the speed bags, the thuds of the heavy bags, and the indistinguishable yammer of coaches yelling out instructions in both English and Spanish came to life as I opened the door. The punch of humid gym air with the smells of worn leather and old sweat hit me. I only noticed it because it was a different type of stink than I was used to back home. It was the same and different all at once.

Rusakov and his crew were on the opposite side of the ring toward the back of the gym, but the energy and attention was focused on the front corner of the gym. All the guys in this corner were Mexican, and they were all shorter and lighter weights. It set up a strange separate-but-equal thing going on at Tocco's with the cold, quiet Russian bastard on one end and the passionate Latinos on the other, separated not just by gym space but by language, skin color, and culture.

I wrapped my hands over by the Mexicans so I could watch the guys train. I remained a couple of feet back from the main circle of fighters because, well, I wasn't in this group, and in boxing gyms you didn't just join up with a group. There wasn't an application to fill out or a college fraternity initiation thing to get through; it was more something you just sensed.

It was a busy day in the gym, and the roster of fighters blew me away. The Medinas were in, but there were also a whole host of other top-notch guys. Juan Antonio Morales, the featherweight champion, was working the mitts with his trainer and dad, Chico Morales. On the speed bag was the 112-pounder Julio Cante, who was not only a champion, he was undefeated and maybe one of the best pound-for-pound fighters in the game. The fact that he weighed 112 meant he was only known in the Latin communities and in the lighter weight countries like the Philippines, Japan, and Korea. He was a huge hero in Mexico but virtually unheard of in the US. I also noticed all of the Mexicans were wearing red headbands that said "JMM."

The bell sounded to let the fighters know it was time for sixty seconds of rest before the next round. I approached one of the taller, light-skinned guys in the Mexican group who was dressed in a fashionable warm-up but not working out.

"Excuse me," I said, "I'm Duffy." By way of response the guy just looked at me, raised his eyebrows, and slightly tilted his head up.

"What's the JMM headband for?" I said.

"Juan Manuel, he was our friend," he said in a heavy accent with the wrong emphasis on the wrong words.

"Oh, the fighter who was murdered," I said. "I'm sorry...uh... lo siento," I said. My Spanish was worse than limited, but I knew a little and I wanted to show respect.

He gave me a nod.

"Can I get one?" I said.

He squinted and looked at me, dug into his pocket and handed me a folded, satiny headband with "JMM" on the front.

"Gracias," I said and got a nod before he turned away to watch the champions work.

I tied my headband on and did a little shuffle-trot over toward the ring I was going to work in, throwing loosey-goosey punches and skipping along to get warm. I bounced from foot to foot while alternating between shaking my arms, rotating my head, and flexing my jaw. This is called "shaking it out" in the sport, and every fighter did it in one way or the other. Mexican guys like to bounce up and down while throwing tight inside punches, black guys move around more with their feet, and white guys tend to hop up and down in a very basic pattern. Rusakov did this methodical stretching and jumping move where he would do a particular stretch, hold it for the exact same count, and then bound up in the air. I think I read where it was some sort of scientific dynamic stretching plus plyometric thing. I'm guessing neither Joe Louis, Jack Dempsey, nor Willie Pep ever did anything remotely like it, ever.

"Next bell, Duffy!" Constantine yelled.

CHAPTER THIRTY-FOUR

I CRACKED MY neck one last time, went up the stairs, and climbed through the ropes. Rusakov was already there, and when the bell sounded he came straight toward me. I was in my stance with my guard high, and when he stepped in to throw at my body he wound up wide with his left to get power into his hook. It was a fundamental mistake. It left him wide open on his left side. I countered with a hard jab with my right that hit him below his eye squarely on his cheekbone. The shot took him a little off balance, again, a function of his poor stance. I came with my straight left hand behind the jab and that punch landed half on his lower lip and half on his chin.

Rusakov staggered awkwardly then went down with a thud on the seat of his pants.

It happened like knockdowns always do—in an instant. I stood over him a little confused at first and then a bolt of realization went through my brain.

I had just dropped the number-one heavyweight contender in the world with my left hand.

The gym stopped. The Mexicans turned and looked on silently. Rusakov's men stood rigid, staring. The usual rattle and hum of gym noise stopped, not at the end of a round, but right in the middle. Everyone in the gym looked on like Haley's Comet had just passed in the night sky. This was the stuff of gym legend, and when it was a big deal who touched the canvas, it was news. Fighters would talk, trainers would talk, and it would show up on Internet columns. It was going to be a big thing.

Rusakov knew that and his corner knew that too.

"Keep your guard up!" Constantine yelled at Rusakov. It was a stupid thing for a coach to say. Rusakov was sitting on all the evidence he needed to know he had dropped his guard.

It was also a ten-thousand-dollar thing. That fact began to register in my mind in the same way that it must with lottery winners—disbelief, followed by realization, then excitement. I could feel ten grand like it was shot into me with a hypodermic.

But sparring wasn't over.

He was up and back in the center of the ring. I offered my glove to tap—the universal boxing sign of sportsmanship—and once again, he ignored it. Then he threw a jab and then a hook incredibly hard and I blocked both of them.

And then he hit me as hard as I've ever been hit in the balls.

It usually takes a second or two to feel a low blow, but not this time. He threw it way low so that it hit me in an upward arc in the business area. This wasn't a body shot that drifted south of the border; this was a shot aimed at hurting someone. And it did.

In a flash I was on my side holding my nuts and very close to vomiting. I rocked back and forth and squinted hard in reaction to the pain. After a second or two, I noticed Rusakov's feet were still next to me. I glanced up and saw that he was laughing. Through his legs I could see his corner guys laughing along with him.

"Piece of shit," Rusakov said to me as he looked down.

The gym was quiet again, just like it had been seconds before, but it had a different feel to it—an evil feel, like something was off.

I got to my feet and saw more than one fighter shake his head in disgust.

"You ready, Duffy?" Constantine asked.

"Yeah, I'm ready," I said.

From there, Rusakov gave me a beating with his ten-ounce gloves. There were no more low blows, but he hit me on the break, which is a scumbag move in a real fight, let alone with your sparring partner. He hit me after the bell rang in just about every round and cuffed me with his laces enough so that I had little abrasions on both cheeks and on my neck.

Of course, the fact that I just made ten thousand dollars made them sting just a bit less.

CHAPTER THIRTY-FIVE

I'VE BEEN A paid punching bag before. I know that sometimes the guy you're working with isn't terribly friendly. That's understandable. I'm a big boy and can deal with that. But I'd never had another boxer go out of his way to be a jerk about it. Other guys may have been mean bastards, but they knew I was there to work with them and they didn't want to expend the energy around fouling me. Ignoring me took less energy.

In short, Rusakov was a douche bag. I didn't have a Yourcrackistan-English dictionary on hand, but something told me that "douche bag" might have been idiomatic and not understood anyway, so there was no point in saying it to his face.

Finally we finished the eighth round and I headed to my corner.

"I tried to tell you, boy," Frankie Camden said as he approached me. Without me asking he started to undo my laces.

"What a fuckin' asshole," I said as I struggled to get my headgear off.

Frankie quickly glanced at my face and squinted a little, assessing the damage.

"You want ice?" he said.

"Not here," I said, and Frankie nodded.

I was undoing one of my wraps when I heard a commotion at the gym entrance. Two guys in warm-ups decorated with the Mexican flag crossed with the American flag came in wearing sunglasses and earpieces. They were casing the room. The Mexican fighters stopped what they were doing and looked in their direction, and then some of them waved or gave a cheer.

The two bodyguard types parted and then I saw why there was such a hubbub. Carlos de Grande was behind them, the Mexican-American welterweight-middleweight who had just retired and was now working for HBO along with doing cologne commercials and whatnot. He went by "DG" and was one of the very few fighters who had equal appeal among Mexican and American fans. In his career he had fought everyone, never quit, and embodied everything you wanted in a fighter—courage, heart, power, and speed. For a fighter, he was good-looking. No broken nose, no vegetation on his ears, and very little scarring.

The man was one of my idols. Everything he did in the ring was effortless. (Everything I did in the ring was a huge effort.) He glided and had total economy of movement, and his reflexes seemed automatic. Me, not so much. Just seeing him walk in was a thrill. He represented what I aspired to, but knew I could never achieve.

Next to him was his nineteen-year-old son, a 10–0 lightweight who was being groomed for a title. He looked like his dad, but that's where the resemblance ended. He wasn't given a lot of cred in the boxing world because it was pretty obvious that they were booking easy fights for him to get wins. Hey, that's the way the game was played. If you had money behind you, that's the way it went.

"Wow, Frankie, that guy was the real shit," I said. "He was one of my idols—still is. I'm going to go say hello."

I walked over to the entourage hoping to shake hands. As I got within ten feet of him one of the bodyguards put a hand on my chest. It was firm if not aggressive.

"I just want to shake DG's hand," I said, feeling just a little like a schoolgirl.

The bodyguard looked briefly at DG, who nodded. The bodyguard released his straight arm.

"Hey, Champ—it's an honor," I said.

DG smiled and gave me a nod.

"I'm Duffy Dombrowski. I'm Rusakov's sparring partner."

I got another nod just before one of DG's men handed him a cell phone. I walked back to Frankie like a twelve-year-old who just met Lady Gaga.

"Well, there now, you got to meet a hero," said Frankie. He put a fresh toothpick in his mouth. "Be nice to have his cash. The guy carrying his towel made more money in one fight than I did in my whole career."

Carlos was on the periphery of the Mexican fighters with his bodyguards in between him and the fighters. He waved like a politician, made a fist or two, and gave a couple of thumbs ups. Then he waved and went over toward Rusakov's side of the gym. He gave Rusakov a hug and a kiss and then repeated the hug-kiss bullshit with each of the Russians.

"He hangs with the Russians? What's that all about?" I said.

"El Grand Campion has money in Rusakov," Frankie said.

"Huh?"

"And they say politics makes strange bedfellows," Frankie said.

"Ho-ly shit. That's weird," I said.

"And here's another one for you. Constantine handles Junior. He hasn't fought a man with a pulse yet, and you watch, he'll have a title after twenty fights."

"You gotta love this game," I said.

"The fuck you do," Frankie said.

CHAPTER THIRTY-SIX

THE MEN OF *the Moment meeting was about to begin.*

There were seventy-two members in the Las Vegas chapter. Sixty-eight of them were men, and they ranged in age from nineteen to seventy-seven. Fifty-one of them had military experience; most of them were solidly in the middle class socio-economically, with just a handful in the bottom of the upper class. Not one of them was working class. All seventy-two members were white.

The Men of the Moment mission statement read:

Our one goal is to preserve an America for Americans and to do all we can to stop the forces that threaten that goal.

Andrew Sinkoff was the founder of the Las Vegas chapter and the current president. He was very careful what he said in public and when speaking on behalf of the MOTM. His informal conversations with fellow members, which he considered safe, were a different matter. Before the meeting came to order he was talking to Derek Dobson, one of his young, twentysomething members. Both had served in the Marine Corps. Neither had left the United States during their tours of service.

"That Italian joint in the strip mall off Sinatra has a whole slew of 'em. They're doing the dishes, the cleaning, and the cooking. The

only thing Romano don't have them doing is working on the floor or behind the bar. Fuckin' hypocrite," Sinkoff said.

"Why can't we pay him a visit, Andy? Let them know it ain't okay, no matter whose name is on the sign in front. I'll do it, just give me the word," Dobson said.

Sinkoff loved interactions like this. It reminded him of his days in the corps. He loved the strict chain of command and the uniformity of purpose. Now in his late fifties, the MOTM movement gave him a chance to relive some of that life he had so loved.

"We need to stand down, my friend. We're too visible as it is. There will be a time and a place." Sinkoff winked and smiled at him. He felt very much like a mentor to Dobson and the other younger members. At twenty-five and still in the reserve, Dobson was the perfect younger member. He got the mission but also knew how to keep quiet and under control.

Sinkoff called the meeting to order and the group recited the Pledge of Allegiance. The banquet room of the American Legion was three-quarters full, even though it was 104 degrees that day.

"Gentlemen, I thank you all for coming," Sinkoff started. His tone was formal in the way an officer would address his NCOs. "We are all united and all committed to preserving this nation—the strongest, most righteous nation in the history of this planet—and seeing to it that it does not become overrun with a scourge of parasitic invaders," he said.

Heads nodded and members offered their agreement with "uh-huhs" and "yes, sirs."

"All one needs to do is look at our streets, our grocery stores, our restaurants, our kitchens, or to our landscapers or household workers to see and realize we are being overrun. Then all we need to do is look at our social service agencies, our hospitals, and our civic resources to see that these invaders might as well stick their dirty fingers into our pockets directly to take our money. Furthermore, as their children interact with our children, our future generations are being polluted with this horrid influence!" With this point, Sinkoff brought his fist down on the podium.

The room cheered him.

"We will not sit back, will we?" he asked his audience.

"No!" they shouted in unison.

"What?" Sinkoff replied in mock deafness.

"No, sir!" they yelled, and the room broke into cheers.

CHAPTER THIRTY-SEVEN

TEN GRAND.

Ten fucking grand.

For one shot.

I've gone twelve rounds with my eyes almost closed from swelling, cut in three places, and hit so hard to the body that I'd piss blood for a week for three hundred dollars. I liked Vegas.

Maybe I'd update the El Dorado. Maybe I'd move out of the Blue. Maybe I'd make sure my Elvis collection was 100 percent complete. I don't know if spending it was going to be fun, but thinking about spending it sure was.

After a shower I grabbed a six-pack at the bodega across the street from the gym for the ride to the airport. The combination of yesterday's sparring effects and this last session was starting to weigh on me. I could feel muscles tightening up, joints getting stiff, and the chronic headache I get from sparring getting a little sharper.

The bodega didn't carry Schlitz, but they did have Pabst in the can, which was a pretty good approximation, and they had it in tallboy sixes. That extra four ounces per can may just have been the required dosage for what I needed on a night like tonight.

The traffic around Las Vegas was brutal. I'm sure that the natives knew how to get around it, but I didn't. I was finishing my third tallboy when I pulled up to the taxi zone at McCarran. The air-conditioning in the Lincoln was blessedly freezing and I reclined the seat a little to wait for the boys to appear on the curb as promised. I wasn't there three minutes when someone knocked on the window and jarred me out of my reverie. Apparently I had fallen asleep, so I was a little startled when I heard the knock, and it took me a couple of seconds to roll down the window. When I did, there was a fat guy with a bushy unibrow going across his forehead and a curly toupee that resembled a hairy shower cap. He looked like a fat Henry Kissinger.

"I want a little tiny girl. You got one who will take a big guy like me?" he said. I looked him straight in the eye and cursed the hallucinations that came with my head trauma. "I like the funky stuff too, so she not only has to be tiny, she has to be willing to get funky," Fatso Kissinger said.

I sipped the Pabst.

"C'mon, pal, there's other whorehouses where I can spend my money."

Then I remembered I was driving a pink Lincoln with "Appaloosa Ranch" scripted on the side of it.

"Uh...I'm not in that end of the business, sir," I stuttered. "You can get the ranch shuttle somewhere around here," I said with as much genuine customer care as I could muster.

"Ah, you fuckin' guys. I'm going to the Chicken Ranch. They'll let me back in if I grease them," Kissinger said.

I was sitting there trying not to think of this fat guy on top of some tiny girl who made a bad vocational choice doing something "funky." Then, just as I was drifting into visuals about what the fat former secretary of state could've done to be barred from a whorehouse, I heard my name called.

"Duffy!"

It was Rocco. He was looking from side to side and walking up and down the taxi zone. TC and the Jerrys fell in behind him. I opened my door and yelled to them and they picked up the pace to get to the pink Lincoln.

Rocco was the first to get to the car.

CHAPTER THIRTY-EIGHT

"Geez, Duff, it's freakin' hot out here," Rocco said. Then he stopped and looked at the car. "The Appaloosa Ranch and Spa? What the hell is that?"

"Duff—you dog! We're staying at some sort of fancy spa?" TC said.

"They got booze?" Jerry Number One asked.

"Probably different types of tea," Jerry Number Two said.

"Oh shit, Duffy—I don't want to stay at no healthy joint," TC said.

"New age bullshit, I don't need," Rocco said.

"Damn," Jerry Number One said.

Their bitching was starting to piss me off. I almost lost it, but at the last moment I regained my composure. "It's kind of like a spa," I said without much confidence.

"They got booze there?" Rocco said.

"Of course," I said.

"Cool," TC said.

"What about TV?" Jerry Number One asked.

"Yep," I said.

"Cool," TC said.

With those assurances in place, the boys loaded up into the Town Car and we headed to the Strip. I took the airport ramp out of McCarran, got on the interstate for a couple of miles, and took the Tropicana Ave exit that headed toward the MGM. Rocco was in the front seat acting as a navigator, telling me with fake confidence how to drive in a city he had never been in before. TC was craning his neck in the passenger side of the backseat trying to see everything in Las Vegas. Jerry Number Two had the hump seat while Jerry Number One was right behind me.

"Holy shit! Cher is at Caesar's!" TC said.

"Cher? You're about to admit you're a Cher fan?" Rocco said.

"Oh no, we get him out of AJ's and he gets weird on us," Jerry Number One said.

"What's the matter with Cher? Cher's cool," TC said. He then began to softly sing "Half Breed" to himself.

"Look, Les Folie Bergere at the Tropicana. Longest running show since 1959," Rocco said. "Bet Sinatra did them two at a time," he added with displaced pride in his voice.

"Do I want to be looking at a gang of eighty-year-old broads in G-strings with their floppy tits getting in the way of their canes?" Jerry Number Two said.

"Huh?" Jerry Number One said.

"They've been doing that same routine since '59—they got to be looking pretty rough by now," Jerry Number Two said.

"Hey, Tom Jones is at the MGM. Check out the video screen," Jerry Number One said and nodded up to the gigantic video screen on the MGM marquee.

"Oh, you guys are worried about me because I like Cher, and Jerry over here is about to throw his room key at a guy with a pair of tube socks in his pants," TC said.

"He didn't wear fuckin' tube socks," Jerry Number One said.

"C'mon, Jer, that bulge wasn't real," Rocco said.

"Bulge?" Jerry Number One said.

"Well, if you wore tube socks with those loafers the crooners wear they would bulge out of the tops of the shoes. Come to think of it, maybe that's why the guy squirmed so much," Jerry Number Two said.

The light finally turned green at the corner of MGM and Tropicana and I headed right, up the Strip. Jerry was now humming "What's New, Pussycat."

"Who the hell is Terry Fator?" Rocco said.

"Yeah, all over the airport. There's all this shit about him being the top Vegas performer ever," Jerry Number One said.

"Bullshit, it was Sinatra," Rocco said.

"Sorry, Rock, it was my man Elvis," I countered.

"I thought it was Wayne Figton," TC said.

"Newton," Jerry Number One said.

"No, thanks," TC said.

"Actually, I just read it was Celine Dion," Jerry Number Two said.

The Lincoln fell completely silent. It stayed silent as we went past Paris and the Bellagio.

"That just ain't fuckin' right," Rocco said.

I took a right at Bally's on Flamingo and went down two blocks and parked. I figured we'd have a few drinks at Bill's. I picked Bill's because when I walked past it the day before it looked like it had the minimum of frill and some old-fashioned Vegas charm. I wanted to break the boys in gradually, and I figured you didn't do that at one of those gigantic joints.

Rocco wanted to look at the front of Caesar's before we went in so we went around to the Strip entrance. The entire Foursome was looking up at what the Vegas skyline had to offer. Jerry Number One was fixated on the gigantic picture of the backside of a showgirl on the billboard for Jubilee!, Bally's titty show; Jerry Number Two had his head twisted at a weird angle trying to get the Eiffel Tower into focus; TC stared at the Flamingo's flashing marquee, while Rocco looked reverently at the pools and entrance to Caesar's.

While my friends gawked, I heard the familiar *snap-snap* of the slappers. I looked at the three guys on the corner, and it dawned on me that they were the guys who were with the Mexican who was killed. Their buddy was shot the night before and they were back in business the next day. I walked over to the trio.

"*Hablo inglés?*" I said to the middle guy.

He handed me a baseball card with a blonde bent over holding her ankles, her face right above a pair of five-inch pumps.

"English?"

The guy to his right handed me a card with two girls on it, one wearing Lucite heels and a G-string with stars covering her nipples, the other a blonde with pigtails and a Catholic school uniform. The uniforms at this school apparently ran on the small side.

"No English?"

The trio just stood, their eyes obscured by their shades, handing the cards to the masses of people cruising around me.

"*Lo siento para su amigo,*" I said. I was trying to say "I'm sorry about your friend," and I hoped it was a reasonable approximation.

The guy in the middle put his hand down for the first time and looked at the other two men, who did the same. Then the guy in the middle looked back at me.

"*Gracias,*" he said.

Maybe it was the counselor in me, but I stood for a moment as if we were going to "share" on the topic before I remembered we didn't have any idea what the other was saying.

He went back to passing out the cards.

CHAPTER THIRTY-NINE

WE SAT AT the long bar and for maybe the first time in their lives the Foursome was quiet as they looked, listened, and tried to soak it all in. Bill's sounds blended together with the *ring-a-ding-dings* of the slot machine melding together with the craps dealers calling out numbers and the craps players alternating between cheers and groans. The cocktail waitresses added to the orchestration with the rhythm of their monotone "Cocktails...Cocktails."

The bar horseshoed around to a small lounge area. A video came on of a four-hundred-pound guy calling himself "Big Elvis." There was a montage of him singing, usually seated. He did the usual Elvis voice approximation and could hold a tune, but other than that he wasn't very good. Any caricature of the real Elvis was offensive to me. Then, just when I thought I had had enough disgust, the video cut to a news story where the fat guy claimed to be Elvis's illegitimate son. This broke the Foursome's silence.

"What you think of that, Duff? We're going to see the King's son," Jerry Number One said.

"Bastard," I said, mostly to myself.

"That's what he said. He admitted it," TC said.

"Speaking of bastards, where's Al the bastard hound? I thought he was with you," Jerry Number One said.

"He's back at the house. Trust me, he's in good hands," I said.

"Where the hell we staying?" Rocco asked.

I thought about it for a second and realized now was good as any time to tell them. They were here, after all. They couldn't go back.

"Fellas, we're staying in a house on the grounds of the Appaloosa Ranch—which just so happens to be a whorehouse," I said. Then I waited.

The four of them looked at me for a long time.

"You're speaking ephremzimbalastly?" Rocco said.

"Efremzimbalastly? What the hell does that mean?" Jerry Number One said.

"Wasn't he the guy on that FBI TV show?" TC said.

"Junior," Jerry Number Two said.

"Who you calling Junior? I'm old enough to be your father!" Rocco said.

"Efrem Zimbalist Jr. was the star of the TV show *The FBI*. It used to be on Sunday nights in the seventies," TC said.

"That was *Mannix*," Rocco said.

"I thought Mannix was the stuff the doctor gave me when I was nervous about flying. He told me to take ten milligrams of Mannix but not to drink with it," Jerry Number One said.

"Xanax," Jerry Number Two said.

"That was the movie with Olivia Wayne Newton and John Travolta. It bombed," TC said.

"*Xanadu*," Jerry Number Two said.

"You're welcome," Rocco said.

It was both a runaway train and like a bad car wreck. I just looked on for a while. Eventually I had to step in.

"We're staying in a brothel outside of town. It's legal out here and the place is nice. The girls are mostly friendly or at least they aren't obnoxious," I said.

"I like whores," Rocco said.

"I've always noticed no matter what pickup line I use on them it always seems to work," TC said.

TC and Rocco were debating about whore opening lines when I looked down at Jerry Number Two. He was oblivious to the conversation and totally absorbed in the action on the casino floor. He went to take a sip out of his cosmopolitan, and there was a noticeable tremor to his hands. His complexion blanched whiter than usual and he actually drooled a little bit out of the left corner of his mouth.

"Hey, Jerry," I said. "Jerr-y…" I sort of sang it. He didn't register any acknowledgment. The other guys started to notice as well.

"Jerry!" Rocco snapped.

Nothing.

TC put his hand on Jerry's shoulder and shook him. His head flopped a little bit, forcing drool to spill out of his mouth.

"Is he having a stroke?" Jerry Number One said.

I got up and walked over to Jerry Number Two and stood in his field of vision. His eyes were staring straight ahead and he didn't acknowledge me.

"Jerry! Jerry! Jerry!" I said, each time getting louder with more emphasis.

He blinked, took a shallow breath, and jerked his head back. Then he squinted hard and shook his head from side to side.

"I thought it had been long enough. I didn't think it would get to me like this," he said in a hushed tone.

"What, Jer? What is it?" I said.

"The action, Duff, the action. A long time ago I was addicted. It was bad," he said. A little sweat had beaded up on his upper lip.

"Addicted?" Rocco said. "To gambling?"

"Yeah, it almost killed me," Jerry Number Two said.

CHAPTER FORTY

ME AND THE boys talked Jerry through his fears, but he never quite chilled out. We switched locations and went to an older, dumpier place called Fitzgerald's, then to an even dumpier place called the Casino Royale that, just for the record, did not in any way reverberate with the spirit of James Bond. The problem with the smaller, dumpier places was that the gambling action was right next to the bars. The blackjack tables, roulette wheels, and craps tables were all right up to the backs of the barstools, and now that I had become acutely aware of their impact on my buddy, I heard the never-ending melding of sounds that had to trigger a craving for jumping in. Sometimes it was the croupier yelling "Seven!" followed by hoots and hollers from the players. Other times it would be "Thirty-five—black!" and a round of cheers, or a "Twenty-one!" from the blackjack tables.

"Jerry, why did you come here if you thought it was going to be this bad?" TC said. He wasn't being critical; he was being, at least for TC, compassionate.

"I haven't been here since the eighties. I haven't been in a casino at all since then, haven't played a horse, a lottery ticket, or even got in a football pool—I thought it was time," Jerry Number Two said.

"Why is it so bad?" Rocco said.

"They say it's an addiction, but I don't know. If I was shooting something in my veins like heroin I could see how my body would get used to it and crave it, but this isn't anything you put in your body," Jerry Number Two said.

Then the conversation was interrupted.

"Holy fucking shit! Holy motherfucking shit! Bless you, Jesus! Bless you, Jesus!" A very large woman was jumping up and down next to a slot machine. The machine was whistling, bells were going off, a light spun, and coins were jingling out of the machine like a brook entering into a river.

"On the other hand..." TC said.

The woman had a huge chest, and as she jumped around the kinetic energy created a certain torsion in her body fat that, to say the least, wasn't pleasant to look at. It looked like she had several very overweight cats stuffed in her T-shirt who were all fighting.

"I don't know if it's related to something like that," Jerry nodded in the direction of the woman who was now on the floor hyperventilating. "I was into the strategy of beating the casinos."

"Whaddya mean?" I said.

"Me and a few buddies had a system. It wasn't illegal, but we knew how to win and win consistently," Jerry Number Two said.

A security guard had the lady doing deep breathing exercises and had placed one of those chemical cold packs on her forehead. She rolled over on her belly and kicked her legs and arms violently.

"Thank you, Jesus!"

"So what happened?" Jerry Number One said.

"Security at the Stardust figured us out. They intimidated us, roughed us up a little, and we went home." Jerry looked straight ahead. "We lost the money we invested in planning, plus our gambling stake, and we were humiliated."

"That doesn't sound like an addiction, Jer," I said.

"That came after. I spent too much time in Atlantic City trying to get back what I'd lost, but I got compulsive. I was drinking and high all the time. It got bad."

The group had gotten a bit somber, which defeated the purpose of having them out to Vegas. We just quietly sat there at the Casino Royale, drinking. After a few minutes, Jerry spoke again.

"Guys, I'm sorry. I'll be alright. I swear." He paused. "I think I'm just tired and wasn't prepared to be in the middle of the action again. I'll be okay, really. Drink up."

We all clinked glasses and smiled, but it seemed a bit forced. Jerry still didn't look right and he didn't feign happiness well. I felt for him without fully understanding what he went through. Sometimes you don't have to know the details to know someone is just plain hurting.

After that we took our drinks and headed out to the sidewalk and watched as the Mirage's volcano went off across the street. Sidewalks on both sides of the street were jammed with mouth breathers watching the fake spectacle of fire and smoke, and the whole thing seemed kind of stupid in a really grand way. It went on for about ten minutes with a crescendo explosion at the end.

"That's pretty fuckin' ridiculous," TC said.

"That's gotta cost a mint," Rocco said.

"How do they make it change colors?" Jerry Number One asked.

"That's the polytechnics," Rocco said.

"Pyro," I said.

"No thanks. I'm not really hungry and I hate that Greek shit," Rocco said.

A crowd was gathering at the next casino, the TI, the one with the pirate theme.

"Fuckin' fake volcanoes, this shit is ridiculous," TC repeated.

"Hey, let's go see the pirate ship thing," Jerry Number One said.

"Cool, let's do it!" TC said.

The gang, like the lemmings they were, started to head over to the TI's pirate ship extravaganza when Rocco called everyone to a stop.

"Where's Jerry?" he asked.

"Right here," Jerry Number One said.

We all realized who Rocco meant and we all froze.

Jerry Number Two had disappeared.

CHAPTER FORTY-ONE

I THINK I read somewhere that a quarter of a million people visit Las Vegas every week. It was going to be tough to find one ex-hippie who drank cosmopolitans, wore tie-dyes, and had a bad gambling jones in that big of a crowd.

"How much money did he bring?" I asked the boys as we walked through the lobby of the Mirage.

"He didn't say, but how much could he have?" TC said.

"It wasn't like he splurges on his wardrobe," Rocco said.

"He ever tell you about his life in computers?" I said.

"I just glaze over when anyone starts talking about bytes and bits and that shit," Jerry Number One said.

"He fixed computers or some crap, didn't he?" Rocco said.

"Fellas, Jerry was in on the ground floor of AOL and sold off just as it got big. Jerry is a millionaire," I said.

On cue the three of them stopped in their tracks. We were in the Mirage, standing by a waterfall in what appeared to be some sort of tropical rainforest complete with recordings of birdcalls.

"A millionaire?" Rocco echoed.

"No way," Jerry Number One said.

"Jerry?" TC said.

"Probably," I said.

They all looked at each other. I could tell they were a bit uncomfortable.

"When was the last time he bought a round?" Rocco said.

"A round? When was the last time he bought us all a car?" TC said.

This was a path I didn't want them going down. If the Foursome minus one got material like this they could go on forever and I needed to intervene.

"Guys, let's focus on finding him," I said.

We walked past a theme bar with a four-piece band booming out something by Sheryl Crow, I think. We went past the "Let It Ride" tables toward the buffet and, to the left, a Brazilian steakhouse, whatever that is. We followed signs that directed us toward the pool and the Danny Gans Theater and went past a bunch of shops selling tropical shirts, coffee mugs, and other bullshit for what I considered to be highway robbery. We kept walking and wound up back by the band that had been playing Sheryl Crow and was now playing something by Bonnie Raitt.

"Isn't this where we started?" I said.

"How could it be? We headed that way," Rocco said.

"Yeah, but we're here," Jerry Number One said.

"Maybe the band moved," TC said.

"I don't think so," I said. "I think these places are designed to confuse you so you don't know how to get out when you want to. Let's follow the signs to the lobby and try the next place."

We went to the TI, the Venetian, Caesar's, and the Bellagio, and it started to feel more and more futile. It was now two in the morning, which meant it was five in the morning back East. I had to fight in a little while and the guys were dragging.

"Alright, look, he knows the name of where we're staying, he's got money—he'll find us. Let's just head to Duffy's place," Rocco said.

It didn't feel quite right, but I couldn't think of a better solution. We walked back to the car and headed to the Appaloosa. The party atmosphere of being in Vegas at night on the Strip with the boys was gone, replaced with worry. The mood in the Lincoln on the way back was somber, and the guys were quiet, which always made everything seem a bit surreal. They were never quiet, they never left AJ's, and the combination of it all tinged the night with a peculiar feel.

The Ranch sign glowed in the distance and alerted the boys to our destination.

"The only other whorehouse I was ever in was in Korea, and there wasn't any neon. There was a big Korean guy that you had to tip to get in. He let you know that there was to be no funny business," Rocco said.

"Isn't that really the only kind of business getting done in a whorehouse?" TC said.

"Good point," Jerry Number One said.

I decided to take the guys through the main entrance, both to give them the full effect and because I was really interested in their reaction. The lilacs hit me when I opened the door and walked toward the velvet curtains. I turned and the guys were standing just a foot or so inside the door, frozen.

"C'mon, guys," I said. "What's up?"

They just collectively shrugged but didn't move.

"What's the problem?" I said.

"No problem, Duff," Jerry Number One said, but they still didn't move.

"Well, c'mon then," I said and went through the curtain. The song "Everybody's Working for the Weekend" was blaring from the speakers. The bar was full and a whole group of the girls were collected on the sectional. Al was in the middle of the sofa getting petted by two women, one on each side of him. The petters were twins I hadn't seen before who wore matching leopard catsuits. They fit with their pulled-back brown hair and fifties-style cat-eye sunglasses for a Julie Newmar Catwoman look.

I looked behind me and the boys had finally come through the entrance and now stood frozen staring at the women.

Lucille came out from the office. "Would you gentlemen be looking for a date?" she asked, snapping her gum as she spoke.

"Lucille, they're with me," I said.

"Doesn't mean they don't get lonely, Rocky," she said and winked while she lit up a butt.

The boys continued to stare at the women like they were zoo animals. It was getting a little annoying, and embarrassing.

"Hey, fellas, there's a bar here," I said.

The word "bar" worked like some sort of hypnotic trance remover. The guys snapped out of it and followed me to the bar where we formed a back row behind the customers getting to know their evening professionals. The bartender raised her eyebrows in lieu of asking us what we wanted and I ordered two beers, a B&B, and a scotch on the rocks.

"Wow, all these women are whores?" Rocco asked *just* as Loverboy was finishing the song. The abrupt end of that song and the long silence before the next song kicked in were ill timed. The four girls entertaining at the bar all glared at Rocco, who nervously sipped his scotch.

"Evening, ladies," Rocco said with a forced smile.

Fortunately the Bob Seger song "Hollywood Nights" started up right after that and the ladies were professional enough to get back to business. I gave Rocco my best dirty look and he took an extra large swig of scotch.

TC was staring directly at Marilyn's cleavage. She was the bleached blonde who looked like a cross between Hot Lips Houlihan and Dolly Parton, except for those really pronounced buck teeth.

"What a pair," TC whispered out of the corner of his mouth. "Her tits are pretty big too," he said.

"There's a certain symmetry to her look, I'll give you that," Jerry Number One said.

I was pondering the depth of my friends' comments when I noticed all the girls at the bar affix their eyes on the front door. Most went silent, one or two let out a quiet curse, and instantly the mood in the bar area changed. You could feel the level of tension rise through the place.

"He's here again," one hooker whispered over the shoulder of her date to another, who looked to the brothel's entrance.

"Oh, fuck," she let out.

I turned to look at the front door and saw whose presence they dreaded.

It was Rusakov.

He stood in the center of the lounge while the girls who were not at the bar formed the traditional line in front of him. When the twins one by one left the couch, Al slowly sat up to see what was going on. He did the tornado hound thing to clear his jowls, and a couple of loogeys landed on the velvet. The girls had their backs to him and he started to whimper at the loss of his latest friends' attention.

Rusakov walked the line and went past Mona, who was doing her best to vamp up her look tonight with leather pants and a skin-tight halter. He reached toward her and squeezed her left breast until she yelped. Rusakov laughed and continued down the line. He stopped in front of what had to be the youngest girl, a strawberry blonde who I think was named Bambi. She was visibly shaking when he put his hand between her legs until she cried out and jumped back. Rusakov thought that was funny too.

The last girl in line was Louise, whose extra pounds were visible in a white, skintight jumpsuit. Rusakov smirked at her and stared right into her eyes until she looked down at her five-inch heels.

"Touch it," he said.

She looked up at him with more than just a little fear. I looked at Lucille, who was watching all of this. She wasn't happy, but she wasn't interfering either.

"Touch it!" He took a step toward her and unbuckled his pants.

"We're not supposed to—" He didn't let her finish. He grabbed her hand and forced it inside his pants. She instinctively resisted for an instant and he backhanded her.

"Do what I say," he said.

She recovered and put her hand down his pants while he ignored her tears.

"Uh, Boris, baby," Lucille interrupted with care. "You can't do that in the public areas, okay?" she said with as much fake charm as she could muster.

"Fuck you, fat bitch," Rusakov said before zipping himself up and motioning to Mona and the young girl that he wanted them both. He had them walk in front of him while he headed down the corridor to one of the rooms.

The rest of the girls shook their heads and muttered "asshole" and other descriptive phrases as they lit up cigarettes and sat down. Clearly it wasn't the first time Rusakov had made an appearance, and it didn't look like it was something that the working girls could easily rationalize away. As they all found their places on the couch I noticed something else.

Al was sitting up straight and growling in the direction of Rusakov.

CHAPTER FORTY-TWO

THE LAST TIME, he took too many chances; he knew that. He acted impulsively, out of the sheer hate for the street Mexicans embarrassing themselves out on the Strip. Still, the police had no leads and no idea what had happened. He took some pride in that, even though he knew it was part luck—and he didn't rely on luck. He relied on hard work, discipline, and commitment.

He had people with like interests he could count on who would be happy to help—more than happy; they probably had the same intensity inside them as he did. But he couldn't take the risk of having others know because that would make him vulnerable. He lived a life where he minimized any weakness. He had been embarrassed before and that had marked him. Never again would he allow it. He was driven to make them pay, now and into the future.

He drove on. Even though it was well into the middle of the night and perhaps even closer to sunup he realized he wasn't at all tired. In fact, he was filled with an agitated energy, the same energy that drove him to kill because after killing and only after killing did he get any sense of calm.

It had begun because he wanted to do something both for himself and for those who came after him, and he'd learned he couldn't rely on the bullshit politicians or the corrupt police officials. They talked, but they didn't get things done and they didn't allow others to get things done. No, he needed to act alone. Only by keeping his secret could his work get done.

But tonight he was just driving and driving and he didn't feel he had accomplished anything. His whole life he had hated that feeling more than anything. When he was just a kid his own father would call him "lazy" or "useless" and he had hated that feeling as much as he hated his father. Even as a child he longed for the day that he could stand up to his father and show him how "useless" he really was.

He did a U-turn. Right now he needed a surefire plan with very little risk. There was an area north of the city where they gathered early in the morning for day labor. They lined up ridiculously early so that they would be the first ones picked. It was so bad, and they were all so competitive, that many got to the street corner before the sun came up, then earlier and earlier. They were pathetic.

It was three thirty a.m. He wondered if it was too early even for them. He was approaching the corner, and because there were no street lights he wouldn't be able to tell if anyone was waiting until he got right up close. When he did, he saw he was in luck—there was what appeared to be a husband and wife team who probably tried to get housekeeping jobs.

The man was very short, not even five feet tall, and when he talked to the woman he showed a missing front tooth. The woman was even shorter, with darker skin that showed Mayan heritage. He slowed his gigantic SUV and lowered the power window on the passenger side. The husband and wife team seemed confused; their usual employers probably came by in dirty pick-up trucks.

The man approached the window with the woman a short step behind him.

"Trabajo?" the man asked as he approached the window.

He pulled the gun from the compartment near his elbow and shot the Mexican once in the center of the forehead.

The woman screamed in shock and put her hands over her mouth, but she didn't run.

He shot her in the head as well and her screams immediately stopped. The noise echoed through the empty streets and seemed to bounce off the faraway canyon and mountains.

Now he felt like he had done something. Now he didn't feel useless.

CHAPTER FORTY-THREE

AL SLEPT WITH me that night. I don't know if I was anthropo-morphizing (I think that's the word when you give human char-acteristics to a dog), but I'm guessing he didn't want to be around Rusakov or at least around his new friends while they were upset. Maybe he just wanted a night off from the girls to rebond with his master.

The next morning I walked to the main building to get some coffee, and at the bar I found TC already up, reading the paper, drinking coffee and fully engaged with the bartender. Elizabeth was a twentysomething redheaded cutie with a Slavic accent who was wearing very tight black jeans and a sleeveless turtleneck.

I asked her for a coffee and traded "good mornings" with TC.

"Elizabeth here is studying to be a hairdresser and she used to be a gymnast," TC said to me but really to let Elizabeth know he had been listening. TC was still working on good lines to use on the Appaloosa women.

"Any sign of Jerry?" I said.

"No, not yet. But he'll be alright," TC said.

"Any sign of the others?"

"They like to sleep in, and yesterday was a long day. I'm guess-ing they'll be down in a bit."

I grabbed my coffee and headed back to the house. As I was leaving I overheard TC tell Elizabeth that he liked the way her red hair brought out the black in her shirt. There was no question the man had all the lines; I just thought it was way too early to be trying to figure out what they all meant.

When I got back to my room Angelina was there making my bed. Al was following every step she took, almost tripping her up he was so close. I watched from the doorway and smiled at how she sang softly to Al and talked to him like a mom would talk to a child. She didn't scold him out of frustration or anything, she just playfully told him what to do. Of course, all that was an assumption because she was speaking to him in Spanish.

"You've taught Al Spanish already?" I said.

She was startled and put her hand to her chest. She looked a lot less comfortable now that she saw me.

"I'm sorry. I am working slow today," she said.

She looked even more beautiful than yesterday. Her hair was pulled back in a bun and it emphasized her almond eyes and her mocha skin.

The TV was still on from last night. I like to sleep with the noise as background. The local NBC affiliate was doing the morning news. They were showing a photo of a Mexican couple. I turned it up.

"Another itinerant Mexican killing overnight, this time a man and woman waiting for day work in the north part of Las Vegas. They were found dead, each with a single bullet hole to the forehead," the male anchor said.

Angelina stopped and stared at the TV.

CHAPTER FORTY-FOUR

"GOD, THIS IS awful," I said.

"Please, Mr. Duffy, do not take the Lord's name in vain. But you are right, it is awful," she said.

We both listened to the rest of the report in silence. Al had lain down at Angelina's feet.

"How bad is it in your country that people work so hard to come here—even when they are treated like this?" I asked.

"Mr. Duffy, it is very hard for Americans to understand. Americans think hunger is something they call for a pizza for, they think sickness is a cold, and they see depression as something that happens when life doesn't go exactly as they want," she said in a hushed tone.

"Doesn't the government help? Isn't there welfare or Medicaid and that kind of stuff?" I said.

"There is nothing like that. Over fifty percent of my country lives in what the United Nations calls extreme poverty. That means more than half of my country lives on less for a year than what someone considered poor makes in a week in your country. There is no medicine, there are no programs—there is nothing, unless you have money," she said.

"There is no work in Mexico unless you sell drugs. Mr. Duffy, I have trained as a singer my whole life. I went to the university to study music and I also have a degree in economics. Before I came here, I sold fruit on the street."

Angelina looked down and pursed her lips. I could tell she struggled to keep what she was feeling in.

"I'm sorry," I said to be saying something.

"You don't have to be sorry. I am here to make as much money as I can to bring back home."

"Why would you go back? Why don't you just stay here?"

"It is not my home, and I have family that needs me back in Mexico," she said. I got the sense that she hadn't talked to anyone in some time.

"Your mother and father?" I said.

"They are both dead. They died from infections because there was no medical care, my oldest brother too. I am here to help my younger brother."

"How old is he?" I said.

"He is sixteen," she said.

"Isn't he close to being able to work himself?"

She got very quiet and looked at her hands. Al looked up at her.

"I am talking and not working. Lucille will not be happy. I must work," she said and went to change the sheets.

I stood up and went over to the bed and gently pulled the sheets from her hands and made sure I looked in her eyes.

"What's the situation with your brother?" I said.

Her eyes filled with tears, but she didn't allow them to leave her eyes nor did she hold up a hand to wipe them.

"My brother has, how do you say it, *el autismo.*"

"Autism?"

"Yes, this. He cannot live alone. He needs me," she said.

"I thought he was the one who worshipped Jesus Medina?"

"He does," she said. "Many Mexican boys do."

I, for some reason, automatically assumed that an autistic wouldn't be interested in what other kids were into. I just looked at her and felt awful.

"Boys with autism have the same likes and dislikes. But they get, ah, I am thinking of the word…obsessed. They do the same things over and over in the same way all the time. Marco can imitate Jesus perfectly. He dances around boxing and repeats 'El Campeón del Pueblo, el Campeón del Peublo!' It is his ritual."

"Ritual?" I asked.

"It helps calm them."

"Is he in a program in Mexico?" I said.

"There are no programs."

"So what does he do?"

"He lives with my elderly aunt who doesn't understand. She does her best, but she believes he needs more discipline, which just makes my brother more confused and makes him worse," she said.

"So you're trying to get him in this country?" I said.

"It is illegal, I know that. I am not legal, but I will do whatever I can to get my brother a life worth living."

"You can't sneak him in?"

"The men that do that are not kind. They want ten thousand dollars to get him in, and he would be traumatized by it. I am here making the money to get him to the United States," she said.

"I don't understand how this all works. Don't you just pay someone and they hide someone in a trunk or something?" I said.

"It's not that simple. First you have to get to the border, which is a couple of hours from where we live. Then you have to trust the coyote to get you to a spot where there is no wall to get over and fewer guards around. Many times they take your money and leave you with no way to get home," she said.

"I had no idea."

"Then, if the coyote has been truthful and you get to a spot on the border where you can walk through, it is a three-day walk in the desert where the temperature reaches over one hundred ten degrees. Mr. Duffy, the body needs two gallons of water per day to survive in that heat, but six gallons of water weighs fifty pounds, and when you are running from the border patrol it is impossible to carry that much water—certainly for my brother it would be," she said.

"So what happens to the people?"

"Fifteen thousand have died in the desert in the last ten years. They gamble their lives to make it here to work the jobs that Americans can't get their own people to work," she said. Angelina had an intense, concentrated look.

"Why doesn't Mexico take care of its people?" I said.

Angelina snorted a laugh that had no humor to it.

"Over fifty percent of the people make less than two thousand dollars per year. Mexico has no welfare system or health care."

"But aren't there wealthy people in Mexico that help out?" I said.

"Some, but not enough. Mexico's upper class is not in touch with the lower classes for the most part. They live different lives, and the government is filled with corruption. There are gangs that traffic drugs, prostitutes, firearms—anything you can think of—and the money is laundered and filtered throughout the economy," she said.

"My God, it is a mess," I said. "How did it get this way?"

"Part of it is our land. Much of it can't grow anything to eat. It is also the way Mexicans have lived for many years. There are different classes and heritages. Part of it, too, is the United States," she said.

"The US, how?"

"In the sixties and seventies, the big corporations built factories all up and down the border, very close to the US. There was very cheap Mexican labor to make products without dealing with unions and labor issues. The Mexicans were happy for the work and the corporations were happy to keep lower costs," she said.

Al was staring straight up at Angelina and didn't even blink.

"I didn't know there were a lot of factories near the border," I said.

"There isn't anymore," she said.

"Why not?"

"Because those same corporations found they could pay Asian people or Guatemalans even less to do the same work. They simply closed them up and moved them. It left many border towns with no resources and no way to earn a living—at least not honestly," she said.

"I had no idea…"

"Americans don't. They also don't realize what will happen to the US if they actually deport the Mexicans already here," she said.

"Well, whether it is the right thing to do ethically, aren't the illegals a drain on the economy?"

"Who picks the fruit? Who works the vineyards? Who works in the kitchens? Who landscapes, picks up garbage…who…"—she started to cry—"…does housekeeping?" She held her hand to her face.

Al whined, shuffled from foot to foot, and then jumped up on Angelina's leg.

I stood there, and everything that came to my mind to say seemed stupid, so I kept my mouth shut and felt even more stupid. I had no answers, and lots and lots of people way more smarter than me didn't seem to have any idea what to do. I swallowed and looked down at my feet.

"I'm sorry to go on…I should work," Angelina said, shifting into what looked like an all-business-no-feeling mode. "I need to work for there to be any hope for my brother," she said.

CHAPTER FORTY-FIVE

THE NEXT DAY when I went to the bar for my coffee there was an envelope waiting for me.

There was a check in it.

It was for ten thousand dollars.

It was a surreal feeling getting a check for so much. It was by far the largest check I had ever received. I looked at it for a long time. There was also a note that said there would be no sparring today. No other explanation. I slipped the check into my pocket.

Ten thousand fucking dollars.

I just slipped a check for ten thousand dollars in my pocket.

I wanted to jump and kick my heels up or do a back flip or something, but that just wouldn't look cool. So I pretended like I got checks for ten grand all the time.

The boys were going to head to the Strip and have some fun and look for Jerry. I decided to go to the gym anyways just to watch some of the Mexican guys train. I didn't figure on getting a lot of chances to come work in Las Vegas and I wanted to make the most of it. Lucille let me take one of the pink Lincolns and I drove to Tocco's like I had been living here for twenty years.

Developing friendships in boxing gyms can be complicated. First of all, there is a thick blanket of machismo to get through even to have a conversation. Second, most fighters are preoccupied with getting in the ring and so there's always a cloud of tension hanging in the air. Third, despite what some philosophers will tell you, race and culture get in the way in boxing gyms. Right off the bat, fighters gather by like and only start to integrate when they get to know each other. I think racial and cultural lines break down faster in gyms, but there's no doubt in my mind that they are still there. Add language to the mix and it isn't actually like a night of speed dating when it comes to getting to know people.

That meant I would go to the gym and gravitate toward the Mexican fighters but not assume they cared about getting to know me back. Over the years I've learned that people may or may not like you and you can't force them to, but you can be yourself and be a decent person. I might not have much in common with those guys, but I was going to ask questions and genuinely show my respect for them. That's all a fighter can do.

I wrapped my hands and started to warm up. I took note that Rusakov was in with most of his crew, and as usual they had removed themselves from everyone else in the gym. I danced a bit and threw some light punches, taking care not to fully extend and stress my joints. When the round bell sounded I'd shift it down and just keep moving to stay warm. The whole time I was in the corner of the gym with the Mexican fighters.

Both of the Medina brothers were in training with the featherweight Omar Vasquez. Carlos de Grande was there, and he gave a quick wave to the Mexican fighters before stationing himself where he could see his son. I was transfixed by him. Rarely are you in the same room with an idol, a man who embodies what you strive for but know you'll never attain. I saw him shake hands and slap one of Rusakov's crew. The son was working on his footwork, moving to his left and cutting off the ring. One of the knocks on Junior was that lefties gave him fits. You cut the ring off of a left-hander by stepping to your left. Looked like the kid was struggling with it too.

The Mexicans used slightly different equipment and their own brand of gloves. Reyes gloves were always known as puncher's gloves, in that they had very little padding over the knuckles, and when you got hit with them you felt almost bare knuckle. Fights with Reyes gloves often led to a lot of blood.

They also used this weird-looking teardrop-shaped double-end ball to train on. They were all good at making it go back and forth. They combined head shots with body punches while the thing wobbled back and forth on a rubber tether. I took a round off and watched Jesus work it.

He stepped in and double jabbed it, let it bounce against his recoiled guard, then countered it with a three-punch combination of a left-right-left and then hooked it and spun away. The entire combination plus flurry occurred in less than two seconds. He did this same combo over and over and it looked 100 percent automatic, like putting one foot in front of the other. It was elegant and devastating all at once.

In the next round, Jesus went to the biggest heavy bag in the gym. It was nearly four feet wide and weighed about three hundred pounds. It was so hard that if you hit it wrong you'd screw up your wrist. I stayed away from it because if I threw too many punches on it I would lose the skin on my knuckles even if they were wrapped.

Jesus, a lefty like me, was doing something unusual. He would step forward and change to the traditional right-hand stance and then throw a short, compact, but hellacious hook into the side of the bag. He did it over and over until the stance-changing step was imperceptible. It was like one fluid motion, and even with the years I've spent doing this sport I wasn't sure what he was doing or, more importantly, why. The result at the end of the shift was what had to be a damaging body shot. It seemed like a lot of work for a body shot.

When the bell sounded I took a chance and approached the champ. It wasn't within gym etiquette to interrupt a fighter—let alone a world champion—while he was working, even during a rest period.

"Excuse me, Jesus," I said. He raised his eyebrows.

"I don't want to interrupt you, but can I ask you a question?"

He nodded.

"I'm a lefty just like you and I've been watching your bag work. What are you trying to do?"

He took his bag gloves off. He raised his eyebrows as if to say, "Watch this." He took his open left hand and dug it into my right side, just a hair under my last rib. A lightning bolt of pain went through my entire nervous system and I felt myself involuntarily jump back.

Jesus laughed.

"What the hell is that?" I said when the ice-pick–level pain finally subsided.

"That's your liver, man. The Mexican punch." He smiled and lifted his eyebrows like Groucho Marx.

I've heard about Mexicans being body punchers and I'd even heard about the liver punch, but I had dismissed it with much of the other boxing folklore.

"I'm a lefty, but you got to hit the liver going upward. You can't do it unless you go orthodox. The hard part is getting the step. Watch," he said.

The bell starting the next round rang but Jesus took the time to teach me. He had me follow him movement by movement so I got the step right. He made the point of saying that if you didn't get the footwork right it would take too long and your punch would never get there.

I watched him do another whole round and mimicked his movement. At the end of that round he took me to anatomy school.

"The liver is protected by the rib." He reached over and curled his fingers around my last rib. "The body is almost all water, so if you hit the area close by the liver it sends shockwaves through it. You do it right, it can kill a man. You do it almost right, he'll get knocked out."

It was like getting a biology lesson. His English was labored, but there was no doubting his knowledge.

"You have to keep the hook short. It has to be coming up when it lands to get the right shock," he said, and to emphasize the point he raised his index finger. "Ask Oscar De La Hoya after he fought Bernard Hopkins."

It was true. De La Hoya got knocked out with a liver shot in that fight. He rolled around on the ring floor for five minutes.

It is difficult to explain, but after Jesus showing me, this technique was already ingrained in me. That happens in boxing, every now and then you learn a simple but elegant nugget that will change how you fight forever. It happens even when you've been doing it your whole life.

"Holy shit," I said like I just discovered gravity.

Medina winked and lifted a glove. I touched it and smiled. Chills went all through me because I knew I was in the presence of a genius.

I spent the rest of the afternoon drilling that move. I did it over and over on the heavy bag, and when the Medina brothers and Vasquez finished with the teardrop bag I worked it there. It was then that I developed a true appreciation for Medina's speed and craft. Every one of Medina's punches landed with perfect force, balance, and power.

I was working harder than I wanted to and was bathed in sweat. The three Mexicans watched and smiled and laughed at my attempts, in a kind way.

"*El Mexicano Blanco Grande!*" Vasquez said, and the three of them laughed. Jesus motioned me over.

"He called you The Big White Mexican," he said, and they all laughed again. With it they all extended the Mexican version of the latest soul handshake hug. I laughed along with them. Their eyes were bright and they laughed with lots of energy.

"*Blanco Grande? Cerveza?*" Vasquez said, motioning like he was sipping a beer.

I was pretty sure he was asking if I drank beer. It made me wonder what the Spanish for "does a bear shit in the woods" was.

"*Vamos,*" Jesus said, and I followed the three fighters out of the gym.

CHAPTER FORTY-SIX

I WALKED WITH my new Mexican friends for three blocks toward downtown Las Vegas and then we took a left turn down a short side street. The Medina brothers and Vasquez spoke in Spanish the whole way, and though I didn't understand a word I didn't feel entirely excluded.

Vasquez led the way into a bar called Mike's, and Jesus held the dirty white aluminum door open for me. The heavy black interior door had fencing over the window and was impossible to see through. There were four or five guys at the smoke-filled bar, and the TV was on to a soccer game broadcast in Spanish. All the guys at the bar were drinking Tecate.

The guy behind the bar was a twentysomething Mexican who went down the line giving handshakes over the bar to my three buddies.

"This is Duffy, good guy," Jesus said to the bartender, who gave me the same handshake.

"Jorge," he said by way of introduction, and he opened cans of Tecate in front of all of us and poured four shots of something clear that I imagined was tequila. I reached into my pocket to get some cash on the bar. I realized that in addition to the couple hundred dollars I had on me I was also still carrying that ten-thousand-dollar check.

"Tecate on us," Jesus said and nodded for me to put my money away.

The fighters didn't throw the tequila down like a bunch of frat boys. They took sips off of it every now and again in the same way guys would take a hit of bourbon. There was no lime or salt or any other affectation.

They explained to me that once they knew they were on weight for their fight, meaning they knew they could make the 135 limit, they celebrated with a single beer and a tequila. It was a tradition with the three of them and didn't affect their training.

Jorge came over with a Spanish newspaper. He turned it around to show the two fighters and pointed at a small article.

"*Que?*" Jesus nearly shouted. He was startled. His brother looked over his shoulder and made a disturbed face.

"*Ayer,*" Jorge said.

Something was up, but it wasn't my place to interfere. I waited. Jesus shook his head. Eventually he looked at me.

"Javy Cano died yesterday. He had some sort of allergic reaction and died," he said.

Cano was in the top ten, a southpaw lightweight. He was scheduled to be on the same card a week from Saturday.

"Holy shit…" I said. "Was he a friend?"

"No, he was from the Yucatan, but we had met. He was training in Big Bear."

Big Bear was in the mountains in California. Lots of fighters liked to train there for the peace and quiet and the altitude.

We stayed quiet for a moment before Jesus turned to me.

"Rusakov?" Jesus said, looking at me. He raised his eyebrows. The other two guys looked my way and stopped talking. It wasn't clear to me what they were asking.

"He hits hard. His straight right has power," I said.

They nodded.

"Asshole," Jesus said with no hint of an accent. The other guys nodded.

"Yeah," I said.

"The money good?" Jesus said.

"Yeah," I said.

Jesus pursed his lips and nodded, letting me know that money can make putting up with an asshole worth it.

Jorge had changed the channel to the Spanish-speaking news and upped the volume. It got the bar's attention. The video was of a demonstration. The only thing I could understand was a graphic that had the words "Men of the Moment" in English and "Andrew Sinkoff, *presidente*." From the signs carried at the rally it looked like an anti-immigration thing.

My friends stayed quiet. I didn't know what to say, but even in the silence I felt embarrassed.

"They don't want Mexicans," Jesus said. "They like the cheap work, but they don't want them next door," he said, not taking his eyes off the television.

"I heard that people die in the heat, that they starve, that they can't find any work in Mexico. This woman where I am staying has a brother with a problem—"

Vasquez interrupted. "Angelina?"

"Yes," I said.

"Appaloosa?"

"Yes."

He nodded.

"She very beautiful. A singer." It came out "sanger." The other three nodded.

"Her brother is autistic—you know autistic?" I said.

They all shook their heads.

"Ah, you know, like slow, needs extra help…" This was tough to communicate between the languages.

They nodded.

"He loves you. Really, really loves you." I pointed to Jesus.

He smiled.

"I am very important in Mexico," he said. He wasn't bragging; it was his weakness with the language that made it come out that way. "Being a champion is very important," he said.

Hector asked his brother and Vasquez a question in Spanish. They shrugged at first, then Vasquez responded. Hector chimed in, seeming to suggest an alternative.

"Hector is going to start training in the evening. He wants his body to get work at the same time. His fight will be in one month. What do you think?" Jesus said.

"You mean, does that make sense?" I said. I couldn't believe they cared about my opinion.

He nodded, and the two others waited for my reply.

"I think it does, but only if you have training partners. If you're all alone or can't get sparring in it's not worth it," I said.

The three seemed to take that in. I was flattered that they listened. I was about to say something else when we were interrupted.

The aluminum door made a crackle followed by a slam. Two young Mexican guys walked in. They were wearing jeans, T-shirts, and work shoes, and they were covered in dusty dirt. The guy on the left was lighter skinned and had a scar running down his left cheek. The guy on the right was missing a tooth.

"Hey, hey, hey, amigos!" Vasquez said, and the two guys smiled. They exchanged soul hugs with the three fighters. Then they spoke in rapid-fire Spanish that I couldn't begin to understand. The light-skinned guy did more of the talking with the one-tooth guy, adding detail from time to time. Vasquez responded conversationally with Jesus adding a word or two but clearly involved. Hector listened intently, occasionally raising his eyes to look at his brother.

Something was wrong. I didn't understand a word of the language, but I could tell by inflection and by the looks exchanged that there was trouble. The light-skinned guy was getting agitated but not at the fighters; it was clear it was the subject matter.

Jesus took over from Vasquez and was having a calming effect—the two young guys de-escalated as the champion spoke. Then the light-skinned guy teared up, and Jesus grabbed him with one arm and pulled him to his side in a rough hug.

"*Mañana por la noche*," Jesus said.

"*Mañana?*" the light-skinned guy asked.

"*Sí*," Jesus answered.

"*Sí? Sí? Gracias, gracias!*" The light-skinned guy's face lit up and he lunged a hug at Juan Carlos.

Hector smiled and shook his head.

"*Tranquillo,* man, *tranquillo…*" Juan Carlos said.

The two younger men nodded a lot and smiled in that awkward way where someone has so much emotion that they aren't sure how to act. They said "*gracias*" a bunch more times and then left.

Immediately the three fighters started talking a mile a minute. Vasquez raised his voice one time and slapped the bar. Jesus gave him a look and a hand gesture that gave him the message to settle down. Jesus mostly listened but was attentive. When his brother asked him something directly he raised his eyebrows to show he was listening and then nodded in the affirmative.

The three got quiet suddenly and I could tell they were thinking.

"*Un momento,*" Jesus said and held up a hand. He turned and stared at me.

"*Qué opinas?*"

"Duffy?" Vasquez pushed out his lower lip and cocked his head to one side in that international language that said, "I'm thinking."

Jesus motioned to his brother. Hector held his hands up as if to say, "Why not?"

Jesus looked at me for a long time without saying anything. His eyes were powerful, and even though I outweighed him by about seventy pounds I felt small. I sipped the empty Tecate in front of me just to have something to do.

"Can I trust you?" Jesus said in a low voice.

I stared back at him. It was one of those man-to-man—shit—person-to-person moments when someone was trying to find out what you were all about.

"Yeah, you can trust me," I said. I looked into his brown eyes and held his gaze.

"Yeah, I think I can," Jesus said. "We need your help."

CHAPTER FORTY-SEVEN

"THOSE TWO GUYS," Jesus said. "They got a family problem."

I just listened.

"They got a sister. She ain't legal. She needs...some help." He was struggling with the words.

I listened.

"She's whoring, well..." He made a look with his eyebrows. "Escorting they call it. The guy won't let her out."

Vasquez and Hector were focused on me.

"We want to go get her out of that shit, but when they see us *Mexicanos* they get suspicious, pull their guns. You, you can go as a customer and they won't suspect. You—"

I didn't let him finish. "I'm in," I said.

"I didn't finish," Jesus said.

"It doesn't matter. I'm in."

"These guys, they're Russian mob or some bullshit. Badass motherfuckers." Jesus looked at me hard.

"So am I," I said.

* * *

After the sun went down I checked into the Lucky 7 motel. It was a dirtbag place across the street from the Mandalay Bay that cost thirty-four dollars a night. It was one of those cinderblock motels built on a slab and the room smelled musty. The view of the parking lot with its empty bottles, discarded escort ads, and various other crap didn't make up for its look.

I was in room twenty-one and Jesus, Hector, and Vasquez were next door in room twenty-two. I dialed the number they gave me and requested "Crystal." The woman with the slight Russian accent said it would be forty-five minutes to an hour. I felt like a scumbag even though I wasn't planning on getting any of the offered services.

I lay down on the sagging mattress and turned on the TV. There was a commercial for Rusakov's title fight across the street and a million miles away at the Mandalay Bay. The local news tease cut to the same demonstration we saw earlier that day at Mike's, but this time I could understand what was being said.

"America for Americans!" the guy named Sinkoff was saying to a mob of several hundred on the steps of some city building. "If you break the laws of this land you don't deserve to be part of it!" he went on.

A knock on the door interrupted my train of thought. It was Jesus.

"Is it ready?" he said.

"Yeah," I said.

"You don't have to do this."

I shrugged.

"When you are ready for us, yell 'now!'" Jesus said.

"How about 'ahora!'"

Jesus shook his head and nodded. Then he looked me in the eye and got quiet. "Thank you, Duffy," he said.

I nodded and closed the door. I went to the vinyl-covered chair and pretended to watch television while I waited. The Atlanta Braves were leading the San Diego Padres 1–0. If it had been the Yankees and the seventh game of the World Series it still wouldn't have held my interest.

Just as Tim McCarver was making my hair hurt with an explanation of the infield fly rule there came a knock at the door. I turned off the TV and went to open it. I suddenly became hyperaware of everything. My heartbeat kicked up, I noticed I could hear the TV in room twenty-two but not in twenty, and I noticed it was dark out with the only light coming from the small parking lot in back of the motel and from the dingy office.

In front of me stood Crystal in white thigh-highs, white pumps, and a lacy bra. Next to her was a guy who looked like an NFL tight end.

"Hello, baby, I'm Crystal," she said with a thick Spanish accent. "Dis is Sergy. He stays outside the door, that's the rules," she said.

"Okay by me," I said. I smiled and motioned Crystal in and closed the door.

"Okay, what you want, baby, I do it—" I silenced her by putting my finger to my lips and she tilted her head playfully.

Then I took two powerful backward steps and slammed my back into the door.

"C'mon, bitch!" I yelled at the top of my lungs, then I slapped my hands together as loud as I could while ramming my back into the door again. "Bitch!" I yelled again and did the slap routine again. Crystal was freaked out and had her hand over her mouth.

I heard the key in the lock. I readied myself just outside of the doorway, bent my knees, and put one foot slightly in front of the other.

The door opened. I didn't hesitate. I stepped one foot in front of the other, jumped, and threw the hardest front kick I had thrown since I left karate for boxing years ago. It was an easy kick to execute and it brought a lot of force with it. I aimed for Sergy's solar plexus and got close enough to do the damage I wanted to do.

"*Ahora!*" I screamed in place of a karate yell as Sergy let out a *hmmf* followed by the moan of a man whose wind had just been knocked out of him. He was on the cement outside my room rolling around when the three amigos stormed out of their door, grabbed Crystal, and ran for their pickup truck. I ran with them, jumped in the back, and Jesus hit the gas while my new friend Sergy was still moaning.

Once I was in the truck there were two things that registered with me.

One was the fact that Sergy had been holding a gun when I kicked him.

The other was that he was wearing a golf shirt with "SHB" on the chest.

CHAPTER FORTY-EIGHT

THE BOYS DROPPED me in front of the Flamingo on their way out of the city. I got some quick thank-yous before jumping out of the truck, but we didn't linger. They were preoccupied with getting off the Strip and somewhere out of the public eye.

My knees felt wobbly and my hands shook a little as I walked in among the throngs of tourists. My heart was beating fast and I could feel my vision getting just a little blurry. I kept walking and did my best to move forward around as many people crowding the sidewalks as I could.

I booked past Jimmy Buffet's place, which was blaring "Margaritaville" for what I figured had to be the zillionth time that day. I broke into a short trot and jogged through the sidewalks in front of the Venetian and then ran up the stairs to the crosswalk to the TI. From there I jogged across to the outdoor mall on the corner and crossed the street again in front of the Wynn. I had to run; there was just way too much going on inside me to expect walking to contain.

My chest was thumping but it wasn't the running—it was the panic. The night's activity ran through my head. Committing violence, especially on someone who wasn't expecting it, just wasn't me. I know I did something for the greater good, but I had hurt another human who I didn't know in the process. He probably—shit—he most certainly had it coming, but I didn't like hurting people. Boxing is different. I know that sounds twisted, but boxing is sanctioned; everyone in the ring knows what they are in for. Kicking a guy who doesn't know it's coming is pure violence, and I didn't like it. The fact that he was prepared to shoot me or Crystal with a handgun didn't change anything. I put myself in that situation, said yes to Jesus, and I didn't have to.

It was for the greater good—my chief and ultimate rationalization.

It worked, a little, but it was also what had set off the pounding that had now moved from my chest up to my head. I was in a full run now and up the street past the tacky strip malls and coming up on the Riviera. Up close, the front of the Riviera was ugly and kitschy and not anything like the glowing façade you see on the Travel Channel.

I didn't stop there. I turned down a side street and went into an all-out sprint. I blew past what had to be the tiniest casino in Las Vegas, called the Greek Isles, and kept pumping my legs with my head down.

Ever since I was kid, when something bothered me I did this. It wasn't running away, it was almost running to get my body to catch up with my thoughts. In the end, the exhaustion of it would calm me. As an adult I often let the ring do it, but when life got weird enough I still got to running.

I ran hard down the sidewalk until a crosswalk made me stop.

I bent over and hyperventilated with my hands on my knees. No one noticed, no one said anything at the crowded street crossing. This was Vegas.

My vision cleared. I looked up, and for the first time I was aware of where I stood. I was in front of the Las Vegas Hilton Casino, formerly the International. I didn't set out to get here, I was just running.

This was where Elvis had lived.

CHAPTER FORTY-NINE

I'M NOT SURE if it was the running exhaustion or the distraction of the Hilton, but my mind slowed.

The Hilton wasn't gigantic by today's Vegas standards, but that made sense because it was built in 1969 when Elvis opened the showroom. He lived on the top floor and, man, I would've loved to be a fly on the wall just one night up there.

There was a statue of Elvis out front just before you got to the lobby. The plaque had an inscription from Baron Hilton saluting Elvis and his record of consecutive sell-out shows. The statue didn't look much like Elvis, but it was kind of like visiting a cemetery; I felt a certain reverence just being there.

The bright, air-conditioned chill of the lobby shocked my system in a not altogether positive way. The casino floor was right off the entrance, and there were ornate cut-glass chandeliers everywhere. The gaming tables and the chairs matched that sixties-seventies feel, and I just strolled around the place taking it in. Toward the back of the casino I saw the sign for the showroom and the marquee read "Elvis…Only Better."

They should know better.

The poster showed a guy in black leather who, I must admit, looked remarkably like Elvis straining to hit a note.

"Recreating the magic of the King six nights a week..." the copy read. There was a rectangular sign across the center of the original poster. It read: "This Tuesday: America's New Superstars Audition Show!" Apparently the Elvis guy was getting a shot on one of those ridiculous talent shows.

Geez.

Tonight's show was three hours away. I tried the door. It wasn't locked. I wanted to see where Elvis performed—better said, I wanted to feel where the man had been. I went in.

My first reaction to the showroom was to note the relatively small size. It held about two thousand seats, which at the time made it the biggest in Vegas, but it seemed way too small for Elvis. Stage guys were pushing equipment into place and running wire and that sort of stuff. I walked to the front of the stage, approaching it like I might walk into the Vatican.

A half a dozen guys were working away and paid no attention to me until I spoke.

"Excuse me," I said, trying to make those two words sound polite.

Two guys setting up a two-step riser half turned. One guy was in his twenties, with a mop of dirty brown hair, a soul patch, and an arm covered in dragon and snake tattoos. His partner looked late fifties and had the build and demeanor of a guy who drove a car parts supply truck. Grey flattop and functionally muscled arms let on that he had done manual labor for a lifetime.

"Yeah?" the young guy said.

"Uh, I'm sorry to bother you, but, uh, can I ask you a weird question?" I heard come out of my mouth.

"Sure," the young guy said. The older guy stopped what he was doing and looked my way too.

"Is there anyone around who worked here when Elvis was here?"

"You're looking at one of 'em," the young guy said and pointed at his partner.

The older guy looked at me without saying anything.

"Yeah, I was. Whaddya want to know?" he said. His impatience let me know for some reason it wasn't his favorite topic.

"Uh, it's just that…uh, well, Elvis means a lot to me…and—"

The guy cut me off. "He was a hell of a nice guy, Elvis was," he said.

"Really?"

"Fuckin' A right he was. The reason I didn't say nuthin' at first was because I've gone sour on the public about it. They all think he was a fat, drugged-out slob, and shit, I know he had trouble, I'm no fool, but the good, no, great times with him far outweighed the other shit," he said.

I didn't know what to say.

"C'mere, man," he said. His partner looked at him funny.

"On stage?"

"C'mon." He dug into his pocket.

I hoisted myself up on the stage and walked where Elvis used to walk.

"He gave me this. Me, a fuckin' twenty-four-year-old stage-hand. Elvis Presley gave *me* this," he said, showing me a gold crucifix with a diamond where the cross met.

"The guy had heard that my mother had died and he came down from his suite right around this time of day before a show and took it off from around his neck and gave it to me. He said that he remembered what losing his mom felt like."

The guy stared right at me, his eyes glazed.

I looked at it and looked back at him. I was in awe.

"So yeah, man, I was here when he was here and just about everyone has a story like that one. He didn't act like no big shot. He was a real guy." He hesitated. "Which makes the fact that I work for this fuckin' clown that impersonates him a fuckin' horror show."

I gave the guy a look.

"Oh, don't get me started. He's all full of himself and fuckin' arrogant. *He's* arrogant and the real guy wasn't—go figure. And say what you want, but Elvis treated people like people."

"That sucks," I said.

"Yeah, and to make matters worse, I have to hang outside his dressing room before each of his shows as *security*. Standing there just waiting on his beck and call. It makes me—"

"Boggsy, shush. Here he comes." The young guy gave him a look.

"Yeah, yeah, yeah…"

A booming voice came from the side of the stage. "Look, you better have this straight by Tuesday. That's what's important, you got it?" Jimmy and his partner turned and watched as a guy who looked remarkably like Elvis berate a young stagehand. He had a finger in the guy's face and the twentysomething hung his head.

"Fuckin' asshole…" Boggsy muttered.

"Listen up, everyone!" The guy called everyone to attention. The stage crew reluctantly gave him their attention. "I said listen the fuck up!"

This guy was easy to hate.

"Look, you have to get this shit straight by Tuesday, you hear me? This audition is my ticket out. I don't want to be doing imitations of that fat fuck my whole life, and this can change all that. If I get all the blue hairs all wet in their granny panties and the network people dig it, I'm set for TV. So don't fuck that up." I noticed none of the crew made eye contact.

I could feel the blood behind my face and it began to throb. I was out of place and out of my element, but that was too bad.

"Watch what you say, asshole!" I heard come out of my mouth. The stage got quiet, and I felt the attention turn in my direction.

"Who the hell is this?" The Elvis guy looked at me in disbelief. "What, are you one of those losers obsessed with him?" He punctuated his words with a mocking laugh.

I took a step toward him and Boggsy stepped in front of me.

"Don't do it, kid. Security will have you arrested."

I could feel my heart beat in my throat, but for whatever reason I followed his advice.

"Come back sometime when we can both talk," Boggsy said.

It was time for me to go.

CHAPTER FIFTY

I TRIED TO cool down with a beer in the Hilton's gigantic sports book. I was still pissed but doing my best to ignore it. I just couldn't let the disrespect from someone like that go. Watching three hundred sporting events on movie-screen-sized televisions didn't do the trick, but the beer was cold and the waitresses who kept coming to the server station next to me had fishnet stockings on legs that went all the way up. It did help distract me a bit.

I called the boys to check in. Still no Jerry. Rocco said they had looked all morning and had taken a break to gamble. They were playing blackjack at the Imperial Palace and they had a Marilyn Monroe lookalike as a dealer. Rocco made the point of saying she was fifty pounds overweight but that she had huge knockers and was better looking than the Britney Spears dealer who had zits and was too tall. I didn't really know how to argue with him. They were on a semihot streak but agreed to meet me at the Star Trek bar in two hours. That meant I had time to kill.

As much as I hated the Elvis guy, I decided I had to see his show. It wasn't so much for entertainment value as it was…I don't know…maybe gathering evidence. It felt like something I had to do. I bought a ticket and headed in.

I sat in the back of the same showroom that Elvis had played and let my mind wonder what this place had to be like in '72 when he was on top. Then I wondered what '76, his last engagement, must've been like and how they compared. I was starting to get melancholy when the *Space Odyssey* theme came on and I sat up.

The fifteen-piece band went through Elvis's opening riff and out the guy came. I almost couldn't believe it: he had the look, the walk, and even the facial expression. Some of the band members I recognized as guys who had backed up the real Elvis—some of my all-time music heroes were playing behind the fake. It felt sad. Then he picked up a guitar identical to the one Elvis used in the concert years and went into "CC Rider."

I didn't want to like it. I wanted to hate it.

He was remarkable, and the crowd responded like he was Him. Old ladies, young ladies, men, kids were all standing and screaming.

"Burning Love," "You've Lost that Lovin' Feeling," "Polk Salad Annie" led into the "Teddy Bear/Don't Be Cruel" medley complete with scarves. Then "Blue Suede Shoes," "Hound Dog," and then he killed with "Suspicious Minds."

I admit it, I liked it.

The guy wasn't just good, he was great.

He did "The American Trilogy" and then dedicated "My Way" to who he called his "inspiration," without mentioning Elvis's name, and I wondered if that was part of the stage illusion or an Elvis Presley Enterprises copyright thing.

He thanked everyone and then closed the show with "Can't Help Falling in Love," the number Elvis ended his show on, and I was on my feet with everyone else giving a standing ovation.

Only I wasn't clapping for the guy on stage; I was clapping for the original.

CHAPTER FIFTY-ONE

AFTER THE SHOW it took me twenty minutes to find the guys. The absurdity of meeting the guys at the Star Trek lounge hadn't really sunk in yet. It was a walk from the showroom and it took me a little while. Along the way I got to see bits of the casino.

The gift shop was selling Barry Manilow stuff, and I felt a little nauseous to think that Manilow was now the headliner on Elvis's same stage. Sure, they did an Elvis tribute, but that was during Barry's vacations and off nights. There were Manilow handbags, T-shirts, and satin jackets and involuntarily the song "Mandy" started to play in my head. I concentrated hard and made myself sing "Don't Be Cruel" to ward it off.

I followed the signs to Star Trek and entered into a bigger-than-life *Starship Enterprise*. Actually, as I thought of it, it wouldn't be "bigger than life," it would be "bigger than fake" or "bigger than imagination" or something. Either way, there was no doubting it was weird.

I got to the bar, and it was there that I thought I may have finally and unquestionably lost it. Rocco, TC, and Jerry Number One were there sitting in order, there was an empty seat next to Jerry where Jerry should be, and then there were three other patrons dressed in Star Trek costumes.

Rocco was talking to a really tall guy in costume.

"So, what do you put on your tax return, Klingon?" Rocco said.

"I don't file earthly taxes," the huge guy said with a straight face.

TC turned and greeted me. "Hey, Duff. Rocco's making friends with the casino's Klingon. The guy has to stay in character and Rocco seems to have a hard time accepting that."

"How long has he been talking to him?" I said.

"About a half an hour," Jerry Number One chimed in.

"Are Klingons dangerous?" I asked.

"Rocco keeps badgering him and this guy might turn dangerous," TC said.

"I got one for you." Rocco was now saying to the guy. "You know what planet Klingons are originally from? Uranus. Get it? Your Anus!" Rocco laughed really hard.

The Klingon didn't, though I don't think it was just a matter of staying in character. He turned and walked out of the bar.

"Geez, that guy was weird," Rocco said.

"How many times a day do you think he hears the 'Your Anus' line?" TC said.

"Whaddya talking about? I made that up," Rocco said.

The three of us just stared at him.

"Any word from Jerry?" I asked, taking the silence as an opportunity.

"Not a word, but we saw him on the Strip," Jerry Number One said. "It wasn't good," he said.

"He was with this really seedy-looking guy, some kind of Mexican," TC said.

"And Jerry looked rough. His hair was all screwed up, his clothes were dirty, and he looked disinorientated," Rocco said.

"Disoriented?" I asked.

"I just said that," Rocco said.

I let it go.

"Why didn't you guys grab him or at least talk to him?" I fished around my pocket to find a twenty to pay for the next round of beers. It came to my attention again that I still had the check with me.

"We were in the TI on the casino floor. TC spotted him way across the casino by the high-stakes blackjack area. We went toward him, but he saw us and he and the Mexican guy split," Jerry Number One said.

"I think the Mexican guy has him kidnapped," TC said.

"Why would anyone kidnap Jerry? I mean what for? Who are they going to call for ransom?" I said.

No one had an answer. We just sat there with nothing to say at the bar filled with Trekkies.

"Oh, Duff, not to change the subject, but they want you at the gym tomorrow at one. Lucille told me to tell you that Stan said that," Rocco said. "She also said something about getting ready because it's going to get hard."

"Get hard? How much harder could it get?" I asked. "Anything else new back at the Appaloosa?"

"Yeah, some guy came in last night all pissed off. It looked like he worked for the outfit. He got in a beef with Stan about getting jumped and losing a girl," Jerry Number One said.

I felt a little sick to my stomach.

"What did he look like?" I said.

"He was big, thick-neck guy, balding on top. He had on a golf shirt," Rocco said.

My stomach felt sicker.

CHAPTER FIFTY-TWO

FROM A DISTANCE *he watched them pull away in their pick-up truck. The big white guy jumping in the back like a fool and the whore pushed in between the two Mexicans in front. He had been following the truck for days and relished the idea of taking them all out and getting it done all at once.*

Who was the big white man and why was he in with this group? Yes, he was a fighter like the others, but he was less than a nobody. Not like the other three who were well known, at least in Mexico. Their status didn't sicken him any less; in fact, he hated them more. He followed the truck at a distance while it went down the Strip and the white man jumped out and started to run. This man was bizarre, and not just because he associated with the Mexicans.

He thought about killing all four in the truck, but the shooting would be too difficult while he drove. He could pick off one, maybe two, but it wouldn't be worth the risk of being identified by the ones remaining. He smiled to himself, smirked actually, at how much he wanted to kill, but also at his self-restraint, his patience, and confidence. They had served him well in the past and they were still his greatest weapons.

There would be a time and a place, and he would kill all three like a predator intelligently stalking its prey. That's what he always had been and it was what he always would be.

CHAPTER FIFTY-THREE

I LEFT THE fellas on the *Starship Enterprise* to go get the Lincoln and then picked them up in front of the Hilton. I was exhausted, and the Town Car stayed quiet the whole route. The Jerry spotting had the gang worried and the tension hung heavy.

We pulled in the gate and I decided I wasn't going to linger in the bar or hang around. I didn't know where the SHB guy fit in with my current employer, but I really didn't want to take any chances. I went straight for bed.

Al was asleep exactly on the center of the bed, and the TV was on the local all-news channel. I was on my way to the bathroom when the news on the half hour turned me around.

"Two Mexicans found murdered execution style, two blocks off of Fremont Street..." was the news teaser.

I stood in the bathroom doorway and listened to the story.

"Two migrant workers were shot and killed on Bridger Avenue just two blocks off of Fremont Street. Each with a single twenty-two-caliber bullet hole to the back of their heads. The wounds are consistent with professional execution. There are no suspects and the two men's identities remain a mystery," the female anchor said.

I didn't get it. Somebody was killing Mexicans for no reason other than to kill them. They weren't taking jobs—hell, they were doing jobs that no one ever wanted, that is except for the fighter, but that seemed like some sort of weird coincidence. Did they want to pass out escort baseball cards or wash dishes or wait at the pickup spot to go do daily labor?

I decided to get a beer to help fall asleep and was headed back to the bar when I saw a woman walking toward me. It was dark, but I could still see she was wearing a long black dress with matching gloves and black pumps. Apparently there was a customer who had an elegance fetish.

The woman and I were headed straight for one another, and when her face came into the beam of the security spotlight I couldn't believe my eyes.

"Angelina? Whoa, you're...beautiful," I managed.

She didn't stop. She wiped a tear and started to run toward the main building.

"Angelina—"

She didn't stop.

I doubled back and went through the employee's entrance to find her and find out what was going on. She must've disappeared into Lucille's office or maybe a bathroom because there was no trace of her. I went through a curtain and came in the back of the bar room. It was a busy night. Every stool was taken by one of the girls, each with a companion. There was a line forming for two more customers, and the place was full of energy.

It was a weird energy. I'm no prude, but it felt kind of sick. I don't care how playful and distant the women got; there was no way that this stuff didn't stain your soul. Lucille was out front charming guests and talking a mile a minute.

I came around the bar slowly but didn't see any sign of my friend with the SHB golf shirt. Trust me—it's easy to go unnoticed in a busy whorehouse.

"Hey, Rocky," Lucille's voice startled me. "Where you been? I need you on the floor keeping an eye on things."

I nodded. I was on the floor anyways, so what the hell.

"Get yourself a beer but stay alert, you got it?" Her cigarette dangled off her bottom lip impossibly as she spoke.

Robin was working the bar. She gracefully slid a bottle of Bud in front of me and went right back to working the crowd. The clientele at the bar ranged from some rich preppy boys with Long Island accents to what looked like a pair of midfifties truckers. There was still no sign of Angelina and I was concerned. I walked back toward the lounge area wondering what could have been wrong when I saw the sign.

"Ever had a true virgin? You can! See Lucille for details!"

I froze. My stomach flipped.

I went straight to Lucille, who was talking to a fat guy with a handlebar mustache and suspenders. I interrupted her rap.

"What's the story with the virgin?"

"Excuse me, Bart. Duffy, you need to show some manners, especially around our guests."

"What's the *story*?"

She paused, excused herself from her conversation with a smile, and turned me by the elbow. She dropped the smile.

"Look, you punch-drunk fuck, there's business going on here. I don't care what's on your mind. Don't you ever forget that."

"What is it, Lucille?" I asked again, looking her dead in the eye.

"This is my business. I don't explain myself to you."

"Angelina?" I said.

Lucille didn't say anything.

"Is it?"

She went to walk away. I grabbed her by her fat upper arm.

"Tell me!"

She turned and looked at me. She hesitated then spoke. "She came to us. She can rake in five figures. That's more than she makes in a year here," Lucille said. She lit a cigarette, pursed her lips, and raised her eyebrows, then walked away.

I had to swallow hard to keep from throwing up.

CHAPTER FIFTY-FOUR

I STARED AT the ceiling the whole night.

Every rationalization, every distancing technique I tried failed. I couldn't get my head around making this okay. I was half sick to my stomach, half furious to the point where my head hurt and my neck twitched.

Stan had left a voice mail to get to Tocco's around one the next day. I had gotten no sleep and my concentration wasn't going to be in the ring. But a job's a job, and since I was getting paid I had to show up. There was no sign of Stan at the Appaloosa, so I checked in with Lucille, who gave me permission to take one of the Lincolns.

It was already unbearably hot even though it was only a little after noon. When I came through the doors, Jesus caught my eye and motioned me over to his side of the gym. He invited me to train with the Mexicans. I sat on a wood bench and wrapped my hands. Across the gym, I saw Rusakov in the ring with his conditioning coach. He was doing his thing, squatting low and then bounding up in the air.

The round bell went off, ending the interval, and the energy in the gym temporarily faded for sixty seconds. I stifled a yawn and Jesus caught it.

"Blanco, thank you for last night," he said.

I nodded my head but didn't look up.

"Hey, you alright?"

I shrugged.

"You better get yourself right," he said.

"I know," I said.

I got up and started to shake things out, but the body just wasn't responding today. I took it up a notch to get warm and to break some sweat. My body came around slowly, and though I got a bit warm, it was a creaky loose.

"Duffy!" Constantine yelled.

It dawned on me how much a professional sparring partner had in common with a piece of livestock.

The bell sounded and Rusakov came at me. I moved to my right and gave him very little to hit. I didn't want to be a punching bag and so I got on my bicycle a bit and went "Hector" on him. Hector Camacho was one of my all-time favorite boxers because he was a brilliant defensive fighter. He'd keep giving his opponent angles and movement and when he clinched, he'd spin the fighter to disorient him.

Methodically I moved to my right, mixed in the occasional feint to my left, and then went right back to moving right. Rusakov was the quintessential Euro fighter; he moved like a stiff water buffalo. He had power, but he had to be planted and set to utilize it. Today I was doing my best not to let that happen.

In the second minute of the round he got frustrated. I turned, faked left, and went right and he threw his right hand. It missed by so much it was embarrassing. This pissed him off even more and he barreled in toward me, actually growling. My movement had him off balance and he made a mistake. He came in with his head bowed looking to punish me.

My footwork had me in position and so did his coming toward me with rage. It wasn't effective rage, though, because his equilibrium was off. He threw a hard overhand right that might've killed me if I had been there for it, but I was already two steps to my right. The force of the punch put him out of position and off balance again. I stepped in and hit him with a three-punch combination. None was super hard, but he was caught with his pants down and in a fundamentally unsound position.

My punches didn't hurt him as much as the other day's knockdown, but they humiliated him even more. He was defeated in the technical chess match part of this game against a nobody. The gym had grown quiet and more attention was being focused on the ring as the training fighters started to watch.

I was in a rhythm and my confidence was gaining, compounded by Rusakov's frustration. He swung with anger to the place where I had been and got twisted up in his own momentum. I stepped in and hit him with a quick right-left and went back to moving to my right. This combination had more steam in it—it hurt and embarrassed him more than the other.

Out of the corner of my eye I could see Jesus high-five Hector and laugh. It felt good to know I had impressed two guys I had so much admiration for. Rusakov had begun to tire and slowed down. He seemed content to let the round run out.

The bell sounded, and I didn't offer my glove to tap in sportsmanship. I didn't even look at him. I just stepped toward my corner like he wasn't there. I was in my own zone. It may have been the absolute high point of my fight career.

That changed when I felt a sharp blow to the back of my head and everything went black.

CHAPTER FIFTY-FIVE

It was getting close to time.

Sure, doing away with one piece of scum after another was productive and worth doing on its own, but it wasn't big enough. No, all of this was just part of the setup.

If he could take out and embarrass a hero, a man of the people, and at the same time serve his own needs, it would be perfect. He smiled just at the thought of it.

He had killed enough of them for this to fit in. It was like he had done everything in his life. He once heard someone describe his military precision, his ability to focus on his goal, as being his greatest strength. He loved that view of himself and took pride in it.

Through his sunglasses he watched the front door of the boxing gym. He could get this close over and over and no one took notice. It was why he often came to the bodega, just to become part of the scenery and to blend in.

He noticed a hush in the gym and then angry yelling. It came in Spanish and there was clearly something wrong. The Spanish was joined with Russian shouts. Something was wrong. Today wouldn't be a good day. He drove off before he was noticed.

CHAPTER FIFTY-SIX

I CAME TO in Frankie's office. Things were soupy and I had an ache that started in the back of my head and spread across my entire skull.

"He suckered you from behind at the end of the second round," Frankie said.

"Rusakov? Why?" I said.

"You took him to school with a lot of movement in the first round. He was embarrassed."

"Hold it. I took him to school?"

"Yeah. You came out with a lot of movement. You turned him, moved to your right, feigned, and went back. After about a minute he was getting tied up with his own feet and you started to land."

"Me?"

"You don't remember, huh?"

I didn't remember anything from the time I left the Appaloosa. I remembered waking up and feeling like shit. I sort of remembered not wanting to take a beating today, but that was about it.

"Hey, what's with you and the Mexicans?" Frankie asked.

"Whaddya mean?" I said.

"After he suckered you they all started yelling at Rusakov. They were cursing him and his team. The Russians all split because it seemed like there was going to be a riot."

I smiled. "I helped them with, uh, a personal matter the other night. I think they are appreciative."

Frankie's eyebrows lifted and he pursed his lips. "Uh huh," was all he said. "Well, it got ugly in here. Your ole buddy Constantine ain't gonna be happy. Probably move out of the gym."

"Fuck him."

"Yeah, but the money's good, ain't it?" Frankie's sarcasm was thick.

"It ain't that anymore, you know that," I said.

We just sat quietly for a long moment. Frankie exhaled hard and put his hands on his knees before getting up.

"It's been a while since I had the gloves on and been in there," Frankie nodded toward the ring. "But I remember. Kid, you get a little older and you start to realize that setting out to prove yourself all day, every day doesn't mean shit."

I didn't say anything back. I didn't want what was on my mind to come out disrespectful. Frankie picked up on it.

"And you just being nice and don't want to tell this fat old fuck that when you get to be his age you can cash it all in and be a pussy."

I didn't say anything.

I couldn't.

CHAPTER FIFTY-SEVEN

I GOT BACK to the ranch, and the Foursome, minus Jerry Number Two, was lined up at the bar in perfect order. The "virgin" sign was still up and I felt a little sick when I went past it.

My head still had that soupy feeling and I felt a little nauseous. When I moved, it seemed like my brain lagged behind and then rushed up against the front of my skull.

"Did anyone ever tell you that you have beautiful skin?" TC was saying to Robin, who was in her position behind the bar. I sat down next to Jerry Number One.

"He's still doin' it," Jerry said.

"Hitting on the ladies and acting like he's got a rap going?" I said.

"Yep," Jerry said.

Robin came down the bar and asked me what she could get me. I told her a double bourbon with one ice cube and a bottle of Rolling Rock because they didn't have Schlitz.

Her eyes went up and she kind of tilted her head.

"Took a head shot today, didn't you?" Rocco said.

I pressed the Rolling Rock to my forehead. I could feel the swelling ease just a bit.

"How'd you know?"

"Shit, kid, you drink with us every night. Every night it's Schlitz unless you get drilled. Then it's Jim Beam."

"I'm flattered you pay so much attention to me, my dear Rocco," I said.

"Thing is, kid, it used to be a couple times a year or after a big fight. Lately you order the bourbon a couple of times a week while you're pressing a bottle to your forehead."

I didn't say anything. It was one thing when Dr. Rudy or Smitty said something to me because it was their job to worry about such things. Rocco was so out of it he once asked me why the Beatles were never on Ed Sullivan anymore. The fact that he noticed my head hurt more often bothered me.

"Do you like to dance?" TC said to Robin.

"I love to dance, but I'm strictly all about the tango," Robin said with an exaggerated wink.

"Meow!" TC said and made a scratching motion with his hand.

Jerry covered his eyes, shook his head, and let his elbows hit the bar.

I slid the empty bourbon in front of me and took a sip out of the half-gone Rolling Rock.

"Another?" Robin asked. She knew it was a yes. She was intuitive, like the best bartenders were. When they also happened to be female and the customers were male, the value of that intuition went up a notch. Add in her other profession and I bet she could open a private practice.

She placed the second bourbon in front of me, and when she did, she let her hand slightly graze mine. I looked up and our eyes met for an instant. It was so quick it left me wondering if I had imagined it.

"Hey, what do you know about this virgin thing?" I asked her.

She put her hand on her hip and faced me. "You interested? It will be crazy expensive," she said.

I gave her a disgusted look.

"One of the maids wants in the business. It's a hell of a way to start. You don't find many virgins in Nevada."

"How's it work?"

"I think they make it like an auction—only kind of playful. Guys bid to drive up the price and the winner gets, you know, a night with a virgin. Bidding ends tonight and the 'deed' will happen tomorrow. Lucille asked me to help escort her to meet the winner."

I gulped the bourbon. "Do you know her?" I said.

"We've chatted. She's pretty naïve, but she definitely wants the cash. She doesn't say a whole lot. She mostly keeps to herself."

I forced another gulp even though the last sip hadn't settled yet. I felt something go bad inside.

"She's got no business doing this. Not her," I said.

Robin pursed her lips, and the playful nature ran out of her instantly. She turned her back and started to wipe down the bar. She lit a cigarette and found a reason to fill a cooler.

It took me a long moment to realize what I had said.

CHAPTER FIFTY-EIGHT

THE NEXT MORNING I got a call that sparring would move to the Mandalay Bay and that I was to be there at one o'clock. Rusakov's fight was a week away. I guessed they were looking to maximize the media coverage so that boxing fans would throw down a mortgage payment to watch it on Pay-Per-View. I also suspected that the ugliness with the Mexicans at the gym may have hurried the move.

I headed to the bar to get some coffee in my system. Al tagged along at my heels, and he wouldn't shut up. He kept a steady bark punctuated by crescendos that would go right through your cranium. Halfway to the main building, I had had it.

"Shut the hell up, would ya!" I screamed. Al didn't even pause. He pointed his nose straight at me and almost seemed to rise up off the ground while he went into bark overdrive.

He matched the intensity of my anger, and I do believe if there was a canine linguist with us fluent in Basset he would say that my dog just told me to fuck off.

I got to the bar and asked for a large coffee. There were no customers there, just Marilyn with the buck teeth on duty. Al continued to bark, now adding in hums and growls.

"What's the matter, pumpkin?" Marilyn came around the bar without getting my coffee. "Baby need a cookie?"

She handed Al a handful of Chips Ahoy.

"Good boy!" she said and scratched Al under the chin, which set off that turbo back leg thing.

"Marilyn, uh, coffee?" I said.

"Oh yeah, sorry."

She slid a black coffee in front of me.

"I have to go to the Mandalay Bay today. Is there an easy way to avoid traffic?" I asked.

Before she could answer, Al kicked in with his barking again.

"What's the matter with him today? He seems so tense."

"If that's the case, he's tense a lot. Do I go right up the Strip or—"

She didn't let me finish. "You should take him to the dog spa at Mandalay. It's awesome. It is really awesome."

"Dog spa?" I let it sink in for a second. "Did you say dog spa?"

"What time do you have to be at Mandalay?"

I was having difficulty tracking the conversation. "Uh, one, but—"

"Hang on," she said.

I sipped my coffee while she disappeared. Al continued to bark so that I couldn't hear what the pretty CNN brunette was saying on the TV over the bar. Without the sound her over-the-top facial expressions looked more ridiculous than usual.

"He's all set for one!" Marilyn said. She was smiling from ear to ear.

"Huh?"

"He's got an appointment at Pawsome for one o'clock."

"Pawsome?"

"That's the spa at Mandalay for pets. He's gonna love it!" She couldn't contain herself.

I decided to cut my conversational losses with Marilyn and find my own way to Mandalay. I really needed to get my coffee earlier in Vegas, and as far as getting Al to a dog spa for some pampering, well, why not?

The Mandalay Bay is an amazing structure. In fact, it is several structures. There's the main casino and hotel, which has gold iridescent windows that reflect the desert sun. There's also an upscale tower simply called "THE Hotel," and there's a nine-thousand-seat arena where the fights were to be held. The Mandalay Bay is one of the largest hotels in the world, but not even the largest on the block. With the MGM, the Luxor, New York-New York, and the Excalibur all within a half mile, the scale of things was minimized.

The doorman directed me to Pawsome.

It was at the end of a long corridor adjacent to the human spa. Al pranced down the hallway and had a certain bounce to his step, almost like he knew he was going to get pampered. On second thought, Al spent his life getting pampered, so his excitement must have been because of all the new smells the Mandalay had to offer.

I pulled open the door and headed to the front desk. The place smelled of eucalyptus, and the staff were scurrying around dressed in fancy pink spa uniforms.

"Good afternoon, welcome to Pawsome," the brunette with the pixie cut said. "I'm Cindi." She was strangely reminiscent of Flo on the Progressive commercials.

"Is this Al?" she said, looking down. She wasn't speaking to me; she was addressing the spa-ee directly.

"Al's spa treatment will be three hundred and fifty dollars." This time she looked up and was directly speaking to me.

My jaw opened and nothing came out.

Nothing.

"Oh, is he with the other bassets? Running a little late?" A different voice jogged me out of my three-hundred-and-fifty-dollar horror. It was a cheerful twentysomething with auburn hair. Her nametag read "Sunny."

"Uh, excuse me?"

"There's a party of five other bassets here, but they got to the spa a half an hour ago," Cindi said.

I didn't know which was more absurd—the three-hundred-and-fifty-dollar fee or the fact that there were already five bassets here.

"I'll bring him right back," Sunny said. "He'll be ready in ninety minutes. Would you like to see the facility?"

"Uh…"

"Aw, c'mon, right this way," Cindi said.

Al, the two spa attendants, and I went through a frosted door. Al's tail was high and wagging from side to side. We entered a large room with dog massage stations, fancy hair dryers, and a dog treadmill. There was a tricolor basset sleeping on the treadmill with a perky attendant cheering him on.

"C'mon, Roscoe! Three more minutes! Just three more minutes!" the trainer said.

I couldn't help but wonder what the previous part of Roscoe's workout was like.

"That's Roscoe's girlfriend, Anna," Cindi said, pointing to a little Yorkie who was watching Roscoe's roadwork. "She likes watching him work out."

I never wanted a girlfriend to watch me work out, not that any ever voiced any desire to.

"Here you can see this beautiful girl, Windy, getting a shiatsu rub." A very nice-looking hound on her side with her eyes closed was getting a shoulder rub. Windy seemed to be purring, and I couldn't say for sure, but she appeared to have a smile on her face.

"Over there Wilbur Johnson III is drying off after his mud treatment."

The hound with the royal name was standing on a table while a very pretty woman combed his fur while blow-drying it. Wilbur barked at the blow-dryer as if he was having an in-depth conversation.

Mud treatment? Al gets mud treatments whenever he goes to the dog park.

"That's Ed relaxing under a sun lamp," Cindi said, continuing on with the very perky tour.

Ole Eddie was having himself a fine time. At least his snoring seemed to indicate so. He was burning as many calories as his friend Roscoe, who was still asleep over on the treadmill.

"And over there is Dylan, he's the basset, and his little brother Harry the cat. They're getting their nails done."

The basset was eating the treat he'd earned for not growling when his nails were clipped. Harry, to his credit, seemed as relaxed as a cat in a room full of hounds could be. He was curled up in a ball next to his brother, who got a biscuit for every nail.

"And finally, that's Cleo in the hot tub."

Sure enough I saw the head of a hound sticking out of a specially made Jacuzzi. Her tongue was out, but she seemed to be quite mellow. Any more mellow and she would be comatose.

"Why is it all basset hounds today?" I asked.

"They do this every week at the same time. Their human companions are all friends and they work for the same basset rescue," Sunny said.

I looked over and saw Al being rubbed down by the pretty auburn-haired attendant. His eyes were closed and he was humming. The sum of three hundred and fifty dollars kept entering my consciousness.

Three hundred and fifty eff'in dollars.

Three hundred and fifty eff'in dollars.

Ah, what the hell. I had an extra ten thousand in disposable income. Still, Al in the Jacuzzi was a tough visual.

I looked at my watch and realized I was late for my job of getting professionally punched in the face.

I left Al and his basset spa friends at Pawsome.

I did my best to not dwell on the irony.

CHAPTER FIFTY-NINE

As I just learned, anything is possible in Las Vegas, including putting a boxing gym in the center of an active casino. The ring was set up in front of a row of slot machines and slightly behind the Let It Ride tables. Across the street, the MGM had a lion habitat to distract the gamblers' concentration, and the Mandalay had us.

A very attractive young blonde Mandalay employee named Heather handed me a shopping bag when I approached the makeshift workout area.

"Mr. Duffy, the sponsors request you wear their gear during the filming," Heather said. Her teeth were impossibly white and her blonde hair was something Brian Wilson would have written about.

"Excuse me?" I said.

"Take a look. It's top notch." Heather probably did very well on her annual performance appraisal in the "customer relations" category.

There was a shirt that advertised a beer/energy drink, trunks that mentioned an overpriced premium cable network, and a warm-up promoting the next movie release from someone who used to be on *SNL*. I didn't like him.

"No, thanks," I said.

Heather's eyes lost their sparkle. "But you have to."

I didn't budge.

"Mr. Duffy, it's on the contracted agreement. You're in violation of your agreement if you refuse."

My wish-they-all-could-be-California girl morphed into a member of OJ's legal dream team before my eyes.

"Contract? I don't have a contract," I said. I was getting annoyed.

"Steel Hammer Boxing certainly does, and you are employed by them. I suggest you wear the gear," she said with a tight, angry smile. She turned and walked away.

I don't like the color orange. I don't like words like "extreme" and "out of hand," and I especially don't like the TV commentators of a certain network. But I was now emblazoned with them as I started to warm up. The money I was getting was good, actually quite a bit better than good lately, and I guessed I could wear the stuff for a few hours.

It registered again how right Robin was. I fit in real well at the Appaloosa.

Over the white noise of slot machines, tinkles, bells, and the occasional cheer of the craps table, I heard a murmur from the crowd that had gathered around the boxing area. The bright light of a handheld camera danced along a moving group of people, and with a quick glance I could see Rusakov's head above the mass. As he got closer I could see DG by his side. Rusakov was smiling, signing autographs and making chitchat with the fans who joined in the procession with him.

He looked like a NASCAR driver his warm-ups had so many advertisements. He bounded up the steps to the ring and actually swung himself over the top rope like a teenager jumping a fence. The crowd cheered him on, and he flashed a bright smile and waved. Apparently none of the fans had ever had him punch them in the balls.

"Duffy, Duffy—come up here, my friend," Rusakov called to me and waved with a happy smile. "Everyone, here is the greatest sparring partner in the world!" He laughed playfully and hugged me when I came through the ropes.

I had felt less nauseous when he gave me the uppercut to my nut bag.

It amazed me how the son of a bitch could turn it on and off. It made him even more evil in my eyes.

We did three rounds of sparring totally for show, just for the fans and the media. He was the perfect gentleman, touching gloves at the beginning and at the end of each round and hugging me when it was over. Everyone ate it up.

The handsome ring announcer emceed the circus act. He introduced Carlos the "Grand Champion" and his son the "Next Grand Champion." The crowd loved them and gave them a huge ovation. DG had a million-dollar smile and a twinkle in his eye. He shook hands and did autographs with just enough fans on his way through the crowd. His son had just signed to fight a washed-up ex-contender on big-time TV. It was a setup and a sure win. Most guys had to fight for years and beat a range of opponents before they could even dream of the chance Junior was getting. Again, it was good to be the champ's son.

After the introductions and fanfare, that was pretty much it for the day. This close to fight night, fighters, especially heavyweights who don't have to worry about cutting weight to make the limit, rest and let their bodies get sharp. For me, it made my life easier and helped my head from continually throbbing.

When you're hired meat you're not exactly in media demand. While they hammered it up I grabbed a shower, threw my product placement gear in the trash, and went to get Al from his spa treatment.

CHAPTER SIXTY

I FOUND OUT that if you drop three hundred and fifty bucks on your hound at Pawsome, the hound gets the privilege of accompanying you on the casino floor for the rest of the day. Al was nice and shiny and proud of the "Casino Dog" badge that hung from his collar. He was prancing as we went up the corridor from the spa and headed to the casino.

When we turned toward the bells and jingles of the slots Al hesitated, then looked up and started to bark loudly. He pulled me in the direction of the center of the casino floor, and when I recovered from being startled and was able to focus, I understood why.

Right in front of us stood Angelina.

She was in a floor-length red dress. The hair that I had only seen up and pragmatically pulled back for maid duties now flowed off her shoulders. She wore makeup but she did so delicately. She was simply elegant.

Robin was with her and also dressed for show, but her sequined minidress was as tired as her eyes. She held Angelina's elbow lightly and escorted her across the casino floor. Robin was on the job, but Angelina was in the middle of a tragedy.

Where Robin's eyes showed tired resignation, Angelina's showed terror. Robin's lot had been cast a long time ago, but

Angelina had yet to discover what this life could do to you. The ends justifying the means, a credo I used as a mantra, failed. Even considering her brother, this wasn't right.

The thought of Angelina with some disgusting high roller treating her like a human slot machine sickened me. She wasn't a whale's comp or a payoff for a double down as part of the what-happens-in-Vegas-stays-in-Vegas lifestyle.

This shouldn't happen.

They stood in the elevated casino bar that rose just off the casino floor and waited. Robin had a Long Island iced tea in front of her. Angelina simply remained rigid. Her beauty wasn't lost on the patrons, and everyone, men and women, craned their necks to take her in.

This wasn't right.

I walked toward the bar not knowing what I was going to say. Angelina was an adult, after all, and she made her own choices. The cruelty of this world narrowed those choices and the obscene excess of this town just put a spotlight on it. The fact that her brother needed help and that this was what it would take to give it to him was all Angelina was focused on.

Those shouldn't be the only choices a good woman got presented with.

I got closer, but through the casino din no one noticed me. Robin had a hand resting lightly on Angelina's shoulder. And I saw her tilt her head and give a consoling smile. Angelina forced a nod and then wiped her eyes.

I felt sick. I stood and watched from the distance wanting to walk closer but just not able to. I was frozen, powerless, and didn't know what to do. I had always despised that emotional combination.

"Hey, Rocky, how was the business of getting punched in the face today?" I felt the slap on my back first, smelled the cigarette second, and when I turned I saw Lucille's face.

"This just isn't right," I said. It wasn't a plea, it wasn't a threat, and it wasn't provocative. It was just how I felt.

"Rocky, this is business. I don't deal in the right and wrong of it, adults making choices on both sides. I count receipts and balance books."

"Choices, huh?"

Something small drained from her face for an instant. Then there was a pull off the cigarette, the darting of the eyes, and she was back in business.

"Hey, Rock, I'm on the job. I got to go to work. Sometime later we'll talk philosophy."

She walked past me, looked at her watch, and then quickened her pace. She took the bar steps two at a time and went over and greeted Robin and Angelina like she was preparing them for a sales call. I watched Angelina take a long, labored breath.

I toyed with making an impassioned plea to Angelina alone or even Robin. Something told me it was useless and it was time to fold my hand. This town lets you know that you can't win, that underneath the action and the glitz reality is waiting for you to bust so it can take away what you have.

This just wasn't right.

Al was a little slow moving, and I had to tug on the leash to get him going. He insisted on sniffing every plotted plant, and when he lifted his leg on the third one I made a quick look around to see if I had been spotted. I just wanted to get out of this place.

"C'mon, Al, would ya. Let's pick it up," I said like I always did. Al did like he always did and ignored me.

Al pulled hard on the leash. He looked up and locked in on something, then let out a short growl before bolting into a sprint that almost forced the leash out of my hands. I stumbled with my grip, yanked back, and tried to right myself.

I finally steadied, but Al commenced with riotous barking. I scolded, cursed, and threatened him to stop, not wanting to be the center of attention in the casino.

Al wouldn't let up. The growling only intensified. I looked in the direction he was barking to see if I could identify the source of his rage. He was staring at a bank of doors up ahead. The doors led down a corridor marked "Employees Only" and a small contingent had gathered there. They were surrounded by the usual collection of casino players, the same players Al had ignored since his visit. What was he going off about?

He added more growl to his bark. I surveyed the field of vision to try to get his point.

Then I understood.

They were in front of the VIP elevator. Something went real bad inside of me.

Lucille, Robin, and Angelina were gathered with the man who won the auction.

It was Rusakov.

CHAPTER SIXTY-ONE

I ALMOST VOMITED.

Al raged on, and I couldn't control him as he pulled the two of us toward the threshold. The doors slammed behind them and they disappeared.

It made sense. Rusakov's luxury suite of rooms was down the end of this corridor. The beginning of it was where the housekeepers and grounds crew punched in, and there were banquet offices and other hotel-business-type office areas there as well.

Inside, it felt like something had died. This, somehow, just couldn't be how things went, not for Angelina, not now. She deserved better, she deserved some light. This was darkness.

Lucille's words came back to me. This was the choice of an adult. Angelina had decided this on her own, no one forced her. She wanted things like this. It wasn't my fight. I'd be better off, and so would everyone else, if I just left and got drunk.

Al continued to growl and bark, but I managed to wrangle him to the first casino service bar. His "Casino Dog" badge got some looks. I placed a pint glass of water in front of him while the bartender placed the double Jim Beam in front of me. Al ignored the water and sat facing the set of doors. He panted and continued the low growl while I threw back the bourbon, trying not to think of what was happening down at the end of the corridor.

The bartender refilled the lowball glass, and I threw it back as fast as he pulled his hand away from it. His eyebrows went up almost imperceptibly, and I thought for a second that even in Vegas some things made people take note.

"Bad luck?" he murmured.

"Something like that," I said.

A group of college-age guys had gathered around me trying to decide on which multishot drinks to order. They were already drunk, but I wasn't really in the position to judge so I kept my mouth shut. Two of them stepped toward the bar to order for the rest, and the lead guy stepped on Al's leash, which snapped my wrist down and forced me to spill my third double shot.

I didn't have time to curse him out because Al took the opportunity to break free and sprint away from me.

He was headed for the doors.

The basset hound was bred to make it through dense brush and rough terrain to get after rabbits, so weaving in and out of a casino floor came easy. Most people barely took note of the blur of black, brown, and white. Hell, they probably figured it was some sort of promotion.

When Al was like this he was impossible to catch. He was already at the doors and barking like a mad dog when I got to him. He barked and growled, looked at the door and back at me. He barked some more at the door, got up on two legs while leaning the others on the door and then looked back at me. He changed the weight from paw to paw, barking all the while, and then looked pleadingly at me again.

I felt his pain, but there wasn't anything I could do. Angelina had made her choice. Plus she would get the money she needed. Who was I to say she was wrong?

Al took it up a level, to a level I didn't know he had. He took a step toward me and growled. I looked down and our eyes met. He growled *at me*, not just in my presence. He had never done that before. It chilled me.

I pushed open the doors.

CHAPTER SIXTY-TWO

AL DIDN'T WAIT. He ran so hard his body twisted as he headed all the way down the corridor passing a dozen or more housekeepers and grounds crew employees at shift change. As Al and I blew past them I heard them speaking Spanish.

Al was way ahead and didn't let up. The corridor transitioned to a carpeted area with more ornate doors and molding, and only then did Al skid to a stop like a Harley. He immediately began to bark and growl again.

When I caught up to him I instantly knew why.

My chest was heaving from the run, but from behind the doors I could hear it.

"Bitch, you're going to like this. My dirty bitch…"

The sound of a woman crying.

"Bitch…" and laughter.

A hard slap echoed through the door.

"Whore!"

Al went up a notch. He didn't show any signs of letting up.

"Fucking noise!" I heard the voice say. "Fucking dog. I will kill that fucking dog!" I heard the bolt slide and the knob turn.

I didn't wait for it to open. I slammed my shoulder into it and blasted in. Al ran straight to Angelina. He positioned himself lengthwise in front of her and lowered his head while he growled at Rusakov. Her face was wet with tears, but she still had on the red dress, and aside from her hair being mussed, she looked intact.

"Fucking Duffy scum," Rusakov said, getting to his feet after the door blast knocked him down. He rushed me, but I was ready for it; I grabbed two handfuls of "Out of Hand" hoodie, pivoted, and threw him out the door into the hallway. He went off balance, but I followed him. I lost my head and went to rush him. He caught me with a jab on the way in. It didn't have all his weight on it because of his stance, but my head lit up and it froze me for an instant.

My head did that weird swimming thing again, but I did my best to shake it off. I knew my reflexes were off when my head went bad. Rusakov swung his world-famous left hook and I tried to slip it, but it caught me high on the right side of my head. It quadrupled the dizziness; my legs weren't answering my head's instructions.

I wobbled in front of him and he pushed me back by the shoulders. I stumbled back into the wall. I saw his sick smile as he went to kick me in the balls. I turned a fraction just in time and took it on the thigh. The pain lit up like fire and I bent over. He came up with a knee to the forehead and I fell back into the wall.

I tried to right myself. Things had gotten soupy, but I could see him in front of me. His brow narrowed over his eyes and his look communicated both hatred and pure evil. He loaded up with his right hand, getting ready to come right at me with the force of three steps. With his power and with this momentum, the blow would kill me.

I wasn't ready to die.

Not at the hands of this scum.

It was time to make things right.

Too much was at stake. Too much was inside of me. Too much was there for too long.

Rusakov let out a guttural growl. He had his right hand loaded and was ready to drive it with full power. I was against the wall, off balance and squared up to take it full force down the center of my face.

His body twisted as his right hand went back. I let him think I remained off balance. His body was a projectile and his cocked fist a piston. The multiplication of the two against my head would be deadly.

Except I wasn't ready to die.

He came toward me and I stepped in on his punch, changing my stance and making my left hand my lead. When he let the punch go, I sidestepped to my left, lowered my shoulder, and dug the hardest left-handed hook that I could. I was looking and hoping for just under the last rib on his right side, and the second it landed I got the feedback I wanted. I hit the soft fleshy area and drove upward. Rusakov's rushing in quadrupled the force of it.

First he let out a sick sound then he bent over at the waist, groaning and clutching his abdomen with both hands.

The liver punch had been self-preservation. The next punch I threw was about justice.

I switched back to the southpaw stance and threw a right hook that landed on the point of his chin. His head whipped around violently. He went down backward and hard, his head bouncing off the floor.

I stood over him heaving, sweating, and unable to think. This was 100 percent visceral. This was automatic.

My breathing didn't slow. The adrenaline rushed through my veins and my senses remained white hot. It took me awhile to notice the world again, things gradually coming into focus.

Rusakov wasn't moving.

About twenty-five of the housekeepers and grounds crew had gathered around. Their eyes were wide, but they all remained silent. Instinct told me that this was going to be a mess. I needed to get out of here.

"Let's go!" I grabbed Angelina. We turned and headed to the service exit. Before I could get there a door opened. Lucille and Robin appeared. Lucille quickly assessed the situation, looking down at the motionless contender.

"Oh my God, Rocky, you're in some serious fucking trouble," she said.

"Yeah..." was all I could say. My chest was heaving and my mind raced.

"Least of which is that you now owe ten thousand dollars for Angelina's services. That's what Rusakov bid. SHB doesn't like messed-up accounts."

I dug into my pocket and pulled out my bonus. "Give me your pen," I said. "I don't think I've ever had a virgin."

Lucille pulled a pen from behind her ear. I signed my earnings over to her. Then I fished around my front pocket and found a mangled dollar bill.

"There you go. I'm the highest bidder. Woo-hoo! I win," I said.

"Uh-huh. You got anything to say about the two hundred sixty-five pounds of meat laying here unconscious?"

"When he comes to, tell him he telegraphs the right hand."

I turned to Angelina. "C'mon, we gotta get out of here."

Angelina looked stricken—it was all too much for her.

"You're going to need to get it together," I said.

I handed Al's leash to Robin. "Can you bring him back to the ranch?" She nodded.

As I was heading toward the door, Lucille yelled to me.

"Keep your head low, Rocky. Stan will be looking for you."

CHAPTER SIXTY-THREE

THIS NEXT ONE *was going to be the riskiest but also the most important. It was what he had been building up to. So far, it had worked perfectly.*

There were less scum around now, less for him to detest, less that made his stomach turn. The city was aware and the law enforcement was vigilant, but he knew deep inside that they didn't really want to stop what was happening. He was doing a service to the city.

He needed to be careful. This one would make the news, probably at an international level. He loved attention, but not this kind. This was the kind that could ruin things.

He knew the routines. He knew where to find the next one, what time, and what to do. He had to be careful, but it wasn't going to be difficult.

For now, he just he had to be patient and wait.

CHAPTER SIXTY-FOUR

IT WASN'T EASY to find the Lincoln. Casinos seemed to be designed to disorient you, and right now, it didn't take much to make me feel off kilter.

Angelina did as she was told and silently got in the passenger side. She was shook-up but she didn't cry, and I got the impression that tears were only allowed under the worst circumstances. Since she was out of immediate physical danger, she wouldn't permit it.

My mind raced. The Strip traffic didn't help the situation. It was all I could do to drive without smashing the Lincoln. It also dawned on me that if you wanted to keep low, driving a pink twenty-foot sedan with a whorehouse's name on the side of it wasn't the way to go. The radio was set to the local Vegas station and the newsbreak came on, interrupting the music.

"It's Tuesday, August twenty-fourth, and..."

I couldn't believe it. In circumstances like this there are no coincidences. My mind raced. I looked at Angelina.

"I know it's been awful, but you'll be able to perform for me, won't you?" I said. I turned to her quickly and she barely nodded. "I paid more than he paid so we should be okay, you understand?"

She nodded without expression.

"Good. This is important."

We drove another twenty minutes in silence. I checked the clock. It was going to be tight, but we could make it. We eventually made the right on Sahara and got down to the Hilton where I parked in the garage.

"This is it. This place is special. Special things happen here," I said to her. She dutifully followed me. We walked past the main entrance and headed down the right side of the casino where the service entrance was. I slowed just a bit as I was sure the incline was tough in her heels.

"I'm just looking for an open door. I have a friend—" A set of double doors opened and Boggsy and his partner came out pushing a dolly. I called to him, trying not to be too loud.

He squinted then recognized me and nodded. He said something to his partner and walked over to the edge of the dock. I filled him in.

He smiled and shook his head. "I could lose my job."

"No one will know," I said.

"Give me fifteen minutes," he said and winked.

Angelina stood straight in silence with her hands properly folded in front her.

She was absolutely beautiful. We waited for the signal and Boggsy came back right on time and gave me the thumbs-up.

"Let's go," I said and pulled on her hand.

She resisted and pulled back for the first time.

"I don't want this, but I will do it for my brother. But you, Duffy, especially you…" Her eyes burned into me and I sensed an anger that encompassed most of her life.

I couldn't for the life of me figure out what she was talking about. It finally dawned on me. "Oh my God! You didn't think… Oh my God! I'm sorry!"

She cocked her head and looked at me like I was crazy, but she didn't say anything.

"C'mon, we can't be late." She stumbled a little as I pulled her.

We went through the service entrance and down an industrial hallway until we reached the dressing room area. It was the second door, the one with the star on it, he'd said, and as I reached for the knob I silently thanked Boggsy. It was open.

"Hey! What the fuck?" the Elvis guy said. He was in there with his guitarist, James, the same guy who had worked with Elvis. "You can't be in here."

I whispered to Angelina to hang back.

"Tonight I need a favor," I said.

"Who the fuck are you?—Oh, I remember, the guy from the stage. Get the fuck out of here! Tonight, my friend, is my *America's Next Superstar* audition. Get the fuck out of here. I go on in five minutes!"

I looked at James, who sort of rolled his eyes.

"Call security!" he barked at the guitarist, *the guitarist who actually had played with Elvis.* The guitarist had a sick look on his face.

"You old fuck, give me the phone. I'll call them myself."

He reached for the house phone on the wall. I stepped in and slapped it out of his hand. He burned a look into me, one that was supposed to intimidate me. It didn't.

He assumed an Elvis-style karate stance and let out a dramatic karate yell. It worked on stage.

It didn't work now, not on me, not with what was at stake.

He threw a lame karate chop toward my neck that landed high on my shoulder. I pivoted and drilled a straight left hand into his solar plexus.

He went down on his ass and threw up on his Aloha jumpsuit. While he rolled around and whimpered I looked up at the guitarist.

"Sorry, man," I said.

"Sorry? Kid Galahad, I've been wanting to do that ever since I met him." He winked.

"Man, you're my favorite guitar player ever, you know that?" I said.

He nodded.

"Uh, what exactly do you have planned?" he said.

I smiled. "My friend over here, Angelina, is a really gifted singer. I know that TV show is here tonight and I want her to perform for them."

He laughed.

"She does Elvis?" He looked at me funny.

"No, but she does 'Amazing Grace' and 'How Great Thou Art,'" I said.

"That we can do. C'mere, honey."

The impersonator had stopped rolling around, but he was in no shape to hit the high notes yet. That, and he was going to need the alternate jumpsuit.

"I'll let the crowd know you're going on after Angelina, alright?" the guitarist said, looking down. He moved the guitar to his other shoulder and stuck out his hand. "Thanks, man, this is going to be fun."

CHAPTER SIXTY-FIVE

"LADIES AND GENTLEMEN, as you know, tonight we have some special guests in the audience," James started the show with the announcement. "We have one more surprise for you..."

Angelina wasn't happy with me. Her lips were pursed and her eyes were very dark. I was afraid to say anything, but I had to.

"Please go out there and sing," I said. "It's really important. Just sing like you always do."

"I don't understand," Angelina said. "I don't understand what you are doing."

"Could you just trust me and go out there and sing? Please?"

James called her name and she walked past me. When she hit the floorboards she broke into a full smile and naturally assumed that stately stage walk that entertainers have. She received a polite ovation.

James greeted her and the two whispered off mic. The silence in the audience began to get a little awkward, and when I spied the network guys they looked a little agitated and bored.

"Oh, Lord..." Angelina began "How Great Thou Art" without any musical accompaniment. James followed her voice, and after she sang the first three lines he began to strum gently along.

"I see the stars, I hear the rolling thunder..." Her voice gathered a subtle strength and the bass player joined in. Angelina was in her element, and it was now impossible to see her making a bed.

"And there proclaim..." Angelina paused, looked down, and seemed to ready herself. "Oh my Go—o—d, how great Thou art..."

Her voice cascaded through the showroom. The audience reacted first with shock and then amazement as she held the note and it ran through the audience. I had chills and could feel my eyes well up. James was smiling from ear to ear.

Angelina held the note for an eternity. The power of her voice combined with the power of the song and the man who had made it famous gave it a transcendent feel.

The TV guys sat forward and glanced quickly at each other. Eyebrows went up and nods were exchanged.

Angelina finished "How Great Thou Art," building to an even more dramatic crescendo with the full band backing her. The last note was endless, and the audience hung on it. When she finished, they were on their feet and the applause was deafening.

She bowed, smiled, and bowed again. She walked off the stage. The applause didn't stop.

It kept going and going. The audience was literally in awe.

I waited for her not knowing how she felt. Now that the adrenaline had slowed I realized I didn't know this woman well and I don't think she took to being controlled and manipulated, which, after all, was what I had done. It didn't matter if it was for the tried-and-true "greater Duffy good." She was principled and she had integrity.

She walked right toward me and the stage smile left her face. For a moment she stared straight into my eyes. It was a glare and it pierced. Then a smile came over her face.

When she hugged and kissed me I was relieved.

"Thank you, Duffy. God bless you," she said.

I went to say something but was interrupted. It was James.

"Would y'all like to hear another one?"

The audience cheered.

"*Señorita, por favor,*" he said with a Southern drawl.

Angelina hugged me again and smiled. She gathered herself and strutted back across the stage. She whispered something to James, who nodded and smiled.

"A—ma—zing grace, how sweet the sound..." The audience cheered their approval. She was gifted.

By the second verse I felt something. Here I was, in the same building, on the same stage listening to someone from the wrong side of the tracks sing to God. Something came over me, went through me, I don't know exactly what it was. It was hard to express and one of those things that I probably wouldn't ever mention to another human.

She was almost through the last verse when Boggsy appeared next to me. I looked at him and his eyebrows went up in approval and he nodded toward Angelina. She finished her song and another standing ovation began.

I applauded while tears ran down my face.

Angelina took her bows and began to walk off the stage, but James gently grabbed her wrist.

"Oh, I don't think so..." He kidded her, and the two began a repartee on stage that the audience enjoyed.

"Is this your doing, kid?" Boggsy said.

I shrugged.

"Not bad, kid, not bad," he said.

James and Angelina continued to discuss her third number. My eyes were on Angelina, but I had to ask Boggsy something. I had to.

"Boggsy, do you ever, I mean, can you sometimes feel like...I mean it sounds crazy, but do you ever feel like..."

He cut me off. "A presence?"

I turned and looked at him with my eyes filled with tears.

"What do you think, kid?" He smiled.

I just looked at him for a long time.

"I'll tell you this, though, never as much as tonight," he said.

Angelina began to speak to the audience. "Thank you...*gracias.* I would like to sing this next song to a special friend..." She cued James, who smiled and nodded.

"Oh, Danny Boy...the pipes, the pipes are calling..." Angelina broke the stage rule and looked away from the audience while she sang the Irish standard directly at me. Elvis had recorded it shortly before he died.

I felt a hand on my back. Boggsy leaned over and whispered in my ear. "Nice job, takin' care of business." He winked and walked out.

CHAPTER SIXTY-SIX

ANGELINA STOPPED AT three songs and the hotel decided on an intermission. During the break three TV types came back and talked to Angelina. She got signed to appear on their show. They said they'd be sending her a check for twenty-five thousand dollars.

She couldn't stop shaking, and though tears didn't come out of her eyes, I could tell she was crying on the inside. I cried for her.

She looked at me and I didn't bother wiping the tears that stained my cheeks. She stepped toward me and reached her arms out. I reached back and held her as tightly as I could.

I felt something change inside her. She let go and I could feel her cry shudder throughout every inch of her. I didn't let go. I couldn't. I held her while she buried her head into the side of my neck.

She finally took a deep breath and pulled herself back from me. Her face, a wet mess, and her mussed hair didn't dampen her beauty.

"Why?" She looked at me with a sense of bewilderment.

"Why what?" I said.

"Why did you help me?"

I looked down at my running shoes. I swallowed and then I looked back up. Her stare was fierce. I shrugged.

"Why?" she asked again.

"I don't know. It seemed like something that needed to happen." It was the best that I could come up with.

"You are nuts." The fierceness let up and she giggled when she shook her head.

"I get that a lot."

My cell phone rang. It was Rocco.

"We need to get out of here, right away," he said. There was no irony in his voice.

"Take it easy Rocco. I—"

"Duffy, I'm at the ranch. They know it was you that helped that hooker get away."

"Shit. I'll deal with that."

"That's not the worst of it," Rocco said, the intensity rising in his voice.

"What?"

"I was at the bar with that Stan fella. He's really pissed."

"Rocco, everyone in the boxing business is pissed all the time."

There was a pause.

"Duffy…"

I waited.

"Rusakov is dead."

I felt the wind go out of me.

"What?" I said.

"You heard me. And Stan just ordered someone to kill you."

CHAPTER SIXTY-SEVEN

I IMAGINED THAT Stan was probably pretty good at making people dead. It also dawned on me that when a high-profile professional fighter gets killed at the hands of his sparring partner, the police are probably interested.

Oh shit.

I decided I needed a plan. I walked past the sports book, and all the TV stations were reporting on Rusakov's death. They mentioned the police were looking for me, and my photo flashed on the screen.

My mouth went dry. I was in trouble. I stood back from the bar, grabbed a discarded *USA Today,* and held it over my face like I was reading. I glanced around at the half-dozen customers and the bartender and no one was paying attention. Thank God for video poker and burned-out bartenders with BlackBerrys.

I headed out of the casino as fast as I could, trying not to draw attention to myself. In front of the Hilton is a circular drive where the valets receive and park cars. After getting through the revolving door I had to run through a group of picketers. They carried signs saying stuff like "America for Americans!," "Secure the Border," and "Don't Hire Illegals." I recognized the guy Sinkoff from the TV at Mike's. He was clearly their leader and the most vocal one of the bunch.

I didn't really have time to debate the issue and instead I headed for the tram that ran behind the Strip with my head down. When I got there I bought a ticket and buried my head in my paper again. There was one young couple in the car and a group of three twentysomething guys out partying. They showed zero interest in me. Still, I kept my face in the *USA Today,* and when my heart rate slowed just a bit, the paper I was staring at came into focus.

The sports page feature was on Carlos de Grande, "El Gran Campéon." There was an old photo of him when he was a fighter and he was wearing a big, ridiculous sombrero.

The interviewer had asked him about his son and the prodigy's chances at a title. He had also asked him about the son's weakness against left-handers, fighting other Mexicans, and if he thought he got unfair treatment because of his championship. El Campéon bristled during the interview, it said.

It went on at length about a recent trip to Big Bear and some of the other fighters he handled. The article said he was arriving in Las Vegas to oversee his son's ongoing training.

DG's son was an average fighter at best and everyone knew that. He was totally confused by lefties, and if not for his father, he'd be nothing. In fact, if two left-handed fighters hadn't recently died there'd be no way he'd be in the top five. When Hector got a chance to fight him, Junior would get destroyed. Hector was not only hard hitting, he was a southpaw and would embarrass the kid.

I thought of my new friends and how kind they had been to me. Hector and Jesus began their nighttime training this week and were alone at the gym. This late at night it seemed like a crazy time to train, but boxing was a crazy business and you did whatever you could to get an advantage. You did what others weren't willing to do, what they didn't think of doing—and the more outrageous, the better. It was what gave you the mental advantage.

That's when it came over me.

Holy shit.

No.

God, I prayed I was wrong.

I left the tram station when it got to mid-Strip and headed to the gym as fast as I could.

CHAPTER SIXTY-EIGHT

THIS WAS THE most important one.

This was what the rest was all about. Not that eliminating scum went against his principles. It was more like a fortunate byproduct of the main project. He liked the killing part. It fulfilled that longing like nothing else could since he had changed professions.

Downtown was dark. Away from the Strip, Las Vegas was a dirty town like any other, maybe dirtier. Boxing gyms were always found in these parts of town, at least the good ones. His target made it so simple to carry out his mission.

He watched the two fighters pull in. This was going to be easy. Easy and satisfying.

CHAPTER SIXTY-NINE

I SPRINTED OUT of the cab, running as fast as I could toward Tocco's. Now it seemed so obvious I couldn't believe I hadn't put it together before. I just prayed that the Medinas didn't feel up to training, that they took a day off or were late tonight—all things that would go against their character.

When I turned down the short street I saw the lights were on and felt my stomach flip over. I was going to be too late. I tore the front door open and bolted inside. Jesus was in front of the mirror and Hector was on the speed bag. It was the middle of the round and they were working. My chest heaved up and down and the sweat made the shirt stick to my back. They were oblivious to me as the loud tejano blared from a boom box.

I panted, feeling ridiculous. Absolutely nothing was happening here. The two brothers were training with just a couple of days from a big fight. I couldn't distract them with an outlandish claim based on nothing but speculation. God, I was a jackass.

The bell sounded and the brothers backed off of their stations but continued to bob in place. They were both wearing plastic sweat suits in order to lose water to make weight. The weigh-in was in two days.

"Blanco!" Jesus called to me with his glove in the air. Hector waved his hand and smiled. They were both covered in sweat. "*Que pasa!*" Hector said.

I smiled and began to speak when the round bell sounded and the brothers went back to work. I just leaned against the ropes of the floor ring and shifted my attention to the brothers training. They were amazing to watch. I heaved a deep sigh of relief.

Suddenly the lights went out and the music went off as the power in the building died. The gym went pitch black and silent.

"Fucking fuses," Jesus said through his accent.

"No! Jesus, don't move," I yelled.

The sound of footsteps could be heard near the front of the gym.

"Who's there?" Hector yelled. I heard the tension in his voice.

A metallic clickety-clack accompanied the footstep sound. My mouth went dry.

"What the hell, man, who is it?" Jesus said with more anger than fear.

I removed my shoes and stepped in what I thought was the direction of the door. The footsteps had stopped and the gym was silent again. The ambient street noise was distant in the background. The figure clicked on a powerful flashlight that first only illuminated the bottom of his pants and shoes. The light stayed there only for an instant then it was shone in Jesus's eyes.

"What the fuck?" Jesus's hands were high, shielding his eyes from the light. Through his voice I heard the clicking sound again. The shadow's arms rose toward Jesus.

I lunged at him, swinging a chop as hard as I could at the pistol. The deafening shot echoed around Tocco's cement walls. The flashlight crashed and skidded across the floor, the light going out with it. I had gone down hard on my right knee and the pain went through me like an electric shock.

The shadow figure uttered a muffled exhale and made noises that sounded like he was trying to right himself. I stepped forward in the darkness and bumped into him. It startled me, but not nearly as much as the hard body shot that followed it. I had no chance to tighten my abs and the wind went out of me. The muzzle flashed, offering an instant of light and another deafening blast to the ears. I instinctively rolled and covered my head, my stomach still aching from the body shot.

Another shot rang out, but not in my direction. This one gave off a slight glow that showed the shooter standing about five feet to my left. I righted myself and with every ounce I could muster threw my shoulder in that direction. I felt my body land hard into the rib cage exposed by his raised arm, and this time he went down hard and I heard the gun clatter from his hand.

Something banged through the front door, followed by the light of several flashlights.

"Police! Freeze!"

The lights and music suddenly came back on.

Four cops at the front of the gym looked at Carlos de Grande sprawled on the floor next to a gun, Jesus Medina standing in shock, and Hector Medina at the fuse panel.

"Hands, hands! Hands where I can see them!" the lead cop yelled. Another cop stepped forward.

"Dombrowski—face down, hands out in front. Now or I blow your head off!" I didn't argue.

"Get him out of here!" the lead cop ordered.

I felt my arms roughly pulled behind my back and handcuffs clicked on my wrists. Then I was pulled to my feet, the hard tug straining my shoulders and elbows at a weird angle.

"C'mon, asshole," the cop said.

"What the hell is going on?" I said.

"Shut up, asshole. You're under arrest for the murder of Boris Rusakov."

CHAPTER SEVENTY

As the squad car pulled up in front of the Clark County Courthouse a phalanx of reporters, TV lights, and cameras was waiting to greet me. My hands were still cuffed behind me and the two cops in the car made a bit of a show pulling me out of the backseat, holding my head down and then pretending to rush me through the crowd.

Microphones were stuck in my face and lights blinded me. I felt like Lee Harvey Oswald on November 23. The booking process was long and tedious. No one seemed to like me very much, and I guess, given the circumstances, I could understand why. I was formally charged and read my rights, including the part where I was told I would be assigned a court-appointed attorney free of charge if I couldn't afford one of my own.

I had no idea what to do. I couldn't call the Appaloosa, I didn't know how to get a hold of anyone at the gym, and I had no idea where Jerry, TC, or Rocco were. It dawned on me that I didn't know where Al was except that he was in Robin's hands. I've felt screwed in my life before, but nothing came close to this bad.

They said it might take a few hours to get my free attorney because it was the middle of the night. In the meantime they let me know that no bail would be set and that I might as well get comfortable in my new place. I got one of those desperate-looking orange jumpsuits and the little loafer sneakers. Then they shackled my wrists and ankles before two guards escorted me to my cell.

It was ten feet long and about six feet wide with a stainless-steel toilet. The bed was a concrete slab built into the wall with a two-inch-thick rolled-up mattress sitting on top. A set of sheets and the thinnest pillow I've ever seen lay next to it. I got a very sick feeling in my stomach that this was what life was to be for a long, long time.

The sound of steel doors being locked and unlocked and slammed was punctuated with the other jail sounds. A guy down the hall was making up his own tuneless rap with the vilest vocabulary directed at women that you could imagine. That was tough to listen to, but the guy in the cell right next to me who cried so much that I thought he would choke was worse, probably because he expressed exactly what I was feeling.

I stared straight ahead into the grey cell wall. Graffiti there told me I was "a no good mother fucker" and requested that I perform an unspeakable act on the artist in question. The noise wasn't letting up and I couldn't imagine ever sleeping in such an environment. Still, I unrolled the bedroll and put the sheets on it. Then I climbed up on it, doubling the pillow over. It still put my neck and head in a funny position.

The crier kept on and the rapper started to rhyme lyrics making fun of the guy who was weeping. Even in here it seemed particularly cruel, but a sinking feeling reminded me that my new world wouldn't represent the best of humankind. I drifted, not into sleep as much as into a defeatist trance. A voice startled me out of it.

"Dombrowski!" I've never heard my last name uttered with such clear disdain before.

"Your attorney," was all the guard said, and he began to unlock my cell. He shackled my wrists and ankles again and brought me

to a small room with a glass window just like you see on *Law &
Order.*

A middle-aged guy with a shaved head and a rumpled suit was
waiting for me, pacing in a tight circle. He turned toward me and
I noticed his glasses rested crookedly on a nose that looked like it
had been broken more than once.

"I'm Phillip Fowler, the court appointed me to act as your
attorney."

"Duffy Dombrowski," I said.

He took a seat across the table from me and tried to look me in
the eye. He began to fumble through some papers and then patted
his pockets and opened his jacket looking for a pen.

"Shit, uh, Dombrowski, you got a pen?"

The fact that I was behind impenetrable Plexiglas made the
question seem a bit absurd.

"Of course you don't, uh, sorry," Phillip Fowler, Esquire, said.

Apparently Johnny Cochran wasn't coming to the rescue.

He gathered himself and went over what he thought was going
to happen. I'd be arraigned first thing in the morning. He'd try for
bail, but that was unlikely. He'd get some preliminary information,
but tomorrow we'd get a chance to talk for a longer period and he'd
start building my defense then. He told me I was the only case he
currently had so he could devote all his energy to it.

I didn't take a lot of solace in that.

The guard came for me and ushered me back to my cell. As the
night wore on I started to feel it. I threw up until I had nothing left to
heave. I had killed a man, a man who deserved to die, but now the rest
of my life I was going to spend like a caged animal. My back ached
and my hands shook. The visceral adrenaline rush that fueled me over
the last forty-eight hours was replaced by a nausea-inducing despair.

And Al was alone. That stuck in my head and punched me
in the gut. He didn't deserve to be alone, not after all he'd been

through. In fact, I got him because his original owner, Walanda, went to prison and got murdered while on the inside. It just wasn't fair.

It just didn't seem possible that my life was gone. No AJ's, no clinic, no Trina, Rudy, or Monique. What would I ever tell Smitty? What about the clients that I actually helped? Oh God, how I fucked up. I went to the toilet to throw up again.

I spent the night alternating between looking at the ceiling, choking back tears, throwing up, and wondering why I hadn't minded my own business. Five a.m. in a jail cell has got to be the loneliest place in the world. Lonely with a torment that I didn't think I could ever get used to.

Time had stopped. They'd taken my watch, and as I lay there I didn't know if seconds went by or hours.

CHAPTER SEVENTY-ONE

"DOMBROWSKI!" A NEW voice called to me.

I turned without saying anything.

He unlocked the door and slid it open.

"C'mon. My shift is ending."

He secured my wrists and ankles and walked me through a series of doors and gates back to the same conference room. Apparently Fowler got up early, but I wished he hadn't. Seeing him was worse than seeing no one. It just reinforced to me the hopelessness of my situation.

A sixtysomething corrections officer who looked like he started smoking after he took his first steps was sitting at a table looking down at a file.

"Your possessions: one pair of jeans, socks, underwear, one T-shirt, a watch, a wallet with twenty-eight dollars and no credit cards. Please sign and attest that you've received them," he said with a complete absence of eye contact.

"Didn't I sign this when I got booked?" I said to be saying something.

"Yep."

After I signed the form he handed me my possessions. The other guard spoke.

"C'mon, Dombrowski."

I got ushered into another area with four steel desks, all manned by officers. The guard delivered me to the first desk on the right.

"You got some friends, huh?" the guy said, looking over the top of his reading glasses. He was bald on top and looked a little bit like an angry Carl Reiner. "Seems as though when you delivered the killing blow to Mr. Rusakov you did it in front of a group of people."

"Yeah, I know. So?"

He smiled and shook his head. "Off the record, it sounds to me like this guy was a real asshole."

I shrugged.

"Well, champ," his sarcasm was heavy, "it's good to have friends."

"What the hell are you talking about?" I said.

He laughed. "When the courthouse opened this morning at seven there were twenty-five people in line waiting to get in. Twenty-two Mexican housekeepers and facility workers from the Mandalay Bay showed up."

"What?"

"Oh yeah, and the lightweight champion of the world and his brother." He looked at me and smiled.

I had no idea what was going on.

"Kid, they all came in and one by one offered eyewitness accounts that you defended a woman from an attack, that you, yourself, were in life-threatening danger and that you were merely defending yourself and the woman." His eyebrows went up.

"The fact that three-quarters of the Mexicans were illegal and still insisted on giving testimony seemed pretty significant."

"You mean…"

"Yep, the charges have been dropped, thanks to your friends."

I just sat there for a second. Then a smile came across my face.

"Kid, illegals risking deportation for a gringo? You live an interesting life."

"I get that a lot."

I got ushered out the front door, and the sunlight hit me as soon as I passed through the threshold. When my pupils adjusted I heard the applause and the hoots and hollering.

In front of me on the stairs were Jesus, Hector, and a bunch of what looked like staff people from the Mandalay. Robin and Angelina were there with Al, who began to bay. Jesus and Hector took turns hugging me.

"Blanco! Our amigo!"

"You guys did this?" I felt my voice crack and my eyes well up. They just smiled.

"And your other amigos." Hector nodded toward the crowd.

"We don't forget, Blanco," Jesus said.

"What was the deal with DG?" I asked.

The two brothers got a half-disgusted, half-sad look on their faces.

"He was killing off the left-handed lightweights in his son's way." Jesus pursed his lips. "That's how bad he wanted Junior to be champ. He knew he couldn't handle the left hand, so he murdered them. He was the one who poisoned Cano at Big Bear. Crazy shit."

"And the other Mexican victims?" I asked.

"He confessed to all of them. He ranted on about hating Mexicans, Mexicans being scum, all that kind of shit," Hector said.

"He hated his own people. How the hell do you explain that?" I said.

"Amigo, money does funny things. El Gran Campéon stopped being Mexican a long time ago," Jesus said.

The three of us stood there shaking our heads.

"Hey, fellas, what's with all the housekeepers and Mandalay staff?"

"Well, you and Rusakov got into it right in front of them," Jesus said.

"They came here on their own, even the undocumented ones?" I asked.

Jesus looked at Hector and smiled.

"You forget, we're heroes. They also heard about how you helped us. It didn't take a lot of encouragement."

It brought a smile to my face.

"You guys fight tomorrow. You better get home and get some rest," I said.

"*Sí, sí.* You coming?" Jesus said.

"I don't know how welcome I'd be."

"You better be there. I want you to lead me out," Jesus said.

"Then I'll be there," I said.

"Blanco, if you ever need another favor, you let me know." The two of them started to walk away.

Something went through my head. Something crazy.

"Jesus!" He turned and waited for me.

I told him my idea.

"Whew, Blanco, that won't be easy," he said.

"I know."

He looked at Hector for a long time. Hector shrugged.

"*Por qué no?*" Hector said.

"I'll call the promoter and tell him I won't fight unless he gets it done. I'm the main event and he's screwed without me."

He and his brother smiled and walked away.

CHAPTER SEVENTY-TWO

I MADE SURE I said *muchas gracias* to my new housekeeping friends. Angelina told me she had a ticket for New York in a week and that she'd never forget me. I was feeling pretty good.

Robin came up to me with Al. "Stan wants you dead. You have to get out of town," she said. Her comments quelled my euphoria. Al sniffed me, made sure I was who he thought I was, and lay down at my feet.

"Yeah, I know."

"You can stay at my place." She looked me in the eye for a long moment and then broke the glance. "He won't look for you there, and I got plenty of room."

I didn't respond right away. Not because it wasn't a good offer.

She felt the awkwardness. I saw the sadness for an instant then it got replaced with anger. "Forget it. If staying with a whore is less appealing than getting killed, then fuck you." She turned.

Immediately I felt it. That hypocrisy. Mr. Human-Services-Accept-All-Guys caught standing in judgment. My stomach sickened just a bit.

"Can Al come?" I said.

She half turned to look at me. Her shoulders remained slumped and she didn't make eye contact. "He can definitely come. You, I'm not so sure about." She cracked a wry smile. It was like she decided to take the insult like a body shot, not fire back and know she lost the round. I bet she spent her life honing defensive skills.

She drove the two of us in her late-model Passat into a suburban area and pulled into a very new, nondescript townhouse. The neighborhood surprised me—it looked middle to slightly upper-middle class.

She parked and got out. I must've lingered too long in my seat. "Jesus Christ. Let me guess. You were expecting a red light in the window and lots of crushed red velvet window treatments?" she said.

"No…I…"

"Fuck you again, Duffy." This time there was humor in her voice.

The place was decorated in beige with rich dark brown leather furniture. Her artwork was what I think they call "impressionistic" in that it featured lots of blurry ponds, lilies, and streams.

"Have a seat. You must be hungry," she said. Al jumped up on the sofa with me. It was substantial leather with deep stitched seams and it had that buttery softness that forms around you.

"I'm starving now that you mention it. You want to order a pizza?"

"I like to cook. Do you trust me in the kitchen?" she said.

"Of course."

She gave me a look letting me know I wasn't fooling her. I had never before met someone who could read people as well as she could. There was no point in lying to her because she just looked inside you. I felt silly.

"If you don't like it, we'll call Dominos," she compromised.

I grabbed the remote and flipped on the fifty-two-inch flat screen. Al began to snore. I could hear Robin mixing and chopping and pots and pans clanging. Every now and then she'd pop her head in and make conversation. One of the times she slid a cold Corona in front of me with a neat bourbon.

"Sorry it's not Schlitz."

"I'll make do," I said.

I don't know if it was the alcohol, the not being in jail, the not going to prison for the rest of my life, or something else, but I found myself with that warm, comfortable feeling you get when you're at home away from your actual home.

"It's ready," Robin said.

We sat at a breakfast bar topped with a beautiful black speckled granite counter. She slid an oversized plate in front of me, poured me a glass of red wine, and offered me some warm bread.

"It's pasta with spinach, fresh tomatoes, and gigante beans in a Sangiovese reduction."

"Hmm, what a coincidence. I make this all the time at home."

She punched me in the shoulder. It had something on it like she knew how to punch.

"Hey—ow! Where'd you learn to throw like that?"

"I told you. My brother was a fighter."

"And where'd you learn to cook?"

"Culinary school. The Culinary Institute of America Executive Chef Program, class of 2007," she said and twirled a little pasta onto a fork.

The meal was exquisite.

"You didn't ask, so I'll tell you." She started without emotion. "I came out here for a job. I could only find line cooking jobs and then I got laid off when the market crashed. I got a little too into cocaine and after I met Stan I found out I could make a ton of money dancing. I didn't mind that too much, and so I took it to the next level."

I sipped the wine. I don't know shit about wine, but with the dinner it was terrific.

She sipped hers and continued.

"I got this sense of power when I was dancing. Like men were there for me to exploit, not the other way around. In my head, selling myself for sex seemed like the logical extension of that. The money is ridiculous."

"Really?"

"The house you're sitting in is paid for."

"Better than getting punched in the face for a living."

"Doesn't mean I like it or that it's good for me."

"How so?"

"You ever meet a prison guard?"

"Yeah…"

"What are they like?"

"The ones I just encountered seemed angry, racist, and unfeeling."

"They have to be, right?"

"To do that shit, yeah."

"Well, having sex for money breeds a similar outlook. My view on men, relationships, life—hell, everything—has been tainted."

I nodded. I wasn't sure what to say.

"Be honest. You've pictured what it would be like to fuck me, right? I know men do that with all women, but it's a whole lot easier with me. That makes you either a man to exploit, if I'm working, or a man to avoid if I'm just living. Over time I'm either working and using men or trying to stay the hell away from them."

"That's its own mortgage payment, isn't it?" I said.

"Hell yeah, it is." She filled her glass and topped off mine.

She looked thoughtful.

"I guess we all make choices," she said. We had both cleaned our plates. "Look, I wasn't counting on a lot of psychotherapy. You want to watch a movie?"

I smiled. I found myself really enjoying her company.

"Sure."

"I'm going to slip into something more comfortable, okay?" She said it with a wink, a bad Mae West impersonation, and seductive head tilt. She touched my shoulder and let her fingers run lightly over my arm. She went into the bedroom.

I sipped my wine. What was I in for? I had never been with a professional and there was no doubt Robin had a body a man would always remember. What she could do and, shit, what she would expect. I felt my anxiety rise with my curiosity. The moment passed like an hour.

"C'mon in the bedroom, honey," she said.

I finished my wine and self-consciously walked into the bedroom as though being lured into sex by women happened to me all the time.

She was lying on the bed in a baggy pair of grey Champion sweat pants and an even baggier hoody. She had on thick wool socks.

"I know it's Vegas, but the air-conditioning chills me. C'mon up here. I promise not to take advantage of you. And is it okay if I call Al?"

Al came running into the bedroom and jumped up between the two of us. Robin rolled over and spooned with Al.

"Have you seen *Casablanca*?" she said.

"Nope."

"Oh God, you're going to love it."

She hit a button on her remote and a television screen came out of what I thought was a blanket box at the foot of the bed. She turned off the rest of the bedroom lights and it was like being in a personal movie theater, only in bed.

"Congratulations, Duffy."

"Congratulations?"

"You're the first man to lie in this bed."

I let that simmer in my head. The three of us watched the movie with rapt attention. Humphrey Bogart was lamenting about all the bars in all the lands when I felt Robin's hand on mine.

Nothing spoken, no look exchanged, just a hand reaching out.

CHAPTER SEVENTY-THREE

WHEN THE CELL phone rang I was barely awake, and I didn't recognize the accented voice in my ear.

"It's taken care of."

It was seven thirty a.m. I was alone in Robin's bed.

"Huh?" I said.

"I work for Jesus. He asked me to call. That request. Jesus wanted you to know it's taken care of."

"You're kidding me."

"He wants you to come by tonight and wish him luck too."

My head was starting to clear. "Tonight? Tonight's the fight."

"*Sí*. Jesus wants you there. There will be passes for you and the girl at the will-call."

"I'll be there."

I couldn't believe he had pulled it off.

I got out of bed and headed toward the bathroom. The shower was running and Al was lying in front of the glass door. I could faintly see Robin's figure through the opaque window.

Al sat up and barked at me, like he was guarding the door. He gave me a dirty look, looked back at the shower and then back to me. He barked again.

"There's coffee in the kitchen," Robin said through the sound of running water.

I headed toward the kitchen, stopping first at the bathroom off the great room where I had watched TV yesterday before dinner. My dog was protecting the decency of the hooker in the shower. The hooker I spent the night with—holding hands.

Some shit you just can't make up.

Robin came out of the bedroom with her hair up in a towel wearing an oversized robe that said "Bellagio" on the breast pocket.

"What did you think of *Casablanca*?" she asked as she poured herself some coffee.

"I felt bad for Lazlo."

"Lazlo? Why?"

"Because she was ready to leave him because the crumb who left her wanted her back."

"Geez, you're a killjoy."

"Yeah, you ever been a Victor Lazlo? I have too many times."

She just looked at me. "You're a different kind of man, Dombrowski." She held the glance and shook her head while breaking into a smile. The glance made me feel warm.

"You know, I just wanted you to know—" The phone interrupted her.

The smile left her face when she answered. "No, no, I haven't seen him." She got a look of panic.

"I wouldn't lie to you…Stan, don't say that. Stan, you know I'm grateful for—Yes, I'm coming in—yes, I can be there." Her complexion paled and I recognized the worn-out Robin I saw at the Appaloosa. She hung up.

"You better go. Stan is looking for you. Duffy, get out of town. Now, please. He will kill you."

I swallowed hard and glanced down at Al.

"I have another car, a Jeep. Take it. I hardly ever use it. But get out of town as soon as you can."

She slid the keys in front of me.

"Can you hang on to Al for the rest of the day? I got something I've got to take care of," I said.

"I said to get out of town n-o-w. I meant it."

"There's something left I have to do. I have to."

She exhaled and frowned at me. "Sure, but don't waste time."

I looked at her and we had one of those awkward moments where there was just too much emotion. My eyes felt funny and I was glad when she spoke.

"Be careful. For God's sake, be careful."

CHAPTER SEVENTY-FOUR

"DUFFY, YOU'VE BEEN so good to me," Angelina said. "But I hate boxing. Isn't there someone who would really appreciate going?" Her voice, even through the cell phone, was melodic.

I didn't want to tell her too much.

"I want you to go to see how beautiful it is, really. It's important to me."

"I...I...I know you've been generous, too generous, but I—"

"I insist. Do me this favor. We will leave after one fight if you hate it," I said.

She remained reluctant but finally relented.

Now all I had to do was pick her up, get her to the fight, and not get murdered by Stan. Maybe I was being melodramatic. Stan had never said he wanted to kill me to my face. He seemed even to like me. Maybe everyone was just overreacting.

Of course, I had killed his meal ticket, exposed his illegal prostitution ring, and got a virgin goldmine off the payroll. I guess those things could rub a guy the wrong way.

I pulled up reluctantly in front of the address Angelina gave me. I've been in shitty neighborhoods before. In fact, a lot of boxing gyms are in the worst parts of town, but this was a slum's slum.

We made the ten-minute drive mostly in silence. I could tell Angelina was not happy going to a fight.

We pulled into the Mandalay Event Center parking garage and headed to the will-call window. It was seven o'clock so the prelims had begun, but I wasn't sure if Jesus or Hector would be there yet. Some fighters like to stay in the comfort of their hotel rooms rather than sit around a dressing room getting nervous. Others like to get to the arena and get as comfortable as possible for as long as they can closest to where they are going to fight. When you've been on the big stage as much as these guys I'm sure it didn't really matter.

It didn't seem like a great idea for me to be bopping up and down the Strip or parked in front of a slot machine. If Stan was looking for me it would be to my benefit to get myself to a place with lots of security where you needed ID and a pass to get in. Of course, Stan was part of the promotional team for the fight, so he probably had more all-access passes than anyone.

I gave my name at the will-call window while Angelina stood behind me with her arms folded. She remained polite, but her lips were pursed and her body language screamed that she would rather have been any place else. I got directions to the dressing rooms and headed down the escalator.

It was about a fifteen-minute walk through the large corridors in front of the large ballrooms. Angelina walked just a little behind me to reinforce her lack of enthusiasm for this special trip. We came to an area cordoned off by a velvet rope and a placard that read "Dressing Rooms: Passes and ID Required."

I flashed ours, and the mostly disinterested casino employee undid the rope. We passed through the door to the wide-open unadorned area that made up the guts of the resort through four or five more huge sets of doors to the arena dressing rooms. I could hear the sounds of boxing: buzzers, knocks, bells, and the occasional cheer for the undercard fighters. Since I'm usually in that position I knew that though it sounds really cool at first to be on a big card, you often fight in front of very few fans. The big-time casino fans come in just before the main event. Fighting in an empty or near-empty arena feels weird and kind of lonely.

Handwritten signs directed us down a corridor toward the fighters. Jesus, being the main event, was the very last at the end of the hallway. As we got closer I could hear the tejano music and the Spanish chatter of trainers and the entourage. I stopped before entering and looked at Angelina.

"We're going to go in," I said.

"I'm not going in. It's a man's dressing room," Angelina said with more than a hint of indignation.

"It's not a locker room. They get dressed in a little room around the corner."

She rolled her eyes and shook her head.

I extended my hand. She hesitated, rolled her eyes, and held it. I smiled.

"You're going to like this more than you think."

She let out a heavy sigh to let me know that she didn't agree.

I opened the door slowly to make sure it was okay. Hector noticed me right away, and I realized he must've left his own dressing room to be with family before his bout. Eight or ten other guys from the gym were there, and as I walked by they all gave me the handshake/half-hug that fighters give. They politely said hello to Angelina, giving her the respect men often give beautiful women.

"Blanco, around the corner," Hector said and smiled.

I had to pull gently on Angelina's hand, but she followed. I could hear the familiar chatter of several voices mixed in with the sounds of fighters hitting the pads to warm up. We went around several lockers and I looked at Angelina's face for a reaction.

In front of us were two men, shadowboxing. They both wore identical robes with "Jesus Medina, World Champion, Quiero Mexico!" printed on them. Angelina looked confused. Jesus turned around and stopped shadowboxing.

"Blanco!" He came over and hugged me. "*Encantado,* Angelina." Angelina nodded back politely. Jesus broke into a huge smile and tilted his head toward the "other" Jesus.

The other Jesus kept shadowboxing with intensity. He wasn't as smooth or as rhythmic, but he was copying Jesus's moves.

"Was it hard?" I asked.

"Blanco, being a world champion has its privileges," he said.

I heard Angelina exhale. "Duffy, I think I want to go," she said.

Jesus reached out and lightly grabbed her wrist. "*Un momento, por favor.*"

He smiled and cleared his throat.

"Hey, *campeón del pueblo! Vamos!*" Jesus yelled over the tejano to the other fighter. Only Jesus's voice broke him from his work.

The fighter turned. His head was hooded by the boxing robe, which obscured his face for a moment until he looked up.

That was when Angelina saw her brother for the first time on American soil.

CHAPTER SEVENTY-FIVE

HER EYES WENT wide. She looked at me, then at Jesus for a split second, then back to her brother.

"*Campeón del pueblo! Campeón del pueblo!*" her brother yelled. He looked remarkably like Jesus.

Angelina began to shake and then ran to him and threw her arms around him.

"*Campeón del pueblo! Campeón del pueblo!*"

She hugged him and swayed back and forth.

"*Dios mio, Dios mio!*" she kept repeating softly.

"*Campeón del pueblo! Campeón del pueblo!*"

Marco broke free to continue his warm-up. He spun around and threw a three-punch combination.

Tears ran down Angelina's face and her hands trembled as she brought them to her mouth. She looked at Jesus and at me. Jesus had his hands on his hips and was smiling from ear to ear.

"I just might let him take my place tonight," he said and laughed. The rest of the entourage gathered around and everyone was laughing and smiling.

"How?" Angelina said through her tears. She glanced back and forth between Jesus and me. "My God, how?"

"*Su amigo*, Blanco..." Jesus started to say. He switched to English. "You tell her, Duffy."

"Your brother flew here this morning on Top Fight Promotions's corporate jet."

"What?"

"Jesus called the promoter and said he wasn't fighting unless it happened." I looked at Jesus and he shrugged like it was no big deal.

"Your brother was given a robe, told to keep his head down, and to warm up because he was coming to the fight. Your aunt and uncle got the message and they never hesitated," I said.

"Immigration?" Angelina said softly.

"I am a champion in Mexico. The rules are a little different for me," Jesus said without a hint of arrogance.

Angelina looked confused. She looked at her brother and back at us. She smiled from ear to ear. "I don't know what to say..."

She looked at her brother with obvious devotion.

"I have a favor to ask of you," Jesus said and smiled.

Angelina just looked at him.

"I want your brother to lead me out for the fight tonight. Okay with you?"

She smiled. "Of course."

"See, now you're a boxing fan," I said.

Jesus went over to Marco. He put his hands on his shoulders and looked him in the eye. He spoke softly to him and there was quiet. They each took a knee and after a moment made the sign of the cross. Then Marco threw his hands in the air and spun around.

"*Campeón del pueblo! Campeón del pueblo!*"

Angelina hugged me. She began to cry hard into my shoulder. I thought she wasn't going to let go. She held on tightly for a long time. Finally she broke away.

"I love you, Duffy," she said.

"I love you too."

It was the most natural thing that ever came out of my mouth.

CHAPTER SEVENTY-SIX

WE LET JESUS warm up and get prepared. When the music was cued and the TV lights went on, Marco got out in front of the entourage and entered the arena at the head of the group.

Angelina and I were back behind Jesus at the tail end. Jesus's music came up and the noise from the crowd was deafening. I'd never been a part of something quite like this. Fans were leaning over railings and stretching past security just to touch Jesus's robe.

The jumbo scoreboard television in the center of the arena broadcast the entrance just a few seconds after it started and a roar went up. Out in front, Marco was shadowboxing his way toward the ring in the identical robe and damn near doing the identical moves. The absolute best part was when fans would reach over he'd give them a high five or a fist bump. The fans would go away thrilled that they got to touch their hero.

The entourage snaked around toward the ring, and there was a bit of a bottleneck as the area narrowed for the ring entrance. I could feel my heart beating and took a second to take it in. I'd never get to this level of the sport as a participant, but this was still pretty cool.

I took a deep breath and took one last look around to take the enormity of it all in. I did a 360 of the arena and felt a big smile come across my face.

That's when I saw Sergy, the guy I kicked at the motel, standing near the metal barriers next to the ring. He was with three friends, all just as big, and their eyes were all fixed on me.

CHAPTER SEVENTY-SEVEN

"UH, I GOTTA go," I whispered in Angelina's ear through a cupped hand. The noise of the crowd was deafening.

She scrunched up her forehead and looked confused. I didn't have time to explain.

I jumped the stanchion on the opposite side of Stan's men and ran as fast I could through the crowd, pushing and shoving people out of my way. My heart pounded as I headed for the exits toward the casino entrance. Sprinting through a casino looks a little weird, but, hey, it's Vegas. People don't mind a little weird.

A long corridor filled with designer shops and upscale restaurants flowed into the casino. It was fight night, the place was jampacked, and I could hear the now-familiar casino sounds of bells, coins, groans, and cheers. A quick look over my shoulder and I saw the four guys about fifty yards behind me still in the large corridor heading out of the casino.

I went for the front exit and didn't take the time to tip the doorman. I pushed through the taxi line and ran down the steep Mandalay ramp that led to the sidewalk. Las Vegas Boulevard, the Strip, isn't your average urban avenue and crossing it wasn't easy. I decided to not wait for the traffic to die down and instead ran in between oncoming cars and trucks from both sides, taking curses, screeching tires, and blasting horns as part of the territory.

I got across the street and ran off the sidewalk toward the dilapidated motel where we had liberated Crystal. There was a barbed-wire fence about eight feet high that I had to scale, and I felt the barbs tear into my palms, rip my pants, and dig into the skin on my legs. I managed to pull myself over and landed at the end of the parking lot feeling just a hint of satisfaction that I had pulled it off.

I slowed to a trot and took a turn around the far end of the motel slab. I was halfway down the building when I heard the squeal of tires and saw the glare of headlights coming from around the other side. Three Lincolns made the turn and gunned their engines right toward me.

Before I could react, they had me boxed in against the wall of the motel. Two were pink with "Appaloosa Ranch" written on the sides.

One was white like Stan's personal car.

The doors of the pink Lincolns flew open and I saw the guns. The four guys who had been chasing me got out and immediately pointed their pistols at me. Stan got out last.

He walked to the vortex formed by the two pink cars and stopped. His hands were in the pockets of his suit coat.

"You, you fuckin' piece of shit, you. You had the balls to fuck with my business? Fuck with me? Fuck with the people I represent? A message needs to be sent. When they find your body it will make noise. The noise will serve as a warning to anyone who wants to mess with SHB."

He nodded at the four goons, who stepped toward me. They holstered their guns. Two of them pulled out heavy chains that they could hit me with from a distance. The other two had blackjacks cocked and ready. The message was going to be clear by the condition of my body when it was found.

My plan was to go crazy with punches and kicks when they got close. It was crazy and futile, but I knew it was my only chance. My mouth was dry and I could feel the quiver in my legs.

That was when the four doors of the white Lincoln flew open.

"Freeze, motherfuckers!" came the high-pitched voice.

"Drop your weapons!" another voice said.

The four goons froze and Stan's head swung around.

A shadowed figure stood with a gun trained in the direction of the attackers.

I squinted through the headlights' glare and tried to see. There, standing and holding what looked to be an Uzi, was the silhouette of a strange-looking dude. He stepped just into the light and I noticed he had frizzy red hair and was wearing a bizarre tie-dyed three-piece suit.

"Walk this way, Duff," the voice said.

I did as he suggested and as I stepped toward him I realized.

It was Jerry Number Two.

CHAPTER SEVENTY-EIGHT

"GET IN THE Lincoln, Duff," Jerry said. He held the Uzi awkwardly pointed in the general direction of Stan.

"Hold it, asshole," I heard Stan yell. He had his own gun out and had it pointed at Jerry. "You really think these clowns are your saviors? No way they can pull the trigger."

I glanced at Jerry Number Two and saw a bead of sweat run down his face. Stan was a lot of things, but he could read people. Jerry was a pacifist; he didn't believe in hurting anything. He had lost the drop on Stan and his men. Stan walked toward Jerry.

"I told you," Stan said. He had that big evil smile on his face. The goons behind him laughed, and they all began to walk toward us.

I swallowed hard and looked at Jerry. I could see his hands trembling.

"Nice try, Dombrowski. Get a better army next time and—"

An ear-piercing volley of gunfire blasted through the dark night. Grunts, thuds, and screams came right after it, as Stan and his men were mowed down. Torn flesh, blood, and that putrid cordite smell filled the air. My ears rang.

I looked at Jerry. The Uzi was at his side and he had a very strange look on his face.

"My God, Jerry, you did it!" I went to hug him.

He didn't hug me back.

He looked straight ahead and spoke without any inflection.

"It wasn't loaded," Jerry said.

Jerry looked at the carnage in disbelief. I was grateful to be alive, but I was confused as hell. Then I heard the clicking of heels walking toward us, but the shadows made it difficult to make out the figure.

Whoever it was was holding a gun.

CHAPTER SEVENTY-NINE

THE FIGURE TURNED and gave a short whistle. Then she came into the light.

"I told you to be careful. Now will you *please* get out of town?" It was Robin. Al flopped out of her VW and ran over.

"Robin?" I said.

"Duffy, get out of Vegas *now!*"

"She's right, Duff. I think we've done all we need to do here," Jerry Number Two said.

"Come with us," I said.

She laughed.

"That's just what you need." She shook her head.

"But the police...you'll get—"

"I'm getting out of here, trust me. And as for Stan, well, tonight maybe I didn't get back all of what he took from me, but somehow it feels like I got a little." She smiled out of the corner of her mouth and turned. "See ya, Duff. And remember, we'll always have Paris."

I watched her walk away in the darkness.

She started her car and took off.

I hesitated just a second and then Jerry tugged at my shirt. We piled into the white Lincoln, and some Hispanic guy sitting behind the wheel floored the big sedan.

"Holy eff'in shit!" TC yelled. "That was cool!"

I was about to throw up.

A quick glance around the car and I noted TC, Rocco, and Jerry Number One were all there. I didn't know the guy driving.

"Javi, let's get to McCarran, and I don't think we better stop for a steak," Jerry Number Two said. "We don't know who else might be coming after us."

Al was at my feet staring up at me. He didn't know what the hell was going on—and he wasn't the only one.

"Fellas, you want to kinda fill me in?" I asked.

"We found Jerry Number Two. Er, actually, he found us," Rocco said.

"We went back to the Star Trek place to ask the Klingon guy some more questions." TC nodded at Rocco and rolled his eyes.

"Jerry comes walking in with his buddy, Javi, wearing that suit, throws a few hundred down on the bar, and backs up everyone in the place," Jerry Number One said.

"We still haven't got the whole story," TC said.

Everyone looked at Jerry Number Two.

"Gentlemen, I'll fill you in in a moment. I need to make this call."

He punched the numbers on the cell phone and waited just a moment.

"Yes, Murray, how are you? The children?" I found it a very weird time for small talk. "We will need a plane, a jet actually, something nice for six. It would be great if you could wrangle up some food and a full bar."

He hung up and let out a long, self-satisfied exhale.

"You feel like explaining?" I said.

"We're just about at the airport, Duff. Let's wait till we get on the plane."

"No, let's not, Jer."

He exhaled again, like Winston Churchill or some other fat, important guy. Neither of those two ever wore a three-piece tie-dyed suit, however.

"You remember my meltdown right before I disappeared? During it I started to think what this town did to me and I got really pissed. I couldn't live with myself feeling like a coward. I decided to do something about it."

Javi pulled off at the airport exit and headed toward the private aircraft area.

"I found Javi. We were partners back in the day, and I was surprised to find that he still lived in Vegas. We went back to our old plan, only we spread it out over six or seven casinos. We had our twenty-one system, we had our stake, and we put it to use without sticking around any one casino for very long."

A guy in a tuxedo and one of those orange flashlights was at the security gate. Jerry brought down his window.

"Murray! It's been a long time." They shook hands, and Murray gave Jerry a big smile. Jerry pulled out his wad and started handing Murray bills. I'm pretty sure he gave him five hundred dollars.

"What do I owe you for the jet?"

"Twenty-six thousand even."

"Murray, you are the best!" Jerry took a few moments and counted out the cash from the gym bag at his feet.

Javi pulled out onto the tarmac and we all followed Jerry out of the Lincoln and up the short staircase to enter the jet. Jerry lagged behind. I saw him give Javi a big hug.

"We got 'em back, brother. *Vaya con Dios!*" Jerry Number Two said to Javi.

The pilot introduced himself, and I found a cold Schlitz in the refrigerator. The others poured their faves from the plane's bar.

"Go on, Jerry," I said when Jerry Number Two came up the stairs.

The plane began to taxi out.

"Well, the system not only worked, we got lucky a few times on some splits and double downs. It was—"

The pilot interrupted.

"Excuse me, gentlemen. Are these cars with your party?"

I looked out the window, and Murray was talking to three beefy guys next to a pink Lincoln.

"No, they are not. Meeting up with them would be terribly awkward," Jerry said. I wasn't sure, but he might have affected a British accent.

"Very well, sir. Time to take off," the pilot said.

We were next in line for the runway and I could hear the jet's transmission, or whatever it's called on a plane, kick in.

"Anyways, we got this town for somewhere between one point one and one point two."

The four of us just looked at him with slack jaws.

"Million, that is. One point one, one point two million dollars."

CHAPTER EIGHTY

I RECLINED IN the soft leather recliner and took alternating hits of Schlitz and Jim Beam. The pilot did a long, slow circle so we could take in the Strip. From this height it seemed magical, even after the dirty time I had spent there. He turned around at the Stratosphere and cruised over the volcano at the Mirage, the fountains at the Bellagio, and past the iridescent Mandalay Bay.

His wide, sweeping turn took us past the emerald MGM and over the Flamingo, and he banked the jet to the right. We flew straight toward the Hilton, and I looked hard at the top floor, imagining Elvis and thinking of Boggsy and his mom. Angelina's "Danny Boy" would stay in my heart not far from the place Elvis occupied.

"Hell of a trip," Rocco said to no one.

It broke my reverie. I turned toward the Foursome. I raised my bourbon.

We clinked glasses and toasted.

"Things are different in person," TC said.

"A lot of this town loses its glitz up close," Jerry Number One said.

"I guess everywhere is the same in a lot of ways. The cards you get dealt sure do seem random," I said.

"Of course, there are always things you do to put the odds in your favor," Jerry Number Two said with a big smile.

* * *

Jerry Number Two's jet enabled me to e-mail the photo to Trina, and I asked her to make it an eight by ten, frame it, and put it in an obvious spot on my desk. She was panicked, almost certain that Cheese had been found out. Apparently later in the conference there had been a couple more "incidents."

I wasn't too worried.

The next morning I dropped by the Rocqueforts' house. I squared up the money with Cheese and he gave me the certificate of attendance. A deal is a deal.

"Duff, dude, I ain't ever doing that shit again. Two weeks with social workers just ain't worth the money," he said.

I thanked Cheese and told him I didn't think I would need him in that role again.

When I came through the clinic's front door I could feel Trina's annoyance before I could see or hear it.

"Well, I think you did it this time. You really have a goal of unemployment, don't you?" Trina said even before a "good morning." Her lips were tight and she wouldn't look at me. "She wants to see you when she comes in."

I smiled and went to my desk.

The framed picture of Lucille and me with our arms around each other had come out perfectly. The likeness was remarkable. It was right in the center of my desk and it made me smile.

I heard her footsteps behind me and then her voice.

"Duffy, I need to see you in my—" She didn't finish. Claudia was standing right behind me. She had come in and gone right to my desk before even going to her office. She was planning on firing me right there and then.

I spun around in my office chair. I looked at her, looked at my photo, and looked back at her. I smiled.

"Hey, Claudia, what an experience the last two weeks were. I don't think I'll ever be the same." I said it with as much enthusiasm as I could.

I meant every word.

Claudia had the same look on her face that I bet people who have just seen Bigfoot get.

"Uh, well, uh…good. That was the point. It was about growth and self-improvement."

She squinted again at the frame, acting like she had seen a ghost, and stumbled toward her office.

"Uh, Claudia, Trina said you wanted to see me?" I said.

She gave me a dismissive wave and closed her office door behind her. I took a deep breath and looked at me and Lucille. I felt a smile come over me. I started to think.

Jerry Number Two was right.

Life is a random gamble, no doubt, but there are always things you can do to get the odds in your favor.

ABOUT THE AUTHOR

TOM SCHRECK IS the author of five novels, including *On the Ropes* and *Out Cold*. He graduated from the University of Notre Dame and has a master's degree in psychology—and a black belt. He previously worked as the director of an inner-city drug clinic and today juggles several jobs: communications director for a program for people with disabilities, adjunct psychology professor, freelance writer, and world championship boxing official. He lives in Albany, New York, with his wife.